The Age

PAK KYONG-NI

TRANSLATED BY
Sophie Bowman
Anton Hur
Slin Jung
You Jeong Kim
Paige Aniyah Morris
Mattho Mandersloot
Emily Yae Won
and Dasom Yang

Honford
Star

This translation first published by Honford Star 2022

Honford Star Ltd.
Profolk, Bank Chambers
Market Place
Stockport
SK1 1AR
honfordstar.com

ISBN (paperback): 978-1-7398225-2-1
ISBN (ebook): 978-1-7398225-3-8
A catalogue record for this book is available from the British Library.

Printed and bound in Paju, South Korea
Edited by You Jeong Kim
Cover illustration and design by Sanho
Typeset by Honford Star

This book is published with the support of the
Literature Translation Institute of Korea (LTI Korea).

3 5 7 9 10 8 6 4 2

Contents

Calculations

Hwe-in wore a simple outfit. She flung a black scarf around her neck, opened her desk drawer, and took out a sealed envelope and several hundred-hwan bills. Tucking them into the pocket of her overcoat, she went out through the front gate and walked until she came to the police box, its lights glowing red as rabbits' eyes. Stooping down, she checked the time—5:40. Figuring it would take about ten minutes to reach Dongdaemun, she trudged ahead.

She was on her way to Seoul Station. Yesterday she'd made plans to meet Jeong-ah there at seven, before the other woman was set to leave for Busan on an eight o'clock train. Jeong-ah had come up from Daegu a few days earlier. She'd probably had plenty of other business to attend to, but the main goal of her visit had been to feel out Hwe-in's intentions. Namely, to get a better sense of Hwe-in's feelings toward Gyeong-gu, Hwe-in's ex-fiancé. Still, Jeong-ah was a dear friend Hwe-in had been genuinely happy to see.

So dear, in fact, that she would have seen her off even in the dead of night, instead of in these cold, early hours of the dawn.

Dongdaemun came into view. The sloped rooftop drew closer, looking like something out of an ink painting. Wedged into the stone wall was a streetcar box office as tiny as a crab shell. Hwe-in wondered if someone would be inside selling tickets in the bitter cold at this hour. She went up close to check, but the window was shut tight. A streetcar bound for Yeongcheon went by. Trembling, she waited for the next one.

The streetlamps cast a faint glow on the asphalt, and the stars were dim and watery in the sky where the dawn and the morning seemed to be intertwined. Two boys crossed the streetcar tracks from the other side of the road and approached the spot where Hwe-in stood. They stopped and stood beside her, looking ready to board the streetcar too. The light from the streetlamps shone down on them at an angle. One boy had plump, dark lips, and a face riddled with acne, and though he was quite hefty, the way his teeth kept chattering made him seem silly, like a little kid. He looked sort of like a street rat in his shabby leather jacket. There he stood, yammering away in a North Korean accent. The other boy looked world-weary, like a student putting himself through school, a cloth-wrapped bundle in one of his arms and a bag in the other. His face was pale and hard-pressed, absent of even a glimmer of the youthful spark befitting someone his age. Yet there was a gentleness about him that he seemed to have in common with others who had suffered a great deal in life.

"What're we gonna do if we can't get a ticket?" he drawled, looking worried.

The sound of his accent filled Hwe-in's ears, familiar. She found herself leaning closer to hear more of it. The rich, distinctive scent of her hometown flooded her lungs. The boys must have been students at a nearby school, headed home now that they were on break.

"Hey, don't sweat it."

"But if he ain't there, we'll be screwed, won't we?"

"Ah right, it's Sunday. He might not be on the clock today … but it doesn't matter, since it's close to my house."

From this, Hwe-in guessed the talkative boy was going to buy a train ticket for the other boy at the station and then see him off. But for some reason, the chatty one struck her as unreliable. Seeing the country boy feebly gripping that bundle under his arm, Hwe-in felt a twinge of worry that he wouldn't be able to get the ticket in time and was going to miss the train.

The streetcar appeared then, rattling to a stop in front of them. It was bound for Itaewon. The boys got on board, and Hwe-in followed after.

"I wasn't able to buy a ticket," she said to the conductor. "I hope you'll accept cash." She held out two ten-hwan bills. Right as the conductor reached out to take the money, someone approached them with quick, urgent strides.

"I've got a ticket right here."

The country boy hurriedly placed the orange ticket in the conductor's hand. The conductor looked a bit confused as he rang the bell, studying the boy's face and seeming awed by his generosity.

"Thank you. Here you go." Hwe-in thrust the money at the boy like she couldn't bear to have it in her hands. The thorniness in her voice surprised even her, and she realized she was probably being rude. Obviously, the boy wouldn't accept the money, and even offering it to him must have made her look mean, the sort of person who would heartlessly turn down an act of kindness. But seeing as they had never met before, Hwe-in had no choice but to adopt the cold formality she would in any business transaction. No matter how harsh her words sounded even to her ears, she couldn't let that sway her.

"No need for all that. It's fine," the country boy replied in a prim Seoul accent, his face blushing red. Resigned, Hwe-in took a seat, leaving a good amount of space between herself and the boys.

The streetcar started up again, twisting like a big snake. The air was so cold it felt like it would soon freeze and coil up inside their car, spacious and empty but for the three of them. Outside the rattling windows, the darkness fluttered like a blackout curtain. When she looked into the glass, Hwe-in found her own face reflected back. She quickly looked away. Even the boys were silent now. Hwe-in knew she should say something, perhaps try showing more gratitude; she felt deeply troubled about just pocketing the money and taking a seat. She couldn't very well thank the boy again, yet when she tried instead to feign obliviousness, staring blankly out the window, all her worry rolled itself up into that little streetcar ticket that was spinning around and around before her eyes. Despite herself, she found her gaze returning to the reflection in the glass. She took in her own sad eyes. Turned her head a bit to the side. *All right,* she thought. *Let me buy his ticket. It should be no problem if I ask Sung for help.*

Right—it wouldn't be too hard to get a train ticket if she asked a favor of Sung, who was affiliated with the company where she worked. Hadn't she asked for a similar favor on Jeong-ah's behalf just the day before? Stowing this timely idea away in her mind, Hwe-in lowered her gaze and studied the tops of her shoes. She contemplated how she might casually bring up her intentions to the boys. It was bound to be awkward. Where were the polished and composed words when she needed them? She tutted, annoyed and embarrassed with herself. *Did I ever ask you to buy me a ticket?* She felt restless. All at once, she remembered being in almost the exact same situation a few days earlier.

She had been waiting for someone at a coffee shop called Black Cat. It was around six in the evening, and the café was teeming with people—almost no empty seats in sight. Hwe-in didn't normally frequent places like this, and the moment she stepped inside, she was overwhelmed. Like a lone girl surrounded by a pack of wily boys, she was at a total loss for what to do. She made a reasonable effort to remain calm, but her cheeks burned red. Seeing only one empty seat in the entire café, Hwe-in grudgingly sat across from a man she didn't know. She thought about just leaving and waiting outside, but there were two entrances, plus it would be a hassle to make her way back out to the street now. Besides, she could feel the tearoom waitress's sharp glare burning holes in the back of her head. With no other bright ideas coming to mind, she sat there, suffocatingly close to a stranger. As smothered as she felt in that coffee shop, the atmosphere as heavy as lead, the thing she was most worried about was where to let her gaze fall. She couldn't simply stare at the table or the wall, and she definitely couldn't look at the man across from her. So she studied the entrance to the left, which seemed like a natural spot to watch as she willed the person she was waiting on to hurry and show up. Whenever someone came in, though, Hwe-in's eyes darted around like a startled rabbit's, which served to embarrass her all the more. She felt renewed anxiety about where to look, eyes hopping to a vase, a landscape painting, the wall. Nervous, she brought her hand to the kerchief around her shoulders, absently running her fingers over it.

Just then, a boy selling newspapers came by. Hwe-in was quick to speak up.

"I'll take one," she said.

The boy passed her by, not seeming to have heard. The saliva in her mouth dried up, and even that one request she could manage seemed to have come out as a whisper. She felt embarrassed in front of the man across the table. She sat quietly until the paper boy came around again. This time, Hwe-in called out, "Newspaper, please!"

"Which paper would you like?"

"The *Seoul Shinmun*."

"Which one?"

"The *Seoul Shinmun*, I said."

She reached into her pocket, took out a hundred-hwan bill, and placed it on the table. At that moment, the man across from her deftly snatched up a copy of the *Dong-a Ilbo* and rummaged around in his pockets. His hand came out clutching three ten-hwan bills. He reached into his back pocket again and found one ten-hwan bill wedged between thousand-hwan bills. He fished it out and gave it to the newspaper boy too. The boy, thinking Hwe-in and this man were together, left without taking her hundred-hwan bill.

Hwe-in had no idea why this stranger, someone she had never met prior to this moment, had paid the cost of her newspaper. She couldn't even eke out a simple thank you, her throat was so dry. Hoping to carry on like nothing had happened, she fixed her eyes squarely on the newspaper in front of her. But she couldn't concentrate on the words. Instead, she found herself resisting this stranger's goodwill, wondering why people bestowed such arbitrary kindnesses on others. Because of one newspaper, her plan to distance herself from this man and maintain her own peace of mind had gone right down the drain. Her mood grew more and more sour. Just then, she spotted the person she'd been waiting for, gesturing from the entrance. Without a word, she stood up, leaving the money and newspaper behind.

*

"Where exactly are you headed?" Hwe-in managed to ask, forcing the question out across the distance between her and the boys. "Busan?"

Pulling on their rough-hewn army gloves, they answered almost in unison, "No, Yeosu. On the Honam Line."

Hwe-in faltered for a moment.

"If you haven't bought the ticket yet, I can arrange the purchase of one for you."

"That would be great. Can you really do that?"

"I'm not sure, but I'll try."

Feeling only slightly reassured, Hwe-in turned to look out the window and furtively unfolded her hands to slip one inside her pocket. Her fingertips brushed against the crisp envelope. There was ten thousand hwan inside. When Hwe-in had gotten word from Jeong-ah that her mother had fallen ill, she'd taken out a loan at a fifteen percent interest rate with no real plan for how she would pay it back. She borrowed the money with the desperation of a poor father on Christmas Eve, when he'd be willing to steal anything for his family. She had shut her eyes to the reality of both her mother's illness and the dangerous amount of debt she had accrued, opting instead for denial. Even Hwe-in, who had begun to view all suffering with some degree of pessimism as of late, couldn't bring herself to see her mother's suffering in the same way. That her mother had been in agony, that she had grown old from all her worrying about Hwe-in—these were sobering fears much too hard for Hwe-in to bear. The mental preparations she had done to greet any misfortune she encountered with cynicism were rendered moot when it came to her mom. She'd sought escape from all that suffering. She was trying all the time to purge the thought of her mother from her mind. Even now, as she half-listened in on the two boys' conversation, her thoughts were drifting elsewhere. If thoughts of her mother had been weighing down her mind, the distraction the boys offered was helping her to readjust the scales.

With Jeong-ah leaving this morning, all that old business with Gyeong-gu would be settled once and for all. While the issue was already a year old and nothing to cry over now in Hwe-in's mind, this marked the first and last time she would give Gyeong-gu a hard answer. It was an open secret that Gyeong-gu had spoken about his upcoming marriage to Hwe-in with something like regret in front of her acquaintances—despite the fact that their engagement was the outcome of a romantic relationship they had both willingly entered. It had already been a year since Hwe-in fled her hometown without a word, hoping to escape the complicated tangle of rumors that had surrounded her there. Gyeong-gu tried to sway her with letters or else by asking her mother to bring her around, but not once did Hwe-in cave or break her silence. Stubborn and unyielding, Hwe-in couldn't bring herself to forgive what Gyeong-gu had said, but because she had never put a neat end to their relationship, she'd committed herself to this stubborn stretch of silence without knowing what it would become. Was that why she had so clearly spurned Jeong-ah's suggestions the night before—to resolve the issue and be done with it? Even now, she couldn't say with certainty whether the situation with Gyeong-gu was indeed resolved or not. All she knew was that she felt surer than ever that any semblance of emotional reconciliation between them was impossible.

The streetcar arrived at Seoul Station. Hwe-in and the boys entered the waiting area. Hwe-in looked all around in search of Jeong-ah. She didn't seem to be there yet.

Hwe-in turned to the boys. "Wait here. I'll be right back," she said, scurrying off.

Sung greeted her when she arrived at his office. She had already paid for Jeong-ah's ticket just the day before, so he didn't seem too surprised to see her again.

"Sung, do you think you could buy a ticket to Yeosu?" she asked in a rush.

"Sure, I could."

"Buy one for me, then, please. A relative of mine suddenly needs to go there," she lied. With that, she hurried back to the waiting area. The boy with the Northern accent had disappeared somewhere, leaving the country boy standing alone by the wall, staring at an advertisement like he had nothing else to do.

"I got the ticket," Hwe-in said. "Come with me."

"I'm really sorry you went to all the trouble."

Without another word, he followed Hwe-in down to the office.

*

Once the boy handed Sung the money, he told Hwe-in he would pass the time in the waiting area and left her sitting alone in the office, warm with steam. Hwe-in felt herself growing languid as her body, frozen from the cold, began to thaw. A feeling as warm as a spring day flowed through her heart. A softness, giddy and light, like sheep's wool. But soon enough, it was gone. Such moments of comfort never lasted long for her. Her mother's illness, her decisive split from Gyeong-gu, the agonies that came with living—they lurked deep inside her heart like a nest of thorns. She stared blankly at her own hands resting on the desk. Her neat, clean fingernails. The office clock read seven o'clock sharp. The inside of the room was glaringly bright, light reflecting off all the white walls, so intense that Hwe-in could see a faint jade edge to its glow. There was a bare wall with not even a single landscape painting on it, and a green armband inscribed with white letters hung in one corner like a lone leaf drooping from a stem, along with a tattered black uniform that reminded Hwe-in of a heap of coal glittering next to the railroad tracks in the midday summer sun. An impossibly doleful whistle came riding in on the dawn. Hwe-in put her head down on the cool desk. She tried to hold back tears. It felt like there was a rusted statue tumbling around in the dark space behind her eyes. The tumbling sound echoed off the walls and rang throughout the room, that ringing resounding over and over again, an infinite void opening up inside her head. Then she sat up and shook her head, grimacing as if in pain. Another whistle sounded in the distance. She kept thinking about the night before, the last conversation she'd had with Jeong-ah. She buried her face in her hands, as if covering her eyes to avoid seeing her own sad self. Tears pooled on the tip of her nose. Like a statue of a goddess looming over some Western harbor, forever alone and looking out at the distant sea, the statue of herself Hwe-in had erected in her own unending loneliness vanished into her tears.

Jeong-ah said Hwe-in's treatment of Gyeong-gu had been harsher than winter frost. Hearing that, Hwe-in stared her friend down, eyes flashing with an unusual intensity.

"I see. So you want to argue over the hard facts alone. You think I'm being harsh? Fine. To tell you the truth, I haven't once thought about whether I was handling this situation with Gyeong-gu the right or wrong way. The whole time, all I felt was like giving up on everything."

"Hwe-in, you're being far too immature. Say what you will, but you don't come across someone like Gyeong-gu every day. I'm a realist to the end, you know—don't tell me you're really going to be like this over a few little words? When you think about how worried he must be—"

Hwe-in cut her off, every word of her reply laced with bitter derision. "I know, I know. Everything you're saying, I've heard a million times. You were the one who told me before it would be ridiculous not to forgive him for those few little words if I genuinely loved him, right? Because he'd never once betrayed me aside from that one time? Well, that may be true, but let me turn your words back on you a bit. Let's suppose there's a two-timing husband. Let's say that even though he has several girlfriends, he insists to his wife that he loves her most of all. And at the same time, let's say there's a good-hearted man who carries himself well but caves under the pressure around him and declares his love for his woman only after he's hurt her, in a selfish attempt to defend himself. Would the quantity of the wrongs in these two cases really outweigh the quality? If you put all the blame for our breakup on me, saying the harm done might be big in scale but not in number, you have to admit you're being a downright mathematical woman, no better than a meter or gauge. Relationships aren't something that can be built or resolved using that sort of metric. It would be wonderful if the human mind were so methodical."

Jeong-ah's face had gone red. "I'm begging you," she said. "Let go of that impractical idealism of yours. All you've done, day in and day out, is turn a blind eye to what's flawed and ugly in life—it's such a coward move. You're always fixating on the mental things alone, but do you really think that's the way the world works? We tread dirt everywhere we go. I'd rather try to accept that for as long as I'm alive. Why must you be so choosy? I know you'd say I'm being materialistic, but I'm thinking about the reality. Just what's the point of trying to dig at these invisible things? Emotion will always be the victim of reality. Always."

"Then what'll you do after you've killed off all your emotions and become the even bigger victim of reality yourself?" Hwe-in fought to control her sharp glare, the flash in her eyes. She continued. "You go on and on about emotion this and emotion that, like you think feelings are a problem, but I believe I would have handled those feelings properly if they hadn't been a joke. If you take sufficient responsibility for the outcome, there's nothing to regret. I know when a knot is impossible to unravel, and I don't want a marriage where I hurt the other person or that person hurts me. All your talk about rationality does nothing but pressure and coerce both me and him. And that's not even rationality, it's just one of many ways of being practical. Just earlier, you brought up idealism—you said tolerating even the rotten parts of life is one of the ways we've learned how to look on the bright side of it, right? If everyone were like you, the basis of our society would be lies and selfishness. Things like romance would naturally become obsolete. If marriage consisted of nothing more than a few terms and conditions, all you'd need for one would be a contract, no? And if reality is nothing more than that, then I'm not even an idealist. I'm nothing, just someone who's managed to survive. Someone with no passion—no, more like no aptitude for acquiring wealth and power. If everything that went into dating Gyeong-gu were to vanish, all that would remain would be our parting."

Jeong-ah sat there in silence. She was a simple, easygoing person, as buoyant as the ocean in May. She had sympathy for Gyeong-gu, but she'd thought of Hwe-in's happiness above all else. Though she'd gone so far as to put forth a view she didn't even believe to try changing Hwe-in's mind, Jeong-ah was—counter to everything she'd said—a natural emotionalist who wielded both tears and laughter in abundance. By comparison, Hwe-in might have been as cold as unheated stone floors. Inside her placid, expressionless silence burned the fearsome flame of her emotions—a flame no one could approach by even an inch, one she skillfully managed to keep from surging like a raging sea, a cold smile always on her lips. But that night more than any other, she wanted to tell Jeong-ah every little thing that came to her mind. Hwe-in rambled on like a child because she knew that Jeong-ah, who was so kind despite her simplemindedness, was leaving tomorrow and Hwe-in would be left to her all-consuming loneliness again.

"What happened back then tormented me. Really … When those strange rumors were going around, Jeong-ah, I kept my mouth shut. Even before you came up here, I hadn't opened up about any of this to anyone. Of course I had a lot to say. All these words surged to the top of my throat. But I maintained this painful silence, as if I'd swallowed a thorn. I didn't trust myself at all back then, and it seemed too risky. Like if I made one wrong move, I would fall into this pit lurking right beneath my feet. I thought anything I said at that time would come out as a bunch of nonsense and drivel, that I would burst into tears if I had to face the people who'd resented me, now delighting in my defeat."

A bitter smile appeared on Hwe-in's face. As she cupped her hands to catch the heat of the embers smoldering in the brazier, they trembled from the sharp pain of that memory. Her voice rose steadily as she went on.

"Things don't seem so shaky anymore. Even if you chide me now for seriously misconstruing what was said, who would trust him again? Even if it was a lie or he didn't mean it, is there any redeeming him? If it were all a lie, that would make him one sad magician. Isn't that the most tragic farce you can imagine—a job where your lies are rewarded with an audience and applause? Then again, if what he said was true, that would make Gyeong-gu an unspeakably awful and ignorant person. Could he really be so dense? He said nothing to me when I should have been the first to know, and it remains a complete mystery how that letter of his—where he went so far as to claim his affections were pure and even sacred—reached me almost at the same time he publicly denied his feelings toward me, causing such ripples around us. Maybe it was his extremely delicate nature, but I'm not sure if he really did it to soften the blow against me, the unlucky woman that I was ... That letter ... it was what you'd call a beautiful lie, wasn't it? But he shouldn't have told my adversaries how he felt first. In the end, he went about it in a way that was decidedly *not* delicate or admirable at all, and if he still has those messy feelings now and is going around blathering on about our past together or our sacred love and whatnot, I ought to slap him!"

Hwe-in had been talking in a whisper at first, but at some point, she'd gotten swept up in her own wild emotion. Her face was red, her mouth pressed shut, tight enough that it must have hurt. Jeong-ah felt an inexplicable weight pressing down hard on her chest. She imagined she'd gotten a fierce lashing from a whip. A long silence sat between them like a grave.

As if beating away that silence with both hands, Jeong-ah said, "Of course, I understand how you feel. But is Gyeong-gu really such a bad person?" It had seemed like a rhetorical question, but then she answered herself with a strong denial. "No, he's not—do you really think of him that way? Even if things aren't like they used to be, you have to see that the poor man is miserable."

"I despise Gyeong-gu's penchant for frailty and pretense. I have no desire to shed even one tear for his cheap feelings and lies."

Hwe-in had cooled down now, her voice low and calm, but firm. Her back was to the window, outside of which the winter night drifted wanly by. For some reason, Jeong-ah felt the sudden urge to hug her, wrap her arms around Hwe-in's slender waist and hold her tight like an older sister would. Her forehead was pale and beautiful as if carved from ivory, which was rare for a woman. Jeong-ah wanted to sweep up the bangs that fell over that forehead. Overcome with this sense of fondness, Gyeong-gu's haggard appearance and dark eyes seemed like distant clouds, no longer the tragedy Jeong-ah had thought they were. Instead, all she could see was how sad, pitiful, and utterly defeated the woman before her looked—like an unwavering empress, stubborn in her refusal.

The fire in Hwe-in's haughtily upturned eyes dwindled until

they resembled those of a tamed beast, her own forlorn sadness pooling in the bottomless lakes of her irises. She sneaked a glance at Jeong-ah and chuckled. It was the sort of laugh that might set off a surge of round, fat tears.

"It would be best if Mr. Lee married someone else," she murmured, almost to herself. Her remark might have signaled either a complete return to objectivity or a camouflaging of the sadness that had burst out of her—but as she stared out into the open air, it seemed the traces of that sadness had not completely vanished from her face.

*

Thump thump thump—the sound of footsteps coming down the stairs filled the still office. Hwe-in raised her head. She allowed her expression to return to the same one she always wore. A look of utter calm. Sung came in, ruffling his hair. Hwe-in accepted the train tickets from him without a word, a sweet smile on her face. It would have been the norm to thank him, but such platitudes didn't come easily to her, so that sweet smile had become her standard form of greeting.

Hwe-in hurried up the stairs, almost running. Her heart fluttered, imagining Jeong-ah standing around waiting for her. She'd almost reached the top of the staircase when she stopped like she'd been struck by a thought. She realized Sung hadn't given her the seventy hwan of change after he'd bought the train ticket for the boy. Hwe-in wasn't ignorant of the social customs around pocketing the difference, but she felt bothered by it all the same. She slid a hand into the pocket of her overcoat, feeling like she had no choice but to pay him back herself.

The Age of Doubt

"Ah!"

She let out a yelp. It was almost a scream. The money was gone. That envelope of money. Incredulous, she searched her other pocket as well. Nothing. All that was left was the twenty hwan she was supposed to spend on her streetcar ticket. Dumbfounded, Hwe-in stood holding up the twenty-hwan bill and staring blankly at it, not registering anything in front of her. Without thinking, she touched her pocket again. Even the eight hundred hwan she had planned to give Jeong-ah to buy herself a snack on the train had vanished. Hwe-in stood there for a long time, her mind empty. The green traffic light seemed as faraway as a dream. She started to walk, one foot dragging itself in front of the other. She pushed the heavy door to the waiting area open with her body and stepped inside. Her black scarf had come undone and now swung sloppily against the small of her back. Hwe-in looked around lifelessly, trying to find Jeong-ah. She still didn't see Jeong-ah's green coat. She saw, vaguely, her little country friend running up to greet her, that white cloth bundle swinging from his grip. Without a word, she held out the wrinkled twenty-hwan bill and the train ticket to Yeosu. She knew she should have given him the seventy hwan of change, but she just stood there, utterly blank, like she had forgotten that thought entirely. The boy took the ticket, studying Hwe-in with a quizzical look on his face. She kept her hand out, wordlessly urging him to hurry up and take the money too. But the boy made no effort to do so. Instead, he seemed to falter, his mind on something else. The northerner from earlier was approaching them now, his hat gone and his thick hair flopping up and down.

"Hey, you got your ticket? It was so easy to get one today! Mr.

Kim bought it just like that, no problem! We were up and running around at dawn for nothing." He cut his eyes at Hwe-in. As if to say they shouldn't have stooped so low as to ask this woman for a favor. He seemed hostile toward her, like he thought she'd had the nerve to steal the chance he'd been up and waiting since dawn for. When she heard what he'd said, the two boys' faces wavered into sharp focus as if she was coming back into consciousness after having been asleep. Hwe-in pawed hard at her chest, like she was trying to dig up some hurt that was buried there.

She wanted to drop to the ground right there on the spot. She had been in such a hurry to find and buy the ticket, like it was some incredibly precious thing, when the whole time it could have been done so easily. And in all her hurrying, she'd lost the money she'd been carrying in her pocket at some point without noticing … As if that weren't enough, she stood in front of these boys now looking like a swindler who'd pocketed the country boy's change.

The Honam line train was departing before the one on the Gyeongbu line, and they had already started checking tickets. The country boy looked like he had something more he wanted to say, but he merely gave a polite bow to Hwe-in before heading over to the ticket check area with his northerner friend. The northerner leaned over and said something to the country boy, who murmured a reply.

"Haha! This idiot got ripped off!" shouted the chatty one. "By a black market ticket dealer! Ha!"

Hwe-in heard him, loud and clear. She wanted to shut her eyes to everything then, to cry and bleat like a newborn calf. The chandelier that hung from the dome of the ceiling glittered weakly at the outer edges of her vision. She spun around to leave. Tears streamed down her face, falling onto her scarf.

"Oh, for heaven's sake!" She buried her pale face in the scarf, as if to hide the anger she couldn't unleash. She clutched the train ticket hard in her hand. In the meantime, she had forgotten all about Jeong-ah, who still hadn't shown up. In the hubbub of the pre-departure crowd and the surge of people shoving this way and that, Hwe-in began to drag herself forward, wading through the rush. She came out of the waiting area. A chilly gust of wind struck her cheeks.

There in the station plaza was Jeong-ah, getting out of a car with her trunk suitcase and slamming the door shut behind her. Right away, she spotted Hwe-in coming toward her, grinned, and clapped her hands. But Hwe-in didn't see. She kept going, hauling one foot in front of the other, trudging forward with no destination or goal—as though she didn't even realize she was walking.

Translated by Paige Aniyah Morris
First published August 1955

Black is Black, White is White

Principal Jang presses a hand against his collar and turns his head from side to side, as though the red tie around his oily, porcine neck has a stranglehold on his throat. The tie is too red, too vibrant for his age. His salt-and-pepper hair is neatly combed, and though he is dressed like a younger man, he is well over fifty. He pulls out a hefty pocket watch. It is precisely half past three. The dishes on the table have long gone cold, but Hwang Geum-soon shows no sign of returning.

It has been some time since his last liaison with her—the woman who was once his pupil and is now wife to an official. She is also the loving mother of a student at the girls' middle school over which he presides. One could describe their many illicit encounters as the final bursts of passion in his old age, but this is only the latest dalliance in his extensive record of undetected incidents.

His eyes enjoyed their long-awaited tryst, savoring the lush rose that was Hwang Geum-soon, but the moment their food had been served, she had gone pale and rose from her seat. She had lost the 300,000-hwan check Jang gave her as a loan, she said. She would have to look for it at the import boutique she visited on the way, and if it was not there, then to the bank. As he could not very well go with her, Jang is left sitting alone, backside occasionally peeling from the seat of his chair before flattening down again.

Once more, he pulls out his pocket watch.

It is forty-five minutes past three. When he catches himself wondering why five minutes feels like an eternity, he is stung by self-pity and deprecation. As though to distract himself from his state of anxious boredom, he puts the watch back in his pocket and inserts a cigarette into his mouth.

Three hundred thousand hwan is no large sum for a man like Jang. It is nothing to cause serious concern, especially since it has already been given to Geum-soon and served its purpose. What irritates him is that someone might find the check and publish a found ad in the papers, which would also list the name of the man who wrote the check. Most unpleasant indeed. Puffing cloud after cloud of smoke, he assures himself this is nothing to be worried about. Even if something as trivial as this turns out to be the thread that unravels him, Hyeon is a loyal man who will make quick work of any trouble.

Jang spits a mouthful of phlegm into the ashtray. He is angry at himself for being so easily cowed.

Jang has nibbled away at the school funds for quite some time, but he has recently taken an unusually voracious bite. He now suffers from a bout of nervousness. Though his corpulent form evokes the galling audacity of a master merchant, decades at the instructor's podium have made him fearful and prone to caution above all. The position he built up over the years is everything to him. But the hypocrisy, greed, and greasy pleasures of life that threaten it are by now woven into the fiber of his being. It is no longer a question of whether he *will*, but how much *further* he will go. That is the reason he requires a schemer at his side, the bookkeeper Hyeon.

Jang remembers Hyeon's request and the matter of the new hire at the school, which is already all but confirmed. He is glad for his own foresight, setting the appointment for Monday, that is, the day after tomorrow. Hyeon is unusually clever, diligent, and dutiful, which makes him the perfect man to willingly take the fall. Jang must show generosity and bolster his loyalty, so that the younger man will be always ready and willing to do as he is asked. Convincing himself that Hyeon is a man after his own heart, Jang gives an emboldened clearing of the throat and shakes ash off his cigarette.

Someone sobs. A woman's voice leaks out of the next room over. Relieved, but seized by unexplainable curiosity, Jang presses his portly body close to the wall.

It takes the woman no insignificant effort to stifle the sob. Jang would not have heard her if he was talking with Geum-soon over food. The excruciating cries go on for some time before the woman, now finally calm, speaks in a low voice.

"What are we supposed to do? What are you going to *do*?"

"What do you mean, what am I going to do?" responds a deep male voice, dripping with irritation and annoyance.

"Day after day after day … Oh, I just want to die."

There is a muffled thud, then silence.

The woman sobs again. "I'm terrified the family will find out. Every time I come home, the front doors look like the gates of hell. Please, I can't take this anymore. Just tell me something— tell me to live, die, anything."

"I can't help it, I'm in no position to marry you. Not much for it except going to a hospital … I'll see if I can get you the money."

The sobs grow a little louder, the woman's awareness of her surroundings—a room in a Chinese restaurant—seemingly overshadowed by worry. The man sounds taken aback, and he attempts to console her.

Jang clutches his noose-tight tie and shakes his head left and right. Once more he pulls out his pocket watch. Five past four. Geum-soon must have lost the check and headed for the bank, he thinks. Scruffily dropping his cigarette into the ashtray, he gets up, puts on his coat, and slides open the door of the room.

The next door over also slides open. He comes face-to-face with a long-faced man about thirty years of age. Both startled, they turn away. Though strangers, they are alike in action. The man gets down to put on his shoes, lowering the brim of his fedora. The woman slips ahead of him quick as a chipmunk.

They are on the street now.

Breathing a sigh of relief, Jang studies the couple walking several steps ahead. He is impressed by the woman's slender frame. Her raglan-sleeved coat hangs across curved, swaying shoulders. Jang slowly deflates. Not only because Geum-soon has lost the check, but because he is reminded of her husband's impending return from his business trip—and the terrible interrogation he will conduct concerning her pregnancy. It is a habit of Jang's in his boredom or frustration to press down on his tie and turn his head from side to side as he licks his lips.

He must end this soon, but Hwang Geum-soon is still so young and so lovely.

The Age of Doubt

Hye-sook presses her shins together until her bones hurt. She pulls the fallen blanket back up around her shoulders and urges her fingers back to frenetic knitting.

If only the sky was clear, she could at least enjoy the bright sun while sitting on the maru ledge just outside the door, but for some reason the weather is dreary and the wind raps angrily on the tinplate roof.

The day after her daughter, Gyeong-yi, finished school for the term, Hye-sook's mother took her to her own sister's home. It has been four or five days since classes opened again, but there is still no news. It is heartbreaking for Hye-sook that they have still not sent word after setting out to beg for alms. Her mother probably hasn't secured any money, most likely, but found lodging there with little Gyeong-yi to at least live on scraps for the winter. Probably helping with the sewing, Hye-sook thinks, or even looking after the kitchen with her sister's daughter-in-law in the hopes of arousing some pity … She feels a sting in her eye.

It has been five years now since her husband was horrifically killed in an explosion and their home set was alight during the Korean War. The grueling march from one place of refuge to another and finally to Busan ended when the armistice was signed. Two summers ago, she found some meagre work in the reclaimed city of Seoul. Hye-sook somehow secured a small plywood room under a tin roof for herself, her daughter Gyeong-yi, and her mother. They lived from hand to mouth in sorrow each day.

Even that life of uncertainty was taken away two months ago when Hye-sook lost her job. But poverty has not defiled her character. When disgusted or displeased, she is the sort who spits on the ground and walks away without a second thought.

That does not help her coffers, but she would rather quit her job than tolerate injustice. Her dogged pot-bellied superiors disgusted her, and being treated as an object of licentious advances outraged her.

But that does not mean Hye-sook, a woman with a young daughter and elderly mother to support and years of suffering after her husband's death, is some naïve, sheltered flower. When she handed in her resignation, her plans were already coming to fruition in her mind. Even as her family struggled, she invested a portion of her tiny paycheck into a monthly gye fund. She was up next for the pot. Two hundred thousand hwan was not a fortune, but a large sum for her nonetheless. With it she could start a small corner store to sustain the family; Hye-sook could entrust the day-to-day business to her mother and check on it occasionally, and she for her part could find work in education, which better suited her character. But the plan was quickly ruined. Life is never so predictable as math formulas, especially in these uncertain times. The gye fund manager snatched the pot and handed Hye-sook only fifty thousand hwan, putting off the payment day after day until Hye-sook's fifty thousand hwan was all spent. Now unemployed, she has no better choice.

Winter comes with footsteps of frost and takes its place sternly on the unheated ondol floors and in her destitute pockets.

A gust of wind. Grains of sand clatter against the tin roof. Bundles of radish greens she hung up against the walls to dry flutter with each flurry.

Hye-sook lightly scratches her head with a knitting needle. She threads it again. She continues until she must put her knitting down on her lap and bring her hands together to blow warmth onto them. Thawing out her frozen fingertips, she looks to the wall calendar—and rises with a start to tidy up the room. Then she rushes outside and returns with what few pieces of firewood are left in the backyard, taking them to the kitchen.

It is Sunday.

Hye-sook is due to receive visitors. Yeong-min for certain, but perhaps also Mr. Hyeon. Yeong-min is a former colleague from work, but Hye-sook considers her a sister. She drops by every Sunday without fail. And Mr. Hyeon is a friend of her late husband. He does bookkeeping work for a girls' middle school, she has heard. He would visit once in a while with a tray of eggs—and last time, Hye-sook resorted to asking him to help her find work.

Hye-sook starts a fire in the hearth against the outside wall of the house and stares blankly into the flames. She chokes at the thought of Gyeong-yi, and of her mother—reduced to looking after the kitchen with her sister's daughter-in-law. She remembers Gyeong-yi, always quavering like a small, helpless chick. Most likely clinging to her grandmother's skirt instead of playing with the other children, Hye-sook surmises. If Hye-sook's aunt lashes out at her pathetic state, Hye-sook's mother might gently push the girl away, and tears would run from the girl's big eyes, Hye-sook tells herself. All the while, she hears her mother wailing, *What are we to do?* The heavy thumping of the elderly woman's hand against her already-bruised old chest is the sound of despair. It resounds in her ears constantly, months after her mother's departure. She is tumbling down a cliffside into a pitch-black abyss. Hye-sook looks up from her frightening vision and focuses once more on the sound of the wind. She is in a sorry state, to cling so desperately to the mere offer of a job introduction from Mr. Hyeon.

Hye-sook picks up pieces of firewood and snaps them in her hands. She does not remember when her tears gave way to grumbling. She is the most pitiful of all, she thinks. She catches herself groping for the barest hint of possibility in Mr. Hyeon's tone and expression as he responded, *I'm not sure, I will look into the matter*. It may be that her request—difficult as it is—keeps him from coming this Sunday with a tray of eggs to check up on the family. Having figured out her final contingency plan for employment, she throws the last of the firewood into the hearth. She rises and shakes off her skirt, as though doing the same for her train of thought.

Once inside, Hye-sook again takes up the knitting needles and thinks of another matter that stubbornly stains her memories. She has already settled the matter of employment. Now she considers the coat she swapped with Yeong-min. She will trade their coats back today even if it kills her. That will at least be one small burden off her shoulders.

Last autumn, they went out together to get coats tailored. Yeong-min picked the brown without a second thought, but Hye-sook could not help but hesitate. She did not have enough money. After feeling and shifting through many more fabrics, she decided on the green solely for the reason that it was ten thousand hwan cheaper than Yeong-min's. It was the gaudy color that made it cheaper, but the material was every bit as good as the brown. Once the coats were done, Hye-sook once more hesitated. The green was too ostentatious for a woman her age. At the same time, Yeong-min tried on the green coat and remarked jealously that it looked much better than she expected from the fabric sample. So they agreed to a trade. Once Hye-sook's turn for the gye pot was up, she would pay Yeong-min the difference. But rather than follow up on the promise, Hye-sook lost her job and ended up in her debt. She could think of no solution other than to exchange the coats back. But each time she brought up the subject during Yeong-min's visits, Yeong-min cut her off and said there was no rush.

It is noon when Yeong-min arrives. Three or four years Hye-sook's junior, she has a well-defined frame, like a Westerner. Her clear voice makes her presence doubly noticeable.

Throwing her purse to the floor, Yeong-min plunks down to the floor, legs to the side. She stares wordlessly at Hye-sook, either deep in thought or completely lost. Hye-sook is not oblivious to her troubles. She knows that Yeong-min is seeing a man named Tae-ho, and that Tae-ho is a boorish man. But she was never seriously worried for Yeong-min. The younger woman is clever and quick-witted.

Yeong-min mutters as if to herself, "I just want to die."

"Why would you say such a thing?" Hye-sook asks.

"Because I don't know how I'm going to live, unni," Yeong-min replies, and bursts into unexplained sobs. Swaying, with hands covering her face, Yeong-min wails. And Hye-sook senses something curiously feminine—as though she only now realizes that Yeong-min is a woman—and something painfully tangible that speaks of the deepening of Yeong-min's relationship and its inevitable end.

Wiping away tears, Yeong-min says, "I swear, I didn't know I was a woman until now."

Hye-sook listens silently.

"I think we'll be breaking up."

It pains Hye-sook to hear the silent resignation known only to those who have suffered. Yeong-min is twenty-three years old, and now knows the most painful wound any woman can bear.

"Of course not," Hye-sook says without thinking, wide-eyed and hoping only to fill the strange void between herself and Yeong-min. When she recognizes the emptiness of her own words, hanging unmoving in the air between them, tears stream down Hye-sook's face as well.

It is much later that Yeong-min finally rises. "I'm going to head out now. I'll come again, unni."

Hye-sook quickly gets to her feet and stops Yeong-min as she puts on her coat. She thinks briefly and says, "Please, you must hear me out." She rushes behind Yeong-min and pulls off her green coat.

"What are you doing now?" Yeong-min asks in confusion, but the answer dawns quickly. "... Oh, it's the money again, isn't it? I told you, I don't mind *when*, or if you give me the difference at all."

"No," Hye-sook says firmly, patting Yeong-min on the back. "I'm certain now that I won't be able to pay you back. And consider how I feel. Every time I look at that coat, it weighs on my mind. I won't take no for an answer."

Hye-sook smiles. Yeong-min gives her a pallid look and finally smiles back, sadly. Limp as a doll, she allows Hye-sook to pull her arms into the brown coat.

"There," Hye-sook says, giving Yeong-min one last pat on the back as she comes around in front of her. Yeong-min stands with a vacant stare. But she quickly flips up her collar, as though rousing herself, and walks out onto the maru to put on her shoes.

"Don't forget your scarf," Hye-sook says, picking it up from the floor.

"It's okay, unni. I bought it to match the coat."

Before Hye-sook can even put on her shoes to follow, Yeong-min has made it to the street. Hye-sook watches her disappear with the scarf still in hand.

"I hope that girl doesn't go and get herself hurt," she mutters to herself.

Strangely unnerved, Hye-sook curls up in the middle of the room. She is still. But the violent thrashing of the wind outside gives birth to a new, fearful realization: there is no sign of Mr. Hyeon.

Dusk passes and darkness falls over the world. A new despair sets into the tiny room, and with each passing moment, Hye-sook's body hardens into stone. The abyss flashes before her eyes again and again, and each time, she shakes her head and looks at the ceiling.

The push-up window facing the street rattles in the gust. Hye-sook jumps to her feet, opens the window, and stares into the dark as if searching for a human form. She is greeted by nothing but the howling wind.

She falls stiffly to the floor. Time loses all meaning.

The door rattles. Hye-sook holds her breath.

"Ma'am."

Mr. Hyeon.

Chills run down her back as she rushes to the door.

The moon glows faintly amidst the rolling clouds.

Hye-sook is saddened by her own hurry. She pulls back unruly strands of hair from her face and bows to Mr. Hyeon in greeting.

Once inside, they sit across from one another, Mr. Hyeon's greasy face lit orange by the candlelight. Hye-sook can do little but wait for him to speak. She dislikes the way he keeps his silence, as though to give some sort of weight to his words. The thought that he will do so again tonight sparks self-pity, like she is a little foal brought to an altar for slaughter.

Hyeon stubs out his cigarette in the ashtray and finally opens his mouth.

"I can see that you are in quite an urgent situation, so I considered the matter and spoke to the school I work for. As it happens, the home economics teacher recently married and left an empty post. From the principal's tune, I say your chances are eight in ten, at least. The man can't say no to me."

Hye-sook is elated. Stammering, she tries many times to thank him, but Hyeon goes on with his eyes locked elsewhere. "Come to the school tomorrow around half past ten to see the principal." He looks up at her. The desire he has cleverly hidden slowly rises to the surface. Hye-sook can do little but sidestep it guiltily.

"I'm so sorry for imposing on you," she says, hanging her head. Hyeon looks at her but says nothing in response. "No one else is much of a friend to him now that he's gone," Hye-sook says to cut off unwanted advances and remind Hyeon of her position. She is his friend's wife.

A hint of emotion rises to Hyeon's face, only for a fleeting moment. He quickly recovers his calm, but with a strange hint of a smile—a mockery of Hye-sook's attempt at defense. She flushes with humiliation and defeat; even the tips of her soft ears go red.

Hyeon rises to his feet, hands brushing his suit pants. "By the way, I gave the principal some idea of your circumstance—and told him that you are my cousin. If he asks, don't forget to stick to the story."

Hye-sook bites her lip and replies, "Right."

Once Hyeon has gone, Hye-sook draws some water to wet

her hair and begins to roll up her hair curlers. Her perm has nearly gone out, and she is worried it will look messy tomorrow. But soon another worry stops her hands. Annoyance and anxiety boil inside her at the unpleasant memory of Mr. Hyeon's piercing stare. She tells herself, however, that this time she must put up pretenses and resumes her work—then her hands stop again and a grimace rises to her face. She got her green coat back from Yeong-min. It is too gaudy for tomorrow, she thinks with a sigh, and wishes she had waited to exchange it until after the meeting with the principal. The interview is too important. But there is nothing to be done now, so she resumes curling her hair. Once the curlers are in place, she wraps up her head like an Arab in a white towel. Hye-sook slides into the futon she has laid out on the floor. She tosses and turns on her pillow in discomfort for some time before she finally closes her eyes. Praying in desperation, with all humility. Praying pitifully for a fortuitous dream in which she is employed. But what she sees in the dark are Hyeon's eyeballs, staring at her from every direction with his designs in his gaze.

Jang spins round and round in his office chair before rising to his feet. He stretches, and makes his way one step at a time to the window. As classes are still in session, the grounds are empty— and unusually clean, perhaps thanks to the strong wind last night having blown the dirt away. Now that the gusts have stilled, tree branches reach quietly into the thawing winter sun. Jang pulls his arms back into another stretch and twirls his moustache. He has been mulling over the matter of adding new classes to the school, and considers once more the procedure and methods. It would be best for optics and feasibility to have existing classrooms take on as many students from other schools as they can, and to transfer current students to the new classes. The train of thought is interrupted when a phone screams in his ear.

"Hello? Who is this? Ah, yes. Mhm. Mhm. Perfect timing … What?"

Furrowing his brow, Jang nods. It is Hwang Geum-soon, saying that he no longer needs to worry about the check because she has retrieved it from the one who found it before it reached the wrong hands—and that she wants to meet with him to speak about some matter.

Knowing what the matter is, Jang feels a prickle of irritation. "Then four o'clock the day after tomorrow, at the usual place," he decides, setting the time and place so that he can end the conversation.

"He's back," Hwang Geum-soon says as though clinging desperately, and hangs up herself. By "he," she means her husband.

Jang is vexed. But when he slams the receiver back onto the phone, the vexation has been replaced by worry. Now that her husband has returned, taking care of that niggling matter is of urgent importance. He is afraid, now that he is forced to consider the matter. He walks a lap in front of his desk and goes to the window to look out at the grounds. In the distance is a woman. She walks through the gates, steps pointed directly at the office, green coat highlighted by a bold grey-and-yellow scarf. Even from afar she catches the eye. Tilting his head, Jang stares at the approaching woman. He cannot yet make out her features, but the outline of her face is clear, as is her fair complexion. When the woman reaches the building door, he gives a small gasp, for he sees her profiled face from his window. It reminds him of a particular moment. That coat and the scarf are unmistakably the garb of the woman who slipped out of that Chinese restaurant after she wept, just two days earlier. Without even wondering what that woman might be doing at the school, he thinks to himself, *What a small world this is*. Habit compels him to grasp his tie and turn his head from side to side as he throws himself into his office chair. As though taking out his anger, he rifles through the documents on his desk and pounds his seal on each like a stamping machine. There is a cautious knock at the door. Jang looks up. Hyeon enters, wearing a look of utter prudence. Jang gives a fatherly smile.

"The cousin I mentioned the other day, Mr. Jang," says Hyeon, wringing his hands together. "I hope I'm not interrupting anything."

Jang replies, "Ah, yes! Of course! No, no, nothing to interrupt, now. Show her in."

Hyeon gives a deep bow and steps outside. It is not long before he shows Hye-sook into the principal's office. Jang cannot help his shock. She is the very woman he saw moments ago, the one in the eye-catching clothes he saw crossing the grounds. So taken aback is he that he is briefly stunned into silence. But he quickly notes Hye-sook's unperturbed and demure bearing. *This woman is a shameless vixen.* He looks her up and down with accusing eyes, and when his sharp gaze falls on her belly, an expression of cold disgust spreads across his face.

Hye-sook is discomfited by the way his eyes relentlessly scan her from head to toe. It is degrading, as if she stands before the man without her clothes, and the ignominy turns into a rage that brings a deep flush into her face. She is compelled to turn her measured gaze from the principal to her own hands clasped on her lap.

"Mr. Hyeon has told me everything," says the principal, brusquely cutting off the exchange. "It was good to meet you, and I will have him follow up with you at a later time."

Hye-sook knows in her heart that things have gone wrong. Despair renders her mute; unbearable pain crushes her heart. She looks into Jang's eyes in one last desperate attempt at persuasion, but the sneer in his eyes is spreading even to the corners of his lips. Able no longer to bear her impossible circumstances, she mechanically rises to her feet.

Outside the office, Hyeon responds with confusion to Hye-sook's despondent face. He implores her to wait and knocks on Jang's door.

Face bowed, with only his eyes looking directly ahead, Jang stares at Hyeon. With a look of deep displeasure, he says, "This widowed cousin of yours—her conduct is inadequate. Mark my words, my eyes can tell when a widow is having an affair. I'll have to turn down this request of yours."

Hyeon squeezes his hands together, rubbing palm against palm. There is no answer, only a face slightly paler than a moment ago.

The phone on the desk wails. Slowly, Jang picks up the receiver.

Translated by Slin Jung
First published August 1956

The Age of Darkness

It has been raining for a long while.

Ten days into jangma, the rainy season, a pool of rainwater has collected under the ondol floor of Soonyoung's family store and adjoining home. Some water has found its way through the broken chimney, but mostly it is from the streets overflooding, pouring through the agoongi, the underground coal fireplace in the kitchen. The rooms have begun to fill with humidity and the smell of mold—Soonyoung's family had been keeping their old clothes in a cardboard box in the corner. Days of endless rain has meant that their laundry has accumulated and is cluttering the house even more than usual. In front of Soonyoung's store, a big boulevard split into an H shape. Either the sewer is clogged underneath this boulevard, or it never existed to begin with, but every time it rains it floods, and Soonyoung's store, standing at the corner of a crossing, suffers from water damage.

The store sells some snacks, fruit, and a few bottles of alcohol. It is a meager selection, especially since the livelihood of her five family members depends on it.

While studying literature, at the same time Soonyoung supports her ten-year-old daughter, eight-year-old son, and aging mother. She lost her husband to the war, and along with him all her worldly possessions. After the war, poverty awaited her. Poverty, hunger, and the desperate need not to surrender—swinging from one extreme to another, she was forced to test how strong she could be. But even among all the small and big fights, she finds herself unable to let go of literature—her last, feeble connection to joy and romance.

The rain seems to have died down a little. Soonyoung stands in the store looking outside, toying with her hair. Next to her, her mother sits on top of an empty apple crate, saying nothing, baring her nipples through the thin, rain-soaked linen jeoksam. Soonyoung, running her fingers through her hair mindlessly, goes into the single room the whole family live in, her face grim. It is dark inside, the floor sticky from the humidity. Kids crouch on the floor with coloring books they had gotten for the school summer break. Considering their age, they are quite small. Their tiny backs curve onto the floor like the arch of a turtle shell. Soonyoung watches on blankly.

Pieces of blue sky begin to push through the thick, grey clouds.

The light lands on her face against the darkness of the room. Her pale face turns away from the children toward the small window where the grey-blue sky hangs. She stands like that for a while, watching, and then says to the children:

"Hey, Myunghye! Take Myungsoo and go to Grandpa's, yes? Mommy needs to work."

She deepens into thought while speaking.

The children look up, holding their pale faces slanted like white mushrooms poking out from a rock cleavage. They start packing their books.

The Age of Doubt

"We'll be back soon, Mother!"

They chirp like sparrows and leave.

"Grandpa's place" really refers to a room near the market rented by a student from Soonyoung's hometown who attended C University. And this "Grandpa" figure is actually Soonyoung's dead father's cousin, a third-removed uncle. The uncle had been living between Seoul and his hometown due to some legal trouble, and a few months ago, he'd asked to stay at Soonyoung's place; her family had owed his family in the past, and Soonyoung and her mother found it difficult to turn him down. But though they managed to feed him, there was just not enough room to accommodate him in their household. So, when this student happened to rent a room in their neighborhood, the uncle became his roommate. Since the student went back home for the summer, Soonyoung's uncle had the whole room to himself.

After the children leave, Soonyoung tidies the desk of the paper and the books and drags another apple crate from the store into the room.

Her mother, sitting on top of a crate and watching Soonyoung with her arms crossed, tells her, "You need to boil the glue."

She sounds grumpy.

Soonyoung knows why. She ignores her, and with sternness in her voice, calls out to the girl who helps with the household chores: "Soonja! Soonja!"

Maid by title, Soonja is as good as their kin, having gone through so many ups and downs with the family. As Soonja appears with her rigid expression and a mopping rag in her hand, Soonyoung looks away to the gradually bluing sky, and tells her: "You know wallpapers. Go get five of them, the pretty ones."

And Soonyoung goes into the room.

"What's the point? Just use newspaper. We don't even have the money. Ay, dear God. Whatever."

As Soonyoung predicted, her mother goes on complaining before giving money to Soonja.

Soonyoung has been meaning to store all the clothes in one of the crates, and she means to plaster one of the apple crates today. Sweating in the room, she waits for the glue to boil.

Mother doesn't stop nagging, boiling the glue herself instead of letting Soonja do it. She goes on about how she had to waste glue that one time when it wasn't boiled right.

"So that room is too good to be plastered with newspaper, huh! We don't have the money for expensive wallpaper. Does wallpaper make apple crates glitter with stars? Cham!"

She continues as she stirs the pot of glue, "Aigoo, I hate everything. This is hardly living …"

Soonyoung, sitting in the room, feels deeply frustrated. She wants to argue that she wants them to at least try and maintain a clean, organized environment within their means, but she swallows her words, knowing how impossible it would be to talk to her mother.

Her mother lost her husband at a young age and has since depended solely on Soonyoung, her only daughter. She had lived a relatively stable, financially secure life, until the war took away all the stability overnight and left her a wanderer amongst ruins, a wanderer who remained stubbornly nostalgic about the past and reserved nothing but venom for the present.

Soonyoung starts to plaster the crate with the wallpaper Soonja brought. When she is about halfway through, she hears Myunghye, who has apparently arrived without Soonyoung's noticing.

"Grandma, Grandpa says, we're all going to get sick due to malnutrition. He says that's why Myungsoo wet himself yesterday."

"He'd be better off worrying about himself."

Her mother's words have thorns—she disapproves of her cousin-in-law depending on her family, all the while knowing their difficult circumstances.

"He says when you get sick the medicine will cost you even more."

"*Tsk*, as if we're not eating well out of choice. If we get sick, we'll have no other option than to die."

"Grandpa says to eat this."

"Hush, he and his greasy stomach can't stop thinking about meat."

Her mother scoffs.

Soonyoung, listening from the room, doesn't like how her mother lets the children in on her adult emotions, but remains silent. Myunghye's voice fills the small space of the store for a while, and then it grows quiet. She must have left. Soonyoung stops gluing and stares down on her glue-webbed fingers.

Life marches onwards, like a field without horizon. How long could this go on. As Soonyoung grabs the glue brush again, her mother appears at the door of the room, carrying something wrapped in newspaper.

"What's that?"

Soonyoung asks, glancing at the paper parcel.

"He sent over some meat."

Soonyoung, dipping the brush into the glue, remembers what her mother said about her uncle's greasy stomach and his obsession with meat. He has led a profligate life. As someone nearing fifty who never sweated a day in his life to win a loaf of bread, he doesn't have the capacity to understand the difficulties that others have. The clearest example of this obliviousness is his unwavering epicurean appetite. His face darkens whenever he notices there is no meat or alcohol on the dinner table. Soonyoung does not completely dismiss his higher-than-average intelligence and fair education, but his unrelenting zeal to boast his knowledge and his picky, gourmet appetite has always bothered her. It is more than understandable that her mother finds his obsession with meat ridiculous when they might be facing the threat of starvation soon.

At the same time, Soonyoung doesn't think that sending over a piece of meat via Myunghye was entirely a gesture of his flaunting. Just last month the uncle's wife had sent someone over with five thousand hwan, and this morning, a note arrived asking if they'd received the money and the clothes, noting how sorry she was for everything. So Soonyoung doesn't want to completely dismiss her uncle's rare gesture of courtesy.

Soonyoung's eyes empty as she watches the back of her mother leaving the room to go to the kitchen. Her bare waist, visible between the still-wet jeoksam and the wide waistband of her skirt, looks exceptionally skinny. Her hair has thinned so much that her binyeo, a single-rod hairpin, slips through her sparse, pinecone-shaped bun, streaked clearly with silvery white. Soonyoung looks down at her own hand, plastered with glue.

How long will they go on living like this. She starts to ponder. Pondering ways to escape living this way. The only possible way seems to be to sell her body. What defeats this idea is not the baseness of the thought itself, but the fact that she doesn't know how to do even that. Eyes watering, she grabs the brush and glues the last piece of paper. She can't help noticing that the stock at the store reduces day by day. A dead-end approaches. Her mother, entering the room from the kitchen, nags again.

"It's not like we have a house like a palace, nor any furniture, nor visitors, to justify wallpaper over a crate of apples. It's pathetic. Stop it."

"..."

"I don't care for meat or any of that. How full of himself ... As if this poor old hag has done something so wrong ... Aigoo, please let me slip into death tonight ..."

Soonyoung yells, "Stop it! You're not the only one that longs to die. Who wants to live?"

Her mother's nagging has continued for twenty-five years, without skipping a day.

After Soonyoung finishes gluing, she feels hot. She washes her face, combs her hair, and ties it back, leaving the room to go sit in the store. Her mother is sitting on the apple crate, sewing her sock. The muddy rainwater that had been running like a stream in the morning has now drained away, bearing the bones of the street littered with stray boots and rotten wooden boards. The tireless sun shines over them. A hot, heavy wind blows. Fanning herself, Soonyoung realizes that the rainy season hasn't finished. It depresses her to think about the rainwater puddled under their ondol floor and the humidity in the room. The sun slowly moves its fierce focus over to the window of the small hotel across the street. It must be setting.

Down the street, Myunghye jumps into Soonyoung's sight. She is sprinting.

Entering the store, she yells: "Mother, Myungsoo is hurt."

Soonyoung's mother, who stops sewing the sock, and Soonyoung jump to their feet at once.

"How come?"

"He fell. He hurt his forehead."

Upon hearing it was just a fall, Soonyoung's face gains back some of the color it lost.

Her mother fixes her skirt, getting ready to leave, and asks: "How did he fall? I can't believe this."

"Grandpa took us to the mountain."

"What? To the mountain?"

Before Soonyoung can continue, her mother cuts her off.

"Why on earth did he take them to that slippery slope? He just won't let us be."

Her face looks rotten with anger for the uncle.

Myunghye comes back without Soonyoung's mother, whom she had left with. She says they had to go to the hospital. Then she explains how it happened: they were bored, so they asked Grandpa to take them to Jongno. He said let's go to the mountain behind his house instead. He bought them caramels, and they climbed the hill and played there for a while, and on the way down, Myungsoo, letting go of Grandpa's hand, fell.

Soonyoung is annoyed, expecting Myungsoo to return with her mother any time soon. But time passes and he is nowhere to be seen. Soonyoung starts to feel anxious, thinking she should have gone with them. Now she must wait. More time passes.

"Aigoo, dear God, Myungsoo doesn't even recognize me ..."

Her mother's wails precede her before she enters the store. Soonyoung feels as if clouds gather in front of her eyes.

"We went to the S Affiliated Hospital. They have to operate on him. I don't know what to do ..."

Her mother goes through her pockets while weeping and

puts twenty thousand hwan into a bundle of Myungsoo's clothes. That twenty thousand hwan is the very last of her fortune—it is all she has.

Soonyoung, seeing Myungsoo's clothes, feels as if clouds thicken in front of her.

Soonyoung and her mother, along with the bundle of Myungsoo's clothes and some blankets, get into a taxi.

"Aigoo, dear God, our Myungsoo … Not even recognizing me …"

Her mother stomps her feet anxiously. Soonyoung's face has turned pale blue, her body shakes uncontrollably while her hands clutch the bundle of clothing.

They get out of the taxi in front of S Hospital and go into the examination room where Myungsoo lies.

He seems to have fallen asleep, wearing a bandage round his head.

Blood has puddled here and there on the thin, rubbery mattress of the bed. His feet and the hand he has two warts on are covered in sand.

Soonyoung wipes the sand off his limbs, watching him.

Soonyoung's mother, following her into the room, abandons the bundle of clothes and blankets on the floor, and opens her arms wide as if to hug him.

Soonyoung stops her short, studying the boy's face. Her mother is acting out of her own emotions instead of caring for the injured boy, and Soonyoung has to push her out of the way and force her to sit down. Feeling dizzy, she presses down on her own head to resist passing out.

The boy has lost consciousness.

Soonyoung, clutching her head, feels like the square surgery room is swirling down on her. Her mother rubs her feet together.

Soonyoung lets go of her head.

The boy remains unconscious. He lies on the bed, raised high in the middle of the examination room. It dawns on Soonyoung that before they entered, there was nobody attending the room.

Soonyoung's eyes redden. Her face too.

What would have happened if the boy had started to twist while nobody was watching and he fell from that high bed?

Soonyoung feels cold sweat push out of her forehead. Then her complexion turns yellow with anger for the uncle who hasn't even shown up yet. She wants to tear his face apart.

But when he does appear after a while, looking tanned and swamped, all Soonyoung manages to do is bury her face at the foot of the bed by the sleeping boy's feet and cry.

"Soonyoung, please don't worry. His forebrain is a bit damaged but they're saying it'll be fine with a few stitches."

Soonyoung continues to cry, bent down over the bed. No matter what he says to comfort her, there is no mistaking the severeness of the boy's injury.

Then enter two young men in white gowns, either interns or assistants.

Soonyoung stops crying and raises her head.

They take a cursory look at the boy, and one of them says, "You'll need to go buy some blood. His blood pressure is too low, he might die during the operation."

Soonyoung buries her face by the boy's feet again, avoiding looking at her mother who is thudding her chest with her fists.

As she closes her eyes, she sees a red ocean of blood. Of type AB. Her blood type is AB.

Soonyoung notices the uncle is standing next to her, still like a statue.

She tells him coldly, "Either we go buy the blood or extract mine, but we first need to test the boy's blood type."

Uncle leaves the room, swinging his long arms, but he soon comes back, telling them that a nurse told him to wait.

Time goes by and nothing happens.

It grows dark outside. It has already been a few hours since the boy arrived in the hospital, and yet, after those two interns or assistants, no one else comes by or sends word. It isn't even clear if someone is keeping watch or doing anything at all, if there is even any sort of line of command.

Dark silence pushes into the examination room that is isolated from the big, wide hospital, like a foreign region, where only the patient and his family remain.

"What is going on?"

Soonyoung spits at the uncle, who has remained standing like a statue.

He leaves the room, swinging his long arms recklessly again, and comes back with a nurse.

When the nurse draws blood from the boy's hand, Myungsoo frowns and cries out weakly. But as soon as she takes out the needle, he falls back into unconsciousness.

After the uncle leaves with the nurse, two janitors enter the room with a gurney. They are moving the boy to the operating room.

The janitors take a quick look at the comatose boy, and without acknowledging the anxious family, start moving the boy onto the gurney. They treat him without care or caution, as if his body were some broken object like a desk missing a leg.

Soon as he is laid onto the gurney, the boy frowns, like before, and lets out a weak cry.

Soonyoung and her mother, carrying the bundle of Myungsoo's clothes, follow their boy and the janitors through a long corridor—the longest one Soonyoung has ever walked down.

Through another one, this time curving, and then another, then another.

Every time they turn a corner, Soonyoung sees orange ceiling lights throwing pale shade onto the white walls. She hears the wheels on the gurney roll, the sounds of railroads being laid in her empty mind.

They arrive in front of the operating room.

A nurse, lying on the long bench in front of the room, gets up and opens the door wide. Damp, sterile air from the sanitation station washes over Soonyoung's face.

Soonyoung steps into the operating room, following the boy.

"Don't go in!"

The nurse yells and forcefully pushes Soonyoung's shoulders. She shuts the door in her face.

Holding her hands together, Soonyoung stands still. She can't see anything.

She manages to calm herself down and goes over to the nurse who has sat back down on the bench. In front of this tall nurse who pushed her, Soonyoung bows politely.

"Please, there's no danger to his life, is there?"

Soonyoung looks up at the tall woman as if she were a god in charge of his life.

"Why wouldn't there be, it's brain surgery."

The words slap Soonyoung across her face.

The Age of Doubt

She loses the courage to ask anything further. She wants to beg, but backs down, afraid of annoying her.

Soonyoung sits down on the bench across from the nurse.

Soonyoung's mother, clutching the bundle, takes a seat next to her, and watches the back of Soonyoung's white neck with pity.

"The doctor said it will be fine. That he just needs this surgery to get better …"

Soonyoung's mother knows that the words don't help, but says them anyway.

She sniffles as she speaks, and the tall nurse throws over a cold, demeaning look.

Next to her stands a younger nurse, whom the tall nurse tells, "Miss! Go check on the patient." She orders with authority—the younger nurse must be a student.

As the student passes Soonyoung, she says, "Please don't worry."

She then disappears into the operating room.

Her words warm Soonyoung's mind—*She will look after my poor Myungsoo*—but soon she grows frustrated. She tries once again to speak to the tall nurse.

"Don't you need blood to start the operation?"

The tall nurse stares at her with cold contempt.

"Of course you need blood. Didn't someone tell you to get it elsewhere?"

"Yes."

"We have it here."

"But the blood type …"

"We have type O. It works for everyone."

The nurse says this reluctantly, yawns and stretches her arms, and goes into the operating room.

What on earth are they doing? Have they not even tested his blood type yet? An operation like this would hurt even a healthy man. She can't stop her thoughts. *And the boy is definitely not a healthy man.*

At last the uncle appears at the end of the corridor.

He tells her that the blood type is B.

Soonyoung says, "The hospital has blood …"

"No, we can't count on that. I've been told it's safer to get it ourselves."

He takes some money and leaves.

At this point, six hours have gone by since the boy first arrived in the hospital.

Time passes. People appear in the corridor, only to go into other rooms.

The tall nurse peeks out from the operating room and asks if the blood has arrived yet. Soonyoung gets up.

"Just begin with the blood you already have here."

Soonyoung's mother grabs her by the arm.

"Dear, if we run out of money …"

Soonyoung pinches her, and as if intending the nurse to hear, speaks loudly, "We can get more from my sister."

These were empty words.

Soonyoung's mother shoots a questioning look at her, then shuts herself up, reading Soonyoung's eyes.

"Now that you've gone to get blood anyway, we'll use that up first before we use ours."

The tall nurse then shuts the door.

"Mother, why would you let on that we are tight on money. What are your rings, your silver binyeos for? We can sell them."

Soonyoung snaps quietly, hating how her mother could say such reckless things.

It was sad for her to think about her mother's gnawing anxiety about money, even at a desperate time like this. The single mother who had to manage without a husband, always struggling.

Soonyoung wipes the tears from her eyes and turns her gaze toward the other end of the corridor once again.

Her mother's rings and binyeos are the only remnants of her old life. She has always said that she'll never sell them, but at least this means that they had a last resort after the twenty thousand hwan in cash.

The two young men from the examination room, the interns or assistants, come by. Soonyoung's eyes are fixed down the corridor.

They seem to be flirting with the tall nurse, drawing circles on the floor with their feet. They joke and chat.

They talk about how gynecology pays well, how with that money they could attend their school reunions, they keep on talking. Throwing in English words here and there, they sound vulgar and brash.

Soonyoung is unable to stand it. She pleads with them once again.

"Please start the surgery with the hospital's blood. Please."

"We will use the hospital's blood once we run out. Just let us work."

The tall nurse seems annoyed and returns to her chitchat.

Soonyoung stands in front of the three of them without moving. One of the giggling men stops and stares at her, as if to ask what her deal is.

"Please, the blood, use the hospital's, I would like for you to begin."

"What kind of blood would the hospital have? We don't have any blood."

The man says coldly, and the nurse nudges him. Soonyoung can't fathom the meaning of all this. It all seems like a code. A wave of anxiety arises in her.

The two young men leave, and the tall nurse, her face somewhat softened, tells Soonyoung, "OK, so, the operating surgeon tonight has very good medicine for brain surgery, and I just want you to know that he's going to use it. Ordinary pharmacies don't carry it, so the transaction will be made between you and the hospital."

Soonyoung nods like a doll.

There is noise at the end of the corridor.

Assuming it's the uncle with the blood, Soonyoung springs onto her feet. But she is disappointed once again; it is another patient and his family.

The new patient goes into the operating room next to Myungsoo's, and his family takes over the benches. They all look brave. It must not be a big operation.

Soonyoung finds it impossible to sit still and wait—she goes outside, but the night chill in the garden makes her even madder.

Every now and then a car arrives in front of the hospital, but none of them carry the uncle.

"The blood bank doesn't have it, Baekinje Hospital doesn't either …"

Standing in the garden, she hears these words. She runs to the hospital entrance, where the voice came from.

A driver in a military uniform notices Soonyoung's paper-white face and sunken eyes, then asks,

"Are you the mother of the boy?"

Soonyoung nods.

"I drove your male relative earlier. The blood bank and Baekin-je Hospital had no type B or O. So we went to the Capital Police Hospital and there was nobody on duty there. We phoned someone, and your guy is waiting there still."

Soonyoung feels her legs give in. She sits on the concrete floor.

"Aga, Soonyoung! Where are you? Aigoo, what am I to do."

Her mother comes to the entrance, holding onto the walls as if she were blind.

"No blood in this big, fancy hospital. What can we do for our Myungsoo." She says, rubbing her hands together. "Aga, Soonyoung, draw your blood."

Soonyoung ignores her.

"Aigoo, let's use your blood!" Her mother wails.

"It won't match." Soonyoung answers, still looking away.

"Well then where is she. Let's draw Myunghye's blood."

Mother looks around, searching for Myunghye. She is at home. And Soonyoung remembers when she had her blood tested at school—Myunghye's blood was also type AB. But even if her blood matched, how would they draw a drop of blood from Myunghye's frail body, small and soft like a baby chick.

Soonyoung's mother beats her chest.

"Aigoo, what do we do then." Her mother resorts to surrendering and lying down when even the smallest things go wrong. Once, she went to buy an imported Japanese TV with five thousand hwan, and when the first TV she saw cost fifteen-thousand, she turned around and came home empty handed.

She goes back into the corridor she came out of, groping the walls like a blind person who has lost her way.

Time passes. The uncle doesn't come back.

Leaves shake in the darkness.

Urgent footsteps approach from the inside.

"Myungsoo's mother! Myungsoo's mother!" Someone shouts. "Come to the operating room at once."

Only that voice rings in Soonyoung's head. Nothing else registers in her mind. She can't tell if she's walking or running.

A doctor with a surgeon's white cap appears. Soonyoung feels dizzy, not knowing where she is.

"Are you the boy's guardian?"

"Yes."

"Come and look."

She is now in the operating room.

A nurse pulls on her, telling her she is stepping on something, but Soonyoung can't see what lies under her feet.

The doctor is pointing at Myungsoo's head, cracked open.

"Have a look. It's all a mess in there."

The nurse then pushes Soonyoung outside the operating room and shuts the door on her.

It was only a reddish object that fleeted across her eyes, something like a fantastical red shape you see when you close your eyes.

When and how did the operation begin, even without blood. Mumbling like a sleepwalker, she doesn't notice that her mother is not there. She doesn't know where she is.

Myungsoo's cries.

Soonyoung holds her head in her arms, then starts running down the corridor, away from the cry. But it follows her.

A woman from another family sitting on a bench chimes in,

"It must be bad. They wouldn't bring the family into the operating room otherwise."

Soonyoung keeps on running. Down the corridor behind the operating room, then along the side of the room, but Myungsoo's cry follows her regardless.

Seeing the stairway down to the basement, she heads down, skipping three steps at a time.

Myungsoo's cry seems further away now.

Soonyoung butts her head against the wall. She starts pulling out her own hair.

"Soonyoung! Aga!"

From the corridor, her mother's voice echoes.

Soonyoung keeps on pushing her head against the wall, and as the voice draws near, she lifts herself up, pats down her hair and climbs up the steps.

Her mother says she went to get the medicine.

Soonyoung, looking away from her mother, tells her, "The operation has already begun."

Mother seems to know this already. She says nothing.

No cries from Myungsoo can be heard.

The door to the operating room opens.

The light from the bright lamps in the operating room reaches the bench on the other side of the corridor, and the upper body of the tall nurse peeks out the doorway. Soonyoung's eyes fixate on her face as if frozen.

"Grandma, the medicine you just brought. Fetch ten more packets of that."

Soonyoung watches her mother's small, stout body waddle off down the corridor, and walks over by the window.

She can't see anything outside. Only a giant mass of darkness.

She feels her body as a part of that mass, melted into nothingness.

No noise comes from the operating room.

Families of other patients stare at Soonyoung and whisper among themselves.

Soonyoung sees her mother returning with bottles of medicine and walks away in the opposite direction, going outside.

She can feel her body shaking like a beast.

As she falls into the bushes in the garden, she finds herself saying, "Save him. Please save him." Over and over.

Darkness envelopes her like an unfathomable wall. She cannot see a way out.

Warm wind blows. A wind that brings rain.

Off-duty nursing students in casual clothes pass by, whistling.

They are witnesses of death, yet only their youth seems to exist, and a mellifluous darkness.

Soonyoung gets up and starts back on the curvy path she ran down, towards the hospital.

The footpath seems to go on forever. As she reaches the entrance of the hospital,

"Soonyoung."

The uncle runs toward her with a box under his arm.

Turning her back to the faint hospital light, Soonyoung buries her face in her hands. Tears escape through her fingers.

There is no anger left, nor hatred. Only despair.

"Stop crying. It's all right now."

"What do you mean all right. There is no hope."

Soonyoung breathes out through sobs.

It is nearly ten p.m. by the time the uncle delivers the blood to the nurse.

The Age of Doubt

The uncle sits on the bench outside the operating room and wipes off his sweat. His lips look dry, and his eyes are blank.

He keeps on panting—his aging body seems unable to cope with all the physical and mental shock.

A middle-aged man from another family, looking at the panting uncle with pity, asks him, "You only managed to get the blood now?"

"Yes."

"Where from?"

"I went to the Capital Police Hospital, but there was no one on duty. I've been running around all over the place and only just now …"

He stops to catch his breath, then continues: "Sir, this is not how the world should be. This is wrong. A person's life is at stake and there's no blood and you don't even know if there really isn't or if they are saying there isn't …"

The older man nods. "You are new to this whole business. This is the seventh bottle of blood we bought today. First we tried the blood bank. They tell us there's none left, every time. So I tried negotiating. I filled their pockets with one thousand hwan, some cigarettes, and so forth. Only then they tell me that this was reserved for tomorrow or whatever, and hand over a bottle of blood. You should have tried that, that would have saved you a lot of trouble."

The uncle keeps wiping sweat off his face, saying how wrong this all is.

The door of the operating room opens again. Everyone looks. The nursing student who told Soonyoung not to worry earlier seems to be a messenger.

Muttering to himself like a maniac, the uncle gets up and follows at her heels.

He means to ask how the operation is going.

Swinging his arms, he hurries after the student and then stops her in the corridor before rounding the corner. After a word with her, the uncle returns with a pale face. He lowers his head as if trying to avoid Soonyoung and her mother, who are crouched down on the bench. He sits down, resting his arms on his knees. His pants have blood on them. Soonyoung's mother looks away from him as if he is grim death itself.

Silence takes over. Only the shadows on the wall sway from time to time.

"What time is it now?"

A woman from another family asks an elderly man.

"Eleven-twenty p.m. or so …"

He answers, looking at his watch.

Soonyoung's mother gets up and moves over to the corner and gestures for Soonyoung to come over. She obliges.

"Aga, you'd better go home. You never know what will happen when kids are left alone. You also need to bring the rings and the binyeos tomorrow so that we can sell them and pay for the treatment."

As soon as she is done speaking, Soonyoung runs out, as if to escape. Soonyoung herself doesn't understand why.

Outside, with each footstep heavy and deep, she keeps on muttering, "Please save him. Please save him."

Clasping her hands together in prayer, she lifts them over her head then lowers them, looking up at the sky.

The families of patients and off-duty nurses getting fresh air outside despite the late hour notice Soonyoung's odd movements and sneer.

"Soonyoung!"

The Age of Doubt

Soonyoung continues to walk, her arms moving up and down.

"Soonyoung!"

She turns back and sees the uncle following her.

"I don't know what to say … Please calm down. It's me, it's all my fault …" His voice shakes.

"My boy, my Myungsoo …" Soonyoung stops herself and stares at him. Her eyes fill with hatred. "He's going to die. You have killed him!"

"Please don't say that. This is all because of the money that came in the other day. If I didn't have any money in my pocket, I wouldn't have taken the kids out."

"He's dying. I am afraid of watching it happen, so I'm running away."

"It's me, it's me that should be dying."

Soonyoung cries, thinking in fact she would like him to die instead of Myungsoo.

Sharing the ride with someone else, Soonyoung catches the last taxi leaving the hospital.

Even after the car leaves, the uncle remains standing next to a tree, with his back resting on the hospital's iron gates, his body only a shell.

The night goes on.

The day doesn't break, though she checks more than ten times out the window that is merely an opening in their wood plank wall. From time to time, speeding cars shake the house.

Then, the agonizing night comes to an end.

Soonyoung takes the first tram. It feels like the tram is crawling through the dawn—a minute feels like a lifetime. In the empty tram carriage, Soonyoung rests her hand on her head.

Myungsoo must be lying down in the recovery room. What sins have we committed to deserve otherwise. He must be fine. The worst is over. He must be thirsty. I'll bring him pineapple juice. Some flowers for the room. I'll read him picture books, I'll sing him songs. Soonyoung keeps telling herself, trying to will bad thoughts away.

She gets off the tram.

The hellish red bricks of the hospital building glisten with the blue porcelain light of the morning.

Soonyoung stands at the reception. Words stick in her throat.

The old man at the reception avoids her eyes. His face feels far away, as if in a dream.

"Where's the boy who had the operation last night? In which recovery room?"

The old man doesn't answer. His face goes out of focus.

"I asked which recovery room." Soonyoung starts shaking.

Avoiding her eyes, he says: "He died, probably."

" ... "

"He might be at the morgue ... I'll ask."

The floor underneath her feet swells up and threatens to engulf her. She remains standing nonetheless and doesn't cry out.

Following the old man, her body is stiff like wood.

There are people starting a coal stove in the corridor to make breakfast. As Soonyoung passes, the nursing student from last night grabs her arm.

"Don't cry. You have to keep it together."

Soonyoung shakes her off. She doesn't cry. She just walks, thumping her feet like they were made of wood.

Down a long corridor, then another one, through an annex building, then across a yard—she doesn't know for how long she's been walking. Then she hears her mother's wails, piercing through her consciousness like a stone thrown into water.

Myungsoo lies on top of a tall gurney. A blanket covers his body.

Her mother sprawls on the floor. The uncle is holding onto the gurney, bending over it.

Soonyoung lifts the blanket. An animal wail boils up her throat.

Nothing can be seen on the boy's face, all wrapped up in bandages. All over his arms and legs too, bandages tied up so they won't loosen.

Although Soonyoung tries to hug him, the body won't respond. The stiffness of death has taken over.

Soonyoung holds her mother, sprawling onto the floor with her.

Amid her mother's wail and her own sobs, Soonyoung feels her body dissipate. Only her soul remains, crying and punching the cold walls around her.

The uncle tries to pull Soonyoung and her mother apart.

"You devil! You devil!" Her mother's voice, hoarse from crying, echoes against the morgue walls. "Why did you come to my house! Why did you come to our house! What have we done to deserve this!" Her body shakes as if she's in an exorcist ritual. "You came here to end Myungsoo's life! This wouldn't have happened if you had left long ago, as you should have. Aigoo, bring my baby back!"

The uncle runs out of the morgue.

Soonyoung lifts the blanket again, but she can't see his face. Falling over his body, she buries her face in his stiff waist.

Soonyoung opens her eyes to find herself in the tatami-floored room next to the morgue. Her mother is talking to herself, beating the concrete floor.

"If he was going to die, why did they have to operate on him. Ran their knives all over his limbs and killed him twice. Took flesh off his arms, took flesh off his legs, like he was some calf meat! Aigoo, my poor baby! My poor baby!"

Lying on the floor, Soonyoung's eyes are fixed on the ceiling.

"Myungsoo, my baby! You were just there awake, asking for Grandpa, Grandma, asking me to buy you ice cream. Why did you have to go …"

Soonyoung closes her eyes. She is a mother who ran away. She is a mother who ran away because she was afraid of watching her son die.

"Dirty bastards! Drunk and talking out of their asses while they operated on him. Running their knives over our only baby boy while drinking lemonade, flirting. You call this a hospital? This is a place that kills people, I ought to set this place on fire, aigoo!"

Soonyoung springs up into a seating position. Her eyes widen and shine, and then she falls back again.

This alerts her mother to stop punching the concrete floor and her wailing and to come and help her up. After a while, however, her mother goes back to raving like a mad woman. Then, she tells Soonyoung she needs to let other people know. She goes home, leaving Soonyoung alone.

Again, Soonnyoung lifts the blanket.

Touching the boy's hand. His fingers are crooked. She straightens them, holds them in her hands. The warts on his fingers have traces of red disinfectant.

The Age of Doubt

Touching his head. Can't see his eyes, nose. Can't see his soft, pretty lips.

The uncle, who has just returned, tries to stop her caressing Myungsoo by grabbing her shoulders.

Her body starts to swing and convulse like a carp out of water.

"You're bad luck. Please leave."

He exits the room again.

Soonyoung covers the boy with the blanket and goes to the window.

Outside, leaves hold the blue-green morning dew. Myungsoo is everywhere. He stands in the bushes; he stands in the branches of the tree, his eyes wide as if he's just been caught surprised; he plays with the grass and smiles at Soonyoung; he frowns with a cicada net in his hands. Everywhere she looks, there he is. Soonyoung tries to reach out to her boy. She reaches out and calls his name over and over.

The boy enters the room and stands over her. Soonyoung scrambles to her feet to embrace him, leaps for him, but only falls back to the floor.

She pushes herself up from the floor again—the boy still stands right in front of her. She jumps to touch him, waving her arms in the air, but she only falls again.

"Myungsoo! Stay there, who bought you the cicada net."

Myungsoo has always wanted a cicada net.

"Myungsoo, stay there! Aah, don't leave. Don't go, stay!"

Soonyoung waves her arms, following the ghost of the boy, wandering around the tatami-floored room.

The uncle, coming back out of concern for Soonyoung, sees her in this frenzy and hurries over, shocked.

"Aigoo, this is going to ruin her. Aga, Soonyoung, stay with me."

Soonyoung sits down with her head lowered and listens to her own breathing.

Darkness. Only infinite darkness. She gets up and goes by the window.

It has started to drizzle. The boy stands still in the rain. Further away, over the barbed wire fence, cars and buses pass along the highway.

Soonyoung's friends, alerted by her mother, come over at once to the hospital. A neighbor with a newborn on her back enters the morgue, blotting her eyes with a handkerchief. Everyone cries and wails. Only Soonyoung's first cousin, a Catholic, stays quiet and prays.

Soonyoung, feeling the sweaty hands holding hers and hearing their wails, realizes this hasn't all been a dream.

Her cousin finishes her prayer and brushes a stray hair on Soonyoung's head back.

"Don't cry, Soonyoung, our boy committed no sins in this meaningless world, he will become an angel."

"I wish, I wish there is a heaven. My poor Myungsoo!"

Soonyoung buries her head in her hands again.

"Your crying is not good for his soul." Her cousin says calmly and waves at the uncle. She goes with him into a corner to discuss funeral details.

"We can't put clothes on, not when the body looks like that . . ."

"Should we wrap him in hemp linen?"

"Let's do that. Maybe with silk, like they do in the Middle East," the uncle says.

His need to flaunt his worldly knowledge, just like his lavish appetite, can't be controlled, even in a devastating moment like this. Listening to him go on about Middle Eastern funeral traditions, Soonyoung is full of rage and hatred for him.

It is decided that they will burn the body. Soonyoung resists at first, but sees no other way. Her friends collect money then go pay for the funeral costs as well as the hospital bills. Now that everyone has left to negotiate the funeral preparations and the carrying of the coffin with the hospital, only the neighbor woman with her newborn stays with Soonyoung and her mother, comforting them.

The drizzle has ceased, and the fierce sun has taken over.

Cicadas cry in the cherry blossoms. Soonyoung lies seemingly unconscious next to the morgue, basking in the blazing sun.

Leafy trees in the quiet afternoon draw dark shadows on the morgue building, which is completely detached from the main hospital complex.

Her mother's grievances don't stop. She questions why they had to operate on the boy if he had no chance of survival anyway, why they had to kill him in such a cruel way.

The neighbor has put her newborn down to sleep in the corner and is sat swatting flies away. She gets up and comes over to the side of Soonyoung's mother, fanning the mourning woman's red, bloated face.

Soonyoun's mother says, "Who wants to live? We're all waiting for our time."

Continuing to fan her, the neighbor agrees.

"You know, we can't trust hospitals or doctors at all. Two years ago, my oldest got hit by a car and we went to the free public hospital. It was awful. We went there because it was an American military car that'd hit him. But the longer we stayed there, the more it looked like they were about to let him die. So we bribed the doctor and the nurse in charge. Only then did they start coming in to take care of his wound twice a day. If they hadn't got anything on the side, they'd have only done the operation and not looked in on my child at all afterwards. In the peak of the summer, maggots can start appearing in operation wounds. For the poor, place is a living hell, not a hospital."

Right then they hear a strange noise.

"*Grr! Grr! Grr …*"

Soonyoung and her mother, both lying down, jump to their feet and lift up the blanket covering Myungsoo.

But he remains stiff. No noise comes from him.

It was the neighbor's baby in the corner breathing through his stuffed nose.

Myungsoo's fingernails have started to turn purple.

Soonyoung leaves to go outside.

Holding onto a tree branch, she looks upon the street down the hill, where the tram roars.

She imagines a body crashing against the wired fence, bleeding. She turns away.

Shadows of the trees dance on the windows of the morgue.

Cicadas cry out from the thick foliage surrounding the small morgue building, so far removed from the main hospital building. Their high-pitched buzzing awakens and exhausts every single nerve in Soonyoung's brain.

Shadows of the trees, still, dance on the glass windows of the morgue.

From a certain angle, the tree shadows look like a black horse carriage, with a coachman sitting in the front, dressed in black. Soonyoung stares at the windows, trying to tell the images apart. Perhaps it's the carriage that's come to take Myungsoo to heaven.

The Age of Doubt

The trees continue their shadow dance. The sun leaks in through the leaves—the carriage and the horse's mane become golden.

But all this is a fantasy, born out of her wish to give life back to Myungsoo. There is no carriage. No coachman. No Myungsoo.

Soonyoung grabs onto the grass and sobs. Sobs and sobs, and no Myungsoo.

Her friend's husband passes by her; he's removed his hat.

The cicadas sing, but no Myungsoo, who wanted a cicada net.

By the time the sun sets, the hearse drives a small coffin carrying Myungsoo's body wrapped in a blanket out the rear entrance of the hospital.

Another day dawns after they dumped their child away.

It starts to rain. A drizzle.

Out of the window of their wooden planked wall, a tall chimney of a priest's beautiful house is visible. Plants in his garden bask in the rain.

This is the one refreshing scene that they have access to from their small, dark room.

The uncle has departed without a word, leaving them a note: *I will not take off my mourning clothes until your and your mother's sorrow lessens, even by one hundredth.*

Soonyoung felt a little discomfort knowing he had left after her mother had banged on and on about his faults, but she could not bring herself to feel moved by the dramatic tone of his note, talking about taking off his mourning clothes and whatnot, just like how he went on about the Middle Eastern funeral customs. It would have been better if he had just said sorry. The words in the note felt like an attempt to intellectualize and dramatize his guilt, and it only aroused another inexplicable surge of anger in Soonyoung.

Gazing at the green trees, Soonyoung opens her palm, stares down at it. There's nothing left.

When she raises her head again, she sees Myungsoo sitting on the tip of a leafy branch. He's not only there. At the tip of every branch, other Mungsoos sit. In his old red t-shirt, they look like red berries blooming at the tips of the branches.

Tears in Soonyoung's eyes blur the red of his t-shirt. It turns scarlet, until everything becomes an ocean of red in her eyes. The tears that flow on her cheeks feel like blood.

The sun sets and the darkness comes.

Kim, a cousin-in-law that lives in Seoul, comes by after hearing about Myungsoo.

He speaks to Soonyoung's mother for a while, and turns to Soonyoung with a serious face.

"Who operates on a brain just like that? Had they shown you the X-ray and given you a diagnosis?"

"An X-ray?"

Soonyoung's voice loses all its strength.

"It's only standard procedure to take an X-ray and determine if surgery is necessary. Once you take the X-ray, you can tell if there is any hope for survival, and if not, you don't operate."

Soonyoung stands up.

"What do you mean, an X-ray ... Ah, there must have been an X-ray ..."

In her confused state, Soonyoung continues to get up and then sit down.

With a devastated face, Kim says, "Who on earth would operate on a brain without taking an X-ray first? This is pure negligence."

"Aigoo, so those devils …" Soonyoung's mother starts punching the floor.

"So they didn't even give you a clear diagnosis, didn't take the X-ray, and went ahead with this life-threatening operation."

"…"

"Did they ask you if you consent to the operation, even though it is life-threatening?"

"No, nothing like that."

Kim sighs and lights his cigarette.

"No family members present, no risk waiver signed. No one to witness what actually happened in the operating room."

"…"

"If they judged he needed surgery, then they should have at least guaranteed that the surgery could save his life … But I wonder why they went ahead with the operation even without an X-ray, ending up killing the boy …" Kim throws the butt of his cigarette down and wipes the sweat off his face with a handkerchief.

"If the boy's injury was lethal, there was no need to knife him. It is the doctor's responsibility to let him die in peace. Those imbeciles."

Soonyoung stands still like a piece of paper, like a stone statue.

"Please Mr. Kim, leave us. I can't stand it."

She drops to the floor.

The most prestigious hospital in all of Korea didn't even X-ray him, just like they didn't have blood or medicine.

"There must have been an X-ray!"

She stands up.

It is now the middle of the night.

Myungsoo sits by Soonyoung's head, covered in bandages; his eyes and nose and mouth are not visible.

Soonyoung tries to get up, but her limbs have fallen into paralysis. They grow cold.

Fidgeting with all her strength to break free, she manages to sit up in the dark.

Myungsoo has disappeared like a shadow. Only unknowable darkness fills her sight.

Soonyoung hugs her knees and buries her head, saying: "There was an X-ray machine. Had they used it, my boy wouldn't have had to end up in those suffocating bandages. He wouldn't have had his arms and legs anesthetized or his flesh chopped off."

Cold darkness starts to enfold her.

A night patrol passes by, clapping the wooden batons they use to alert citizens as they approach.

"*Tk! Tk! Tk! …*"

Translated by Dasom Yang
First published June-July 1958

The Age of Doubt

The night before the Second Battle of Seoul, a bomb killed Jinyoung's husband. But before that happened, he had told her about a death he had witnessed, of a North Korean soldier on Kyeong-in Road. The soldier was so young he might as well still have been a boy. This boy soldier lay beneath a tree on the avenue, hordes of flies attacking his exposed entrails like flesh-eating demons. He was begging for a sip of water and calling for his mother in a trance-like state. A fleeing passerby had taken pity on him and left behind a cracked-open watermelon, but the boy was unable to eat it and his breath slowly left his body.

This story foreshadowed his own death, as Jinyoung's husband died in a bombing just a few hours after telling it to her.

Now widowed, Jinyoung, during the Third Battle of Seoul, put her child on her back and left the city with her mother at the last possible moment. But not only did the Chinese army catch up with them before they even reached Anyang, they were bombarded by the UN forces. Countless refugees littered the icy ground. The bull yoked to their wheelbarrow rolled into a ditch along with their belongings. A child cried by a body bleeding out in front of him. Jinyoung turned and ran from the scene as fast as she could.

And now, the nightmarish war was over.

Jinyoung, holding the hand of her son, Munsu, returned to the ruins of Seoul. The ground their house had stood on was a pile of rubble, covering up the normally exposed foundation stones. From among the roof tiles scattered in the weeds, she fished out a single damp and worn book: *A Survey of French Literature*, written in Japanese. This volume had once resided on a bookshelf—the image came to her like a brief, vivid hallucination. She stared for a long time into the empty gaze of her child.

The early summer when Munsu turned nine, Jinyoung dreamed of the boy soldier with his burst-open guts. And this dream, too, was a herald of death, for Munsu died the very next day. It happened on a rainy night.

Jinyoung's mother, widowed young, depended on her only daughter. After Munsu was gone, the old woman repeatedly knocked her head against the threshold of his room lamenting, "It should've been me instead!" Jinyoung herself only stared into space.

The child had been a healthy one. He had happened to stumble on the street and subsequently died in a hospital. If that were all, Jinyoung might have eventually put his death behind her as another wartime tragedy, but that wasn't what had happened. Her son's death had been unnecessary, one caused by his doctor who had neglected to take an X-ray before the invasive neurosurgery and had not even prepared all the medicines her son would need for the procedure. The unanesthetized child had died like a calf in a slaughterhouse. Jinyoung felt as if she had thrown her child into a garbage pit.

The Age of Doubt

Outside, the night rain roars on the avenue.

Jinyoung's pupils, staring unblinking into the ceiling, occasionally flash with the lightning. Her pale cheeks turn red. A fever from her consumption.

The rain continues to fall.

It has barely been a month since the death of her child—a thousand years as far as she's concerned. When she closes her eyes, Jinyoung can still hear her child's wails coming from the operating room, sounding like the cries of a beast.

She gets on her feet and takes a swig of a bottle of wine given to her by a friend who had urged her to take some if she had trouble falling asleep.

As she lies prone on her blanket, her child's wailing echoes in her ears.

She eventually sinks into sleep. In her dreams, she hurries through a maze of alleyways, looking for her child until she sees him wrapped in so many bandages she can't make out his eyes or nose or mouth—she's jolted awake.

Her body is soaked in sweat, and she is shaking.

A new kind of fear, like a dousing of ice water, trickles over her.

The rain has ceased, and the dawn is slowly seeping into her room. Jinyoung stares into space, confused by her jolt of fear. Perhaps her child was haunting her as a ghost. Can a sadder relationship exist between two people? Jinyoung hates herself to the point of nausea.

She hears the ringing of the Catholic church's bells. It reminds her of her ajumoni from Galwoldong whom Jinyoung had asked to take her to mass this coming Sunday. Sunday is today.

Her Galwoldong ajumoni, as promised, arrives just before

eight. She is the wife of a distant relative of Jinyoung's who passed away a long time ago. With no children, she is a zealously devout Catholic, but recently had come into a nasty tangle concerning her gye money-lending circle. Jinyoung had scraped every bit of her money to put in her share of the gye with the aim of receiving a pay-out of 200,000 hwan, but then she had to forego it because her Galwoldong ajumoni, who happened to be the gye manager, urgently needed it to pay off the others.

Wearing ramie clothes as delicate as cicada wings, her ajumoni had comforted Jinyoung's mother when Munsu died, flashing her gold-capped incisor as she made her condolences.

Jinyoung's mother would grab the hand of anyone she met and launch into a lament about her lost grandson. Jinyoung hates her for doing that, but she can't help seeing how devastating it is for her mother, now that she has only a lone daughter to care for her in this world.

"Don't cry, hyoungnim," her ajumoni had said to her mother. "You must concentrate on the living now. Think of how Jinyoung must feel. Please, dry your tears. Let's think of how we're going to face the future."

Jinyoung has no job, and indeed the only future facing her now is one of darkness.

Her ajumoni, comforting Jinyoung's mother with sweet-sounding words, had readjusted her loosened breast-tie—she always wore a fancy breast-tie even with summer robes—and said, "Let's try to live again, shall we … And I have my own plans for you. I will try, hyoungnim, to return your gye money at least, even if just the principal …"

This had cheered up Jinyoung's mother quite a bit.

Jinyoung silently puts on her socks. The three of them come

out into the avenue where the lines of trees along the road create a chilly shade.

Jinyoung's mother was raised Buddhist and should've been reluctant to step into a Catholic church, but it was all fine according to her. Such things were up to her daughter, anyway …

Slipping into the intimate space beneath Jinyoung's parasol, her ajumoni whispered, "As long as we are with the Lord, we can never be unhappy. The Lord loves you, which is why he has called your name. In this human world where nothing has meaning, only the Lord can be the light."

Her ajumoni is always spouting the same things believers say to each other.

Casting her eyes down at the ground, Jinyoung says, "I'm not going because of my salvation. I just want to think there's a heaven, and that my Munsu is happy there."

"Yes, he went to heaven. Such a good child … Yes indeed, he is playing in the flowery hills of heaven as we speak."

She's trying her best, as an elder family member, to comfort Jinyoung, but she's awkward in her attempts.

"Even if the hills have flowers, he will still be lonely. He'll think of his mother," mumbles Jinyoung as she looks up to the sky. The clouds are like withered leaves.

"Don't say such things, just prepare for your first holy communion." Her ajumoni's voice seems to creep towards her from a far horizon. "Did you know that Sangbae got baptized?"

Mechanically, Jinyoung replies, "That atheist … baptized …?"

"He's changed a lot recently."

There's a faint smell of powder. The gold tooth glints from the side of her ajumoni's mouth.

Sangbae is a college student boarder at her ajumoni's house.

Just last spring he had said to Jinyoung, "Do you really believe all that about Jesus walking on water? Ha! Probably he kept putting one foot down before the other would sink!" Impressed by his own clever quip, delivered in his Busan satoori, Sangbae had flared his nostrils as he laughed.

Her ajumoni dabs at her sweat with a handkerchief and goes on to say, "That child will move on soon. His father is relocating to Seoul for business ... So I'd hoped he would get baptized before he left ..."

What a soft and gentle voice.

At the church doors, the leaves of the avenue's gingko trees shatter the sunlight into fragments on the pavement. Light pink gladioli bloom on the flowerbed, bringing to mind the Buddhist symbol of lotus flowers. Jinyoung's thoughts listlessly move on to meaningless musing about the cultural distance between the East and West—she pulls herself together. She is here to meet the Lord for the sake of Munsu, she can't have these cynical thoughts overtake respectful awe, not in the house of God. But the thoughts keep arising from what she's seeing; does this mean there's enough room in her mind, despite the sadness that fills her heart, for such thoughts? Jinyoung feels ashamed of herself before Munsu. She is chastened.

She stares down at her ajumoni's damp bosom that smells of powder.

Children gather in the cool shade of a tree. Next to them is a middle-aged man selling crosses and Bibles laid out on a blanket. Jinyoung stares at the scene before her like a traveler in a strange land. In her mind, which feels utterly separate from the scene before her, cold winds blow.

Jinyoung enters the church. Her ajumoni wraps her shoes in

a cloth and says, "Children come to this mass, and it can get noisy. Come to the earlier one next time."

What catches Jinyoung's attention isn't so much what her ajumoni is saying but the ridiculous manner in which everyone carries their shoes into church. *I went to the house of the Lord to love his son Jesus, and when my eyes were closed, someone stole my shoes.* This mocking refrain echoes in her head. But then, Jinyoung feels a strange sort of fear. To insult a god in his house of worship—feeling guilty, she quickly catches up with her ajumoni.

Mass begins.

"I beseech you my Lord on behalf of my poor son Munsu. With all my heart … I beseech you with all my heart. Please release him from that suffering, please give his little soul peace …"

While Jinyoung mumbles these words with her eyes closed, the mocking voice in her head mumbles more persistently: *Munsu is dead. He's gone forever and ever.* Jinyoung's vision grows dark as the voice keeps whispering. *They cut open his skull with a knife and killed him. They killed him without mercy.*

It's like a scarlet ball of fire is rolling before her closed eyelids. The mocking voice keeps up its tirade. The hoarse cries of a child, sounding as if compressed in a dark and narrow afterlife … Jinyoung, sweating, opens her eyes. Her mother is sitting in front of her, and the smell of sweat wafts from her mother's head. Panic rises in Jinyoung—the white veils worn by the churchgoers bleaching her sight, her mind—

She turns her head towards the children's choir. They look like a line of shelved war rations at a store. The children create a cacophony of voices singing in different keys, ringing in her ears like the noise of an organ that hasn't taken in enough wind.

She pictures herself miserably kneeling amidst this noise. How ridiculous and pathetic she must look.

Once more, she closes her eyes. But she cannot help hating herself. She cannot help but hate how she can't forget herself. She yearns to step away from this objective self-image and struggles to immerse herself in an ideal, in seeing that this God and Munsu's death as equally mysterious, and that no one could criticize such mysteries. That, at least, she believes in.

When Jinyoung had decided to go to the church for the first time, she'd thought that while religion was an artificially created presumption, she would willingly turn herself into a clown or a tumbling doll if it meant it brought Munsu relief. But her forced intentions refuse to set in her heart.

Mass is almost over. Jinyoung spots a collection pouch attached to a long stick making its way towards her among the parishioners. Once her ajumoni hastily tosses in a few coins, this butterfly net of a collection pouch surreptitiously moves on to the row behind her. It reminds Jinyoung of the weathered hats of street performers being passed around onlookers for coins. This thought makes Jinyoung leave before the mass is over.

She sits beneath a tree and looks into her mother's bloodshot eyes as the latter emerges from the church. Various children around Munsu's age put on their shoes before running off to their games.

The church in the summer sunlight wavers ever so slightly under her gaze.

It's morning, and Jinyoung sits on the maru doing nothing. When her mother tells her to stop being stuffed up in the house and go take a walk, the words grate against Jinyoung's nerves so much that she frowns and clasps her head in her arms.

It's not just about being stuffed up. Jinyoung needs to go out and find a job.

Her head still in her arms, Jinyoung agonizes over where she's supposed to go and whom she's supposed to beg for work. Not to mention how sick she is in the lungs …

Jinyoung thinks of Munsu. How pathetic she and her mother must look in their desperate struggle to live on.

Midday sunlight crashes onto their courtyard. The flies that buzzed around the tree have left the shrinking shade to hover around Jinyoung's face. Her mother is by the earthen jars in a corner of the courtyard, starching their laundry. Her mother's profile seen through the wide leaves of the sunflower stalks reminds Jinyoung of jellyfish floating on the ocean's currents. As lethargic as such creatures may be, they still have their survival instincts … they just go on living … How awful she is to have such cruel thoughts about her mother. She waves away the irritating flies and lies down on the maru.

The sky is blue. Clouds float past. The whole expanse suddenly feels like the ocean, and the clouds are jellyfish flowing with the current. Jinyoung is unnerved by the illusion that she isn't on her back but lying on her stomach, staring into water.

The sun moves on a little to the west, lengthening the shadow of the tree in their courtyard by two or three palm widths. Jinyoung turns her body onto her left side and gazes into the dirt of the courtyard.

The gates creak open, and a visitor's shadow enters Jinyoung's field of vision. Her gaze slowly follows it to the visitor herself. A young Buddhist nun carrying a monk's sack. Like a subject in a surrealist painting, the tall nun walks silently towards her, stepping on her own shadow.

Presently, the nun gathers her palms and speaks. "My lady!"

The loud voice of a girl, its bright confidence completely shattering the serenity of her appearance. Her shoulders are bowed from the weight of the sack, which makes her look at least forty—but as Jinyoung sits up, the nun herself is immediately exhausted by the darkness in Jinyoung's eyes.

When she sees Jinyoung's mother wiping her hands on her apron and coming towards her, the nun tries to recover her cheer and says, "Hello!" Her voice is clear and friendly.

Jinyoung's mother sits down at the edge of the maru and sighs. "Back when our lives were better, I, too, followed Buddha and lit candles in every temple I came across, but it was no use. They say a carefully built tower can never fall, but that's a lie—"

In the middle of this well-rehearsed, long lament, the nun blinks as she suddenly cuts her off. "How terrible for you! Oh my ... But I'm not here to ask for alms ... Oh, I was wondering if you would buy some rice ... It's so heavy on my shoulders, you see ..." She seems less interested in sad stories than in striking a deal. How dear even the cheapest form of pity has become in this world! The sight of her mother begging for scraps of sympathy inspires more pity than resentment in Jinyoung.

Her mother, who still has many words left to say, looks somewhat miffed at being thwarted.

The nun puts her sack down on the porch and baldly states her business one more time. "It's just too heavy to carry around! I wish I could lessen my burden a bit before I move on."

Only then does the old woman catch on and rein in her

emotions, brush off her skirt looking the nun directly in the eye, and strike back.

"Well, if you're selling it anyway, why don't we buy some then. Give us a lot extra."

The nun starts to measure out the rice with her measuring box. Jinyoung's mother complains that the measuring box is too small, and the nun pushes away the old woman's hands because they keep trying to pile up the rice on the box. Still, they manage to settle on a deal.

At the end of it, the old woman politely asks, "Where is your temple, sunim?"

"Yes? Oh yes, it's on the hill behind the school."

Not that far of a walk, even with a load of rice on one's back.

Even after the nun has left, Jinyoung's mother remains standing in the courtyard, lost in thought.

"Jinyoung-ah," she calls to her daughter in a low voice.

Instead of answering, Jinyoung looks into her mother's eyes.

"It makes my heart wretched to leave Munsu behind like this. To not even have a gravesite ... Let's put his nameplate on the temple!"

Jinyoung's gaze fixes on her mother's face.

"The temple is close by, and it's new, they won't be too difficult about it ... I feel such pity for my grandson. His soul must be wandering the Earth in tears, looking for a home."

Jinyoung turns her head toward the sunflowers near the earthen jars. After a long time, she says, "Let's do that." She's not really looking at the sunflowers but her eyes remain on them. "But why did you treat that nun like a peddler? When you were thinking of giving the child to the temple—"

"What a load of nonsense. Business is business, and life is life. And can a nun that goes around selling donated rice be a real nun?"

Jinyoung feels a swell of hatred towards her mother. "Then why do you want to go to a temple that has such monks?"

"Who goes to a temple because of the monks? We go because of Buddha."

She isn't wrong. At the same time, Jinyoung remembers how her ajumoni paid back the twenty thousand hwan of her principal while scolding her for not attending mass. Now that she's agreed to go to the Buddhist temple, Jinyoung feels like she's betrayed her ajumoni and feels guilt. Even if the money had been rightfully hers to begin with, she wonders if even this fake generosity can become a debt of sorts. However, if the purpose of Jinyoung's religion is solely to memorialize Munsu, the temple does make a more practical choice than the Catholic church. If she can come up with the money, she might even get them to do a ceremony for him.

Jinyoung gets to her feet.

The sun is about to completely set over the western mountains. She walks out into the street and buys streptomycin at a local pharmacy instead of Y— Hospital, where she stopped going to. Her Galwoldong ajumoni said the doctor at Y— Hospital was a Catholic and could be trusted. But they learned that he would only give them a third of a dose of any injection at a time. They couldn't continue going to him after that.

Fondling her medicine bottle, Jinyoung stands in the street for a long time before slipping into S— Clinic. She knows who the doctor is there because he is her neighbor. But S— Clinic itself is not a licensed medical clinic.

Jinyoung holds out her medicine bottle to the nurse, who is so awkward that it seems she is very new at her job. The doctor is never happy with patients who come in with their own medicine to get shots, ones they can charge for neither medicine nor consultation. Which is why Jinyoung never even gets to see a doctor. But at that moment, when a doctor administering to a patient happens to turn around and show his face, Jinyoung can't help her shock—he is not a doctor! Only some loaf who happens to live in their neighborhood. Just then, the real doctor bustles by with paperwork in his hand, and leaves the room as swiftly as he came in. The loaf, fidgeting under Jinyoung's withering stare, barks at the nurse, "Two grams of penicillin!" and slips out of the room himself.

The loaf probably thinks of penicillin as some panacea, especially for all the diseases he doesn't know how to diagnose.

Jinyoung stands there, stupefied, not noticing that the nurse with unwashed hands is very awkwardly trying to stick a syringe into her streptomycin. When Jinyoung comes to her senses, she can see cloudy liquid in the syringe; the nurse has extracted the medicine without waiting for it to dissolve.

She can stand it no longer.

"No, it hasn't even dissolved yet! Are you trying to kill me?"

Jinyoung barks at the nurse, snatches the bottle from her, and frantically shakes it.

An old woman with the jaundiced face, sitting before them and waiting for her penicillin shot, shoots the nurse a nervous look.

Jinyoung leaves the hospital. It's already night.

She keeps thinking about what happened just now—wresting the bottle from the nurse's hands and shouting, "Are you trying to kill me?"—and thinks how odd that is, for in this un-bearable life so unsparing of tragedy, hadn't she herself longed for death many times?

Jinyoung wants to look up at the night sky and laugh until her belly bursts. But she's swept up in a terrifying intuition that once she lets loose this laughter, her mind will give way to irre-versible madness.

Maybe I'm already mad. Maybe everything I've seen today is an illusion. Maybe it isn't night right now, but broad daylight.

Jinyoung wraps her head in her arms and runs back home.

An iced tea seller in a straw hat silently watches her disappear down the street.

The moon, surrounded by its halo, is almost red. A wind blows, heavy with the portent of rain.

Ever since the visit of the nun with the rice, Jinyoung's moth-er has wanted to visit the temple for Baekjung, or Buddhist All Souls' Day. A day one makes food offerings to the dead.

The day before Baekjung, the old woman gives a photo of Mun-su and two thousand hwan to the temple to make the necessary arrangements. The next day, as soon as the sky begins to light up, Jinyoung sets out with her mother carrying a basket of fruit.

Once they get to the elementary school and walk up the hill, they can see inside the temple courtyard below. It is busy with Baekjung preparations, with many women from the neighbor-hood helping out.

The temple abbot, a big man, sees Jinyoung's mother and beams. "How devout you are, to come at such an early time!"

The old woman brings her handkerchief to her eyes.

"Sunim, please lead the spirit of our child to heaven. I beg of you. That poor thing …" She blows her nose.

The abbot, who has already sat through the lament once before the previous evening, is not to be moved by such words.

"However," he interrupts in a perfectly businesslike voice, "the chief's wife, who said she would go first, isn't here yet. What to do?" He seems to ponder something.

The chief of what? Jinyoung has no idea, but he and his wife must be very important people at the temple.

Jinyoung's mother puts on a humiliating smile for the abbot and says, "Then do take care of my grandson first, sunim."

He stares at her for a long time. "Then maybe you should go first …" Turning, he calls out to a passing nun, "Little Sister!"

Little Sister looks back at who is calling her. Her face is shriveled with wrinkles; she looks much older than the abbot, who still has smooth skin. Even her expression itself is emaciated.

"These people gave us two thousand hwan yesterday, but the chief's wife isn't here yet so why don't we finish them off first?"

His voice is laden with respect for the old nun. Instead of answering him, she gives the mother and daughter a once-over, and perhaps thinking the amount is too small, walks away.

The sun is rising from behind the peak. It is a beautiful morning, but Jinyoung looks upon it as if it's a lifeless mural.

Jinyoung thinks of how shameless it is of her mother to pay the smallest fee but ask for the first service.

A young monk comes in carrying offerings.

"Excuse me," says Jinyoung's mother to the monk, "isn't there a tall nun here?" She means the nun who had come to sell the rice.

"She's not usually at the temple," he replies and goes back into the main worship hall.

The ceremony is about to start. The old nun starts knocking

her moktak and begins to recite a sutra as if talking in her sleep, and Jinyoung is disappointed. It isn't going to be the big, loud-voiced abbot doing the recitation. If one has to do one of these rituals, surely it wouldn't have hurt to have it done by the best . . .

As the nun recites the sutra, she steals a look at Jinyoung, who is stupidly standing next to her repeatedly bowing mother.

The violet dress Jinyoung is wearing accentuates her slim waist. Her face is pale, and her eyes a deep black.

The nun, displeased, continues to steal her looks. Whenever Jinyoung feels her eye on her, she awkwardly bows herself, coming down on all fours. There is an old saying—a bad monk's mind is on the rice offerings and not the praying—but perhaps the saying should go, a bad nun's mind is on the people who don't bow deeply enough and not the praying. Jinyoung grows more and more tired, feeling as if she were battling something out with the nun.

A little while later, the abbot comes rushing into the prayer hall.

"Little Sister, finish up quickly, the chief's wife arrived, just stop wherever you are!"

He quickly puts on an ink-dyed robe that had been hanging in the corner of the prayer hall over his clothes while the old nun moves from the Buddhist statue to the altar for spirits. It is uncertain as to whether she had finished reciting the sutra. The young monk from earlier, who had been moving offerings, comes in with a large dish. He turns to the mother and daughter and gestures for them to come to the altar.

Jinyoung goes to where Munsu's photo is laid and kneels before it. This cold floor is where her hot tears finally begin to spill. She can almost feel the touch of Munsu's hand.

"Oh Munsu. Have as much food as you want. My poor, poor grandchild!"

Jinyoung has never heard her mother's voice sound so sad. Her mother plants some incense and places twenty ten-hwan bills, stiff and new as if they'd been brought straight from the bank. Jinyoung also gets up and places an incense stick. When she turns, she can see the monk craning his neck to count the money. The stiff new bills look like they could each be a hundred hwan; Jinyoung bows her head at the thought, ashamed of what the monk might think later.

The young monk pushes the money aside and says, sheepishly, "The offering is too little. You need money in the next world, just as you need it in this one. Don't you think he wants to have some fun with his friends before he goes on his journey?"

Jinyoung can feel her blood rushing to her head. In her heart, she curses her mother for being so cheap as to offer such little money.

The young monk puts a little bit of each food onto the dish he brought with him. Some greens, tteok, fish, fruit—his hand goes for each plate on the altar. Just when his hand reaches for an especially tasty yakgwa, the nun who has been hitting a moktak all this time barks at him, "Leave those!"

The young monk gives Jinyoung a look as he goes to put the food out for "the little demons."

Jinyoung is infuriated. She is well aware that the whole thing is a business transaction from the start. But now, it's hard not to have any other reaction than anger. She buries her face in her hands as she explodes into tears. This undirected rage inside her pours out in her cries. And in her sobbing, she feels Munsu's arms around her neck holding onto her. The loneliness and longing surges up inside her into near madness.

Returning from having placed the food on the offering stone

outside, the young monk gathers the fruit and says, "You can take these back. Where is your wrapping cloth?" He turns to look at Jinyoung's mother.

With bloodshot eyes, Jinyoung glares at the monk and says, "We don't care. You can have them." Her voice has an edge to it.

The old nun, who has come out of the hall after finishing things up, now asks them, "Why do you not take back what you brought with you?"

Jinyoung refuses to even look at her.

Her mother answers instead, "Well, the thing is …" She carefully glances at Jinyoung's face.

The old nun swallows her spit. "Do you think a monk could eat otherwise?"

Jinyoung's eyes flash.

"Your breakfast isn't ready yet, it's too early for the rice to be done. Please wait," says the young monk before he leaves them.

Outside, her knees almost giving way, Jinyoung manages to sit down on one of the foundation stones of the prayer hall. *You need money in the next world, just as you need it in this one.* Of course it had been a transaction all along. Does that mean the meaningfulness behind Munsu's memorial is calculated according to the amount of money on the altar? As she wallows in this rage and sadness, a well-dressed young woman, probably that wife of the chief, is being led by the abbot into the prayer hall. In a little while, the sound of a sutra being recited comes ringing out, loud enough to wake a sleeping Buddha, a sound coming straight from the gut.

Jinyoung gets to her feet.

"Mother, let's just go."

They're not here to eat breakfast anyway. Jinyoung is already walking away, and knowing there's nothing in her power to make her stay, her mother says to the old nun lingering in the courtyard, "We're off then, sunim."

"That's a shame, you should have breakfast … You're off now?"

She doesn't try to make them stay. Escorting them to the temple gates, she says, again, "Do you think a monk could eat otherwise?"

Jinyoung feels more overwhelmed with the absurdity of it all than angry.

On the way down the hill, she rips out handfuls of weeds as she sobs. It feels like she has left Munsu behind all by himself in a stranger's home without enough money for his board.

Jinyoung touches her forehead, which is burning up.

All summer Jinyoung has been sick. Her tuberculosis, minor at first, has worsened as she neglected to treat it. Other sicknesses are taking hold as well. Drinking cold water gives her stomach troubles. Her eyes got infected, and her lips crack often. Even her ears took their turn getting sick. And the cavities she hasn't dealt with for years ache day and night.

She feels an all-consuming terror as her body unravels, a terror that has a life of its own, like a worm stretched out under direct sunlight.

And now, as she has feared before, her mind is unraveling as well.

Every night she hears the cries of a child and the sound of mountains, hills, and houses collapsing. When she closes her eyes, shards of shattered glass fly through the air and into her face, and she sees the pleading boy soldier with his burst gut, her husband's face, her child's face, pink lights, yellow lights, blue lights, and lastly black lights, lights that overlap each other until an infinite space has Jinyoung completely surrounded like fog.

Hearing and touch and vision—in that order, Jinyoung's senses leave the orbit of her self.

She finally drags her neglected body to H— Hospital, but even then, she only manages to receive treatment for a week before she stops going.

It is also because she needs to spend what little money they have left on survival, but the real reason is because at the hospital, she witnessed empty bottles of imported medicines being sold as new.

Y— Hospital doctored their doses, S— Clinic was fraudulent. And H— Hospital sold empty medicine bottles.

When she saw a nurse counting empty bottles at the hospital, Jinyoung had wondered if they would be sold to peddlers of fake medicine. But H— was hardly the only hospital that sold empty bottles, and no one could say these bottles were going to be used only to sell fake medicine. She knows such bottles are often repurposed as ink or watercolor bottles, or even pepper containers. But it is also true that the street markets are overflowing with fake medicines. And peddlers trumpet these fakes as the realest of the real. As Jinyoung's trust in their profession erodes, doctors, who should adhere to the moral authority of their calling, seem no better than such peddlers. While even these humble bottles are clearly the private property of the doctor, with which he has the right to do whatever he pleases, it isn't such rights that come to mind when Jinyoung sees the empty bottles but the fake medicine that proliferate like the plague on the streets.

The sunflowers have seeds now.

A few days before, just as she had promised, Jinyoung's aju-moni brought her the last ten thousand hwan of the principal she owed. This meant she has finally repaid them the whole hundred thousand hwan amount, but very little of that money that had trickled into the house is left now.

As Jinyoung's ajumoni handed over the money and rose to leave, she expressed her displeasure at their having placed Mun-su's mortuary tablet at the temple. Why do you worship idols, she said. Jinyoung wanted to point out that Christians wor-shiped their idols, too, but she repressed this urge and simply stared blankly at her ajumoni. She did not have a way to explain the contradictions in her own self.

It is now the holiday of Chuseok.

Jinyoung does not stop her mother from going to the temple. If anything, she takes care to put together for her a basket of fruit. Pears, apples, grapes, chestnuts, jujubes, and some sweet treats as well.

As she watches from their gate her mother carrying the basket to the temple, Jinyoung suddenly remembers the nun's words, "Do you think a monk could eat otherwise?" To think that monks would be eating the food that was meant for Mun-su's soul. What a waste. How distasteful. But then, her face grows red with shame. Why am I thinking such petty thoughts …

Jinyoung locks the gate and goes up the mountain behind their house. She wants to cry, or scream.

There are several tiny shacks erected on that mountain. There isn't a single blooming wildflower or green tree; the place is a slum, and this denuded mountain can hardly be called a moun-tain, although the people continue to do so.

The spidery, skinny arm of a little girl, drawing water from a shallow spring, the yellow faces peeking out of the shacks—Jinyoung, who has come up this hill to cry and scream, realizes that here, she is closer to being a lazy woman of luxury.

She keeps climbing and comes upon a large rock, where she sits down.

The city seen from this mountain is a mess. Houses clumped together like aphids on a plant, a sprinkling of temples and churches, and a mix of Western and Eastern buildings as if the city was in transition—the jumble of life that shatters the balance of things.

If this city has a dream, maybe they are the trees along the avenues? Or the clouds sweeping by the violet-hued mountains in the distance?

Jinyoung cradles her narrow chin.

City noise buzzes like a faraway swarm of bees, and an expensive car glides down a road towards a mountain villa. From her perspective on the mountain, Jinyoung sees the city might as well be no more significant than a beetle. A beetle slowly crawling to who knows where . . .

She shakes her head and looks around her. What aimless musings. *But so what*, Jinyoung says to herself, annoyed over nothing. *So what if it looks like a beetle, or aphids, so what about the trees and the clouds . . .*

Jinyoung sweeps her hair back.

All suffering is in me. All contradictions are in me. Gods, Munsu, they are all in me.

But those aren't real things. Like a whore, I bowed my head at two different places of worship. And I made offerings of goods and money. But maybe that was just a transaction fee I was giving to the gods. I'm sure some of those fees went towards a few meals for the monks, at least. I was trying to fool myself though. Munsu was never there, or anywhere now.

Thick wisps of her hair come over her forehead, and she sweeps them back again. Her hand is so pale it is almost transparent.

Mystery, premonitions, dreams, they're all just coincidences. But Munsu's death, wasn't it a clear case of a manmade blunder? And to say that we all die anyway someday … Of course we do, of old age … Even if the child was going to die anyway from the accident, he never should've been killed that way, like some calf in a slaughterhouse … People, it's people I must hate. Why think about a god that we don't even know exists. But didn't I say gods don't exist a moment ago … I don't know. But people, I want to hate people. I want to rebel. I want to curse all murderers, those vandals of life.

Her thoughts are coming out in mumbles, like she's a drunk.

A shadow falls over Jinyoung's pale face. A cloud passes overhead in the deep blue autumn sky. In the city below, people are dressed for Chuseok, looking like bits of colored paper.

Jinyoung stares at them with feverish eyes and gets up. She has nothing left in her, not even rebellion. Only an endless, empty maze that stretches into the horizon.

She sweeps her hair out of her face again and comes down the mountain.

And the yellow faces peering at her make her repeat her previous realization that here, she is only at best a superfluous woman of luxury.

On a cold day right before the Seol holiday, her Galwoldong ajumoni, wrapped in a thick scarf, comes to see Jinyoung. She looks a touch less carefully put together than usual.

"I have something I wanted to discuss with you … I simply cannot believe what just happened …"

Jinyoung gives her a questioning look.

Visibly uncomfortable with what she's about to say, her ajumoni shifts in her seat and says, "You-you know. This person I loaned some money to died, what am I going to do?"

Jinyoung's look turns to one of suspicion.

"He took my money in May, and I never got to receive a single interest payment before he …"

The look on Jinyoung's face makes her ajumoni fall silent. May was the month Jinyoung was supposed to collect on the gye money-lending club, not to mention the last month of the gye. Not only that, there are also several people around her eager to get in on her windfall that will never come.

Jinyoung finally opens her mouth. "How much money did you lend him?"

"500,000 hwan."

Jinyoung hides her surprise. She had thought her ajumoni only had debts because of her gye, but she had been playing with such a large sum of money all this time?

She gives her ajumoni a cold look.

Tears in her eyes, her ajumoni says, "With no husband or child, that money was the last thing left to me. Think of how much money I've lost. If I can get through this, I could at least repay my debts, but if I lose it, then it will be complete ruin for me."

This only makes Jinyoung want to shout at her for her ridiculous vanity, acting like she'd lost a business or something.

Jinyoung's ajumoni wipes her tears and explains her situation. The dead man had been a director of the company that spent her money, and after borrowing 500,000 hwan from her, she hadn't seen a single coin in interest. Anxious, her ajumoni pleaded with the director to give her back her principal at least, but he refused. After discussing it with someone at her church, this someone said her husband, a Mr. Kim, would take care of it for her. This Mr. Kim proved very effective in his methods, and he managed to secure a promissory note in the name of the company's owner, and just a few days later, the director died in a car accident. It was a good thing they'd obtained that promissory note in the company owner's name, but for some reason, this Mr. Kim refused to hand over the promissory note, and it was impossible to discern what he was up to. But it wasn't as if she could openly suspect him or displease him, because the person originally responsible for the money was dead and couldn't corroborate her side of the story, and "being a mere woman, I couldn't possibly go to some company owner and demand the money," says her ajumoni as she pounds her chest in frustration.

Once she has listened to the story, Jinyoung asks, "How do you even know this director whom you lent such a big sum of money to?"

"Well … You know that boy, Sangbae. He was Sangbae's father."

"What? The one you said you converted to Catholicism?"

Her ajumoni's face reddens. Jinyoung can't believe it. Then, she remembers that the father was supposed to move to Seoul for work.

"So he used your religion to fool you into trusting him."

Perhaps finding Jinyoung's fury blinding, her ajumoni lowers her gaze.

"Thinking back on it now, they had planned the whole thing from the start. Even the baptism—"

"Because if you think about it, what better guarantee on a debt than religion?"

Her ajumoni visibly wilts at Jinyoung's mockery, and Jinyoung turns her eyes from her.

To have loaned someone money just because they were sprinkled with some holy water, just because they were so-called believers—how stupid this woman was. This makes Jinyoung look up at her ajumoni again. All desire to mock her for her weakness evaporates.

"So what are you going to do?"

"I don't know. I wanted to discuss it with you."

"I think that Mr. Kim should take care of the situation and you should hold the promissory note."

"But what if he doesn't take care of it for me because I asked for the note?"

"Then we'll know for sure he has other motives."

"If Mr. Kim doesn't comply, would you help me talk to him? I'm just one woman, he won't take it kindly if I make demands …" Her voice trailed off on a begging note.

"Well …"

Jinyoung can't stand messy business like this. But to know a friend's weakness and to not help them seems like a much worse path to take.

So she puts on a nonchalant face and says, "I'll come with you."

That's when her mother, who knows nothing of what they'd just talked about, enters with a low table laden with lunch. Her ajumoni seems to perk up over their meal and becomes chattier as they eat.

"How funny that one still has problems when one has money.

Now I'm so scared of people that I probably won't lend anyone any."

Jinyoung expressionlessly swallows her bite and says, "Forget everything else and open a shop once you get your money back. Leave your pride … Once I get some capital, I'm going to sell things, too."

"But you can get a job instead."

"Do you think that's easy? I'm ready to sell bread on the street if that's what it takes."

"But you're educated, you can get a job if you want to. It's me who should be selling bread. But you know, gye is the best way to make money. It takes no effort at all …"

Her ajumoni puts down her spoon and picks at her teeth with a match.

Of course that's what you think, with your kind of attitude towards life … Jinyoung stops herself from saying this and looks into her ajumoni's eyes. They are clear and bright, without a shade of ill intent.

"In any case, we have to make money. Money is king. That's the way the world is …" Her ajumoni's tone is somehow mixed with irritation and denial of her own recent, self-made mess.

"That's what they say," her mother says approvingly. "Outliving your children only brings you hunger, but money in your pocket makes you feel secure."

A light panic comes over Jinyoung. She shakes her head as if to erase them from her vision.

"Ah, hyoungnim, do you think we'll ever make it to heaven? With all this talk of money, money, money …" Her ajumoni trails off into soft laughter as she puts on her gloves.

Jinyoung detects a whiff of anxiety and discontent in her

laughter. She looks up at her. *What a tortured and lonely person this woman is …*

After her ajumoni leaves, Jinyoung collapses on the floor. She feels her body loosening up like balls of cotton.

She imagines the stove in the room leaking fatal gas. The gas filling the room and her dying in it.

And indeed, she falls into an uneasy sleep.

The boy with the burst gut appears in her dream. Jinyoung does everything she can to wake up from it.

"It's the holidays in a couple of days, I should send the temple a thousand hwan …"

Her mother's voice comes from her side. Jinyoung rolls around to face her and opens her eyes.

"Ghosts are the same as people … Everyone having their share but our Munsu not having any. And he's going to be waiting for his mother."

Jinyoung is completely awake. She stands up, throws on her coat, and comes out on the maru, winding her scarf around her neck.

Jinyoung grabs a matchbox from the kitchen, thrusts it into her coat pocket, and sets out.

She's finally going to do something that she decided to do a while ago.

Her steps make crunching sounds in the snow as she walks up the hill. Jinyoung feels the hairs standing up all over her body like a hedgehog.

Her scarf and coattails flutter in the wind. Snow from the tree branches softly land on the collar of her coat.

Jinyoung is headed for the temple.

When she enters the temple courtyard, the "Do you think a

monk could eat otherwise?" nun happens to be coming out of the sleeping quarters. The temple eerily has no trace of other people.

Jinyoung can feel the muscles on her face twitch as she sidles up to the nun.

"Excuse me, we are moving to the country, and we'd like to take our child's photograph and mortuary tablet with us."

She says this in a low voice with her head bowed. The nun's unfocused eyes finally seem to register who Jinyoung is.

"You're moving? That's fine, just leave those things here. You can still remember him by posting us money over the holidays."

Jinyoung's head jerks upward and she turns to face the nun and snaps, "What I do or don't do is none of your business, just give me back his photograph!"

The nun is taken aback and grumbles as she heads to the prayer hall.

Once she comes back with Munsu's photograph and tablet, Jinyoung snatches them from her and strides out of the temple without so much as a goodbye.

The angry nun narrows her eyes at Jinyoung's retreat. Once again grumbling, she heads for the outhouse.

Jinyoung isn't really angry at the nun. She just wanted to get the photograph as quickly as possible and leave the temple. Her shouting had been from nerves if anything.

Jinyoung follows the twisting path up the mountain. She glances right and left. When she reaches a patch of dry grass behind a large boulder, she flops down. There, she stares down at Munsu's photo and tablet for a long time.

Then, she takes out a match from her pocket, and sets the photo on fire. The tablet follows suit. But the photo stops burning and starts to simply smolder. Jinyoung takes a tissue out of her pocket and tears bits of it to lay on the photo. The flames dance again.

The photo has completely burned away. The yellowish plume of smoke grows thinner.

Jinyoung stares until the last wisps of smoke disappear into the air.

"I only have bitter memories. Dead, miserable memories."

Two strands of tears flow down her calm, almost sculptured face.

The winter sky is so clear, to the point of seeming cold-hearted. The wind blows some snow off a nearby tree branch, and the flakes swirl around her coat.

"That's right. I still have life left in me. I can still fight the fight."

Mumbling this, Jinyoung grabs a tree branch to pull herself back on her feet and marches down the mountain path.

Translated by Anton Hur
First published August 1957

Retreat

Snow was falling over the night streets.

Hyein was at Mimosa Western Dress, her shop at the entrance of Myeongdong. She was cutting pieces from a blue wool she'd spread out on the worktable. There was a hint of desolation in her profile.

Outside, the snow continued its descent.

The shop was empty but for the arced shadow of Hyein's slightly stooped shoulders darkening the opposite wall. A lone mannequin stood watch from a corner behind her. Hyein was working late as the customer had requested that the item be ready by next evening. She could have passed the work on to another tailor if she'd had reason to hasten back home, but she didn't. After a spell of work, Hyein stilled her hands and glanced at the window.

A vague light flitted across her thin, forlorn face.

Biting a yawn, Hyein turned back to the table and lifted her wrist to check the time. Five to ten. With her hand resting on the watch, she thought for a minute, then gathered up the pieces of fabric strewn across the table and placed them in a safe.

She put on her coat and got ready to leave. Just then a sharp blast rang out, piercing her heart. Hyein's hands flew up from her coat collar to cover her head. A cold gust blew in and lashed her cheek: the glass panels of the shop door were shattered. By the time Hyein's eyes found the door, the floor was shimmering with broken glass. She glimpsed movement past the doorframe, a faint scrabbling that materialized into a human figure carefully picking itself off the ground.

Frowning heavily, Hyein pressed the bell that connected to the tailor's lodging upstairs.

The fallen figure turned out to be a drunkard, a common enough sight in Myeongdong. The tailor was taking his time though, and now the drunk swung open the smashed door and shuffled inside. He was very tall. Powdery flakes of snow skated off his coat in quick succession and dissolved over the concrete.

The man doffed his hat, bowed slightly. "My sincere apologies. I'll have to reimburse you for the broken glass …"

Hyein caught a whiff of alcohol as she stood bolted to the floor, but the man spoke respectfully enough. Not a complete lush then.

Averting his eyes from Hyein's silent face, the man smacked his lips. "I've had a few, I'll admit, but the street was out of sorts."

As the man spun round to gesture at the street, the light picked out his face. A glint of light off his spectacles. Hyein realized the work on the sewers a few days back, when they'd dug up part of the road and filled it in later, had left the ground higher than before. Then she noticed something truly remarkable, and her face stiffened. She stared intently at the man standing in the light, managed to lick her dry lips, and asked, "Aren't you Mr. Kim Byoung-gu?" Her voice was barely audible. Hyein quietly clenched her hands.

"I'm sorry, who are you? Yes, I'm Kim Byoung-gu." The smell of alcohol drifted in her face as Byoung-gu asked in return, mystified. Hyein smiled her odd, biting smile. "It's me, Kang Hyein. Kang Sook-in's sister. Do you not recognize me?" she asked.

"Kang Sook-in!" Byoung-gu shouted, as if this had immediately sobered him up.

Hyein averted her eyes from Byoung-gu's face as it distorted in astonishment, relaxed her hands, and absentmindedly picked up the key to the safe from the cutting table.

That was when a youth of about twenty appeared on the stairs. Hyein turned to look at him, her hands fiddling with the key. She rooted down through her legs.

"The pane's shattered. Sleep with the shutter closed tonight, and I'll get the glass fixed first thing in the morning."

The youth appeared to have just woken up and glanced in confusion at the broken glass, then at the stranger. His steps faltered and he came to an awkward stop.

"I'll be off now, so shut the door and do clear up the glass." Hyein slipped the key in her purse and looked over at Byoung-gu. "Shall we?"

Hyein wrapped a shawl around her head as she stepped out, Byoung-gu following behind without a word. The youth cocked his head a few times in puzzlement, then crouched down and began picking up the shards.

"We could go for tea if it weren't so late …" Hyein said, readjusting the shawl that had slipped off her head.

Reaching a featureless tree on the edge of the sidewalk, Byoung-gu hailed a passing taxi and looked silently at Hyein. He had his coat collar up, and Hyein saw that his eyes were tense behind his glasses. She dusted the snow off her coat and got into the car. Byoung-gu got in next to her. Once inside, he grabbed a cigarette and rummaged around for a lighter with the cigarette dangling from his lips, then finally said, "I'll see you home. Are you still in Hyehwadong?"

In lieu of an answer, Hyein ordered the driver: "Drive to Palpandong."

After that they were silent. Neither was in a position to speak.

By the time Hyein thought they must be passing the bell pavilion in Jongro, the roadside lamps and trees of Gwanghwamun were gliding outside the window in successive flight.

Under their faint light, Hyein's face trembled ever so slightly. Byoung-gu went on smoking.

Hyein stepped out of the car just past Joongangcheong[*], at the mouth of the narrow street that led to her place. It had stopped snowing in the meantime, and tall willows reared in the dark along the back wall encircling Joongangcheong.

"Please give my regards to your father." Byoung-gu's voice was still low.

"Father, family … They're all gone now."

Hyein clasped her purse aslant her body with a detached expression, as if what she was relaying had nothing to do with her. Byoung-gu flicked his cigarette out the car window and, avoiding Hyein's face, mumbled, "Oh I see." His voice was serene, as if he didn't need to be told how or why.

"Cheongpadong, please," he said to the driver. The car started and Byoung-gu, still averting his eyes, dipped his head briefly.

---

[*] Joongangcheong (중앙청) was the former administrative building of the Japanese colonial government of Korea. It was renamed Capitol Hall by the US Army Military Government in 1945; Joongangcheog is a translation of Capitol Hill. The building was demolished between 1995-1996.

The Age of Doubt

The taxi turned and disappeared down the snow-bright road. Hyein stood and stared for an eternity, a snow person in the blotted street.

Hyein had met Byoung-gu a year before the troubles. Byoung-gu was Hyein's sister Sook-in's lover. Hyein and Sook-in were half-sisters. More precisely, Hyein had been born out of wedlock. During his student days in Japan, Sook-in's father Kang Sangho had started up with a fellow Korean student by the name of Youngsook. He was reckless, playing with fire when he already had a wife. Upon Hyein's birth the only response he'd mustered was one of bewilderment, and the woman, confronted with this failing in the man, had taken her own life. Sook-in's mother, of the surname Yoon, was a sharp and intelligent woman. Even so, when she felt her husband searching for a trace of the dead woman in Hyein's eyes, Mrs. Yoon would insert herself between them and weep. For she could tell the woman continued to live on in her husband's thoughts through Hyein. It was in such strained circumstances that Hyein grew of age. Sook-in, who was two years older, went on to medical school while Hyein, an avid reader of literature, went to S University to study home economics, following Mrs. Yoon's wishes. If Hyein inclined toward literature, Sook-in tended toward logic.

As for Byoung-gu, Hyein first saw him at the beginning of her final year at university, in early spring. Sook-in was in her graduating class as well, having completed a two-year premed course prior to medical school. When her sister first introduced Kim Byoung-gu to her, Hyein detected a rugged element in the young associate professor of politics, a trait he seemed to share with Sook-in. But seeing him smile—for reasons she could no longer recall—she had felt deeply moved. It was a good-natured smile, almost boyishly ingenuous. Each time she saw it light up his face, Hyein felt a smoldering sorrow and a nostalgia for humanity, and these feelings came to characterize Hyein's love for Byoung-gu. She would stand by the window and tremble at the realization that she and Sook-in had inherited the unhappy fates of their mothers and were snared in an orbit around one man. There wasn't a soul who knew how Hyein felt. She was destined to suppress her feelings.

A year passed. Hyein graduated and found a teaching job at a girls' school. Sook-in graduated but remained at the university hospital as an intern.

It was around then that the troubles began. With the breakout of conflict, it transpired that Sook-in was a strict communist. This was a surprising turn, but knowing Sook-in's character, Hyein thought it made sense. Among the moments that illustrated how fervid a communist Sookin was, Hyein could never forget the incident with Younghwa. Younghwa was the daughter of a paternal aunt and the same age as Hyein. She lived right next door. She had studied Western painting and married a man she'd shared amorous feelings with shortly before the troubles began. Her husband, who was in service to the military but now unable to leave Younghwa behind, was labelled a straggler; he was eventually executed by the communist army. Younghwa had come to them then and wept, collapsing at their feet, only to have Sook-in look at her coldly and say, "What did you expect would happen?" These were the words she offered her younger cousin. Hyein, embracing Younghwa to help her up from the floor, had glared at Sook-in.

As soon as Sook-in became active in communist affairs, a man named Bak, who was said to be from up north, started shadowing Sook-in wherever she went. As it was, communications from Byoung-gu had ceased following his work trip to Daegu days before the troubles.

And so with Seoul's recapture on September 28, Sook-in fled north. Right before she left, the two of them had sat together on the maru, Hyein listening to the falling shells, Sook-in staring up at the clouds. Eventually Sook-in had placed a hand on Hyein's shoulder and said, as if to herself, "Say it was just sentiment, though I'll never say it was untrue."

Hyein knew full well toward whom that sentiment was directed.

"Kang Sook-in comrade, we have to hurry." The man called Bak came in looking anxious. He had a gun; his eyes were bloodshot. Sook-in stood without a word.

"Unni, where are you going!" Hyein bolted up and shouted without thinking. A desperate urgency stifled her heart.

"Quit it, I'm busy." Sook-in said, even as she stopped to turn back. She looked at Hyein, then walked back toward her.

"It was just sentiment … make sure to say it." Her steady gaze faltered. Abruptly she turned and grabbed hold of the man's arm. The stern echo of footfall filled the otherwise quiet street, which was stained with the setting sun.

Whenever Hyein thought of Sook-in, Sook-in who had loved Byoung-gu but was matched with and left with the man called Bak, Hyein was reminded of the characters in *The Loves of Three Generations*, a novella by the red Soviet Union woman writer Alexandra Kollontai. The story depicted three generations of women and the love they experience against the backdrop of the Russian Revolution, detailing each woman's attitude to love as shaped by shifting social forms. It seemed to Hyein that the situation of the daughter character in the story echoed Sook-in's own circumstance. The daughter loves two men, one with a pure love and the other with a comradely love for a shared ideology. The dilemma for her, then, stems from the fact that she loves each man in equal measure.

Hyein witnessed what a scrupulous communist Sook-in was through the war. Yet she loved Byoung-gu, a liberal at odds with her own values, while also voluntarily transgressing the line of comradeship with Bak; it was in her demonstration of these two forms of love that her predicament resembled that of the daughter in *The Loves of Three Generations*. Hyein thought that both Sook-in and the daughter were romantic women. But in the novella, by the granddaughter's time, romance has become a thing of the past: love is understood as a physiological act; emotions grow increasingly mechanical. Hyein wondered whether Sook-in was headed away to a world of mechanical affect or coming closer to a world suffused with human nostalgia. For some reason, Hyein preferred to think of Sook-in as a woman who could not turn her back on the latter.

Amid the retreat of the communist army and the cacophony of distant artillery fire, Byoung-gu returned to a Seoul razed to rubble and stood in their yard. Hands digging into his coat pockets, wordless, unmoving. Only his hair lashing at his forehead in the wind's agitation.

He did not visit the house again.

The house where Hyein lost not only Sook-in and her half-brother Young-in, but also Mrs. Yoon, who had strove to be generous to Hyein. Young-in and Mrs. Yoon died in the bombings the night before the Army re-entered Seoul. Later, her father, Kang Sangho, suffered a cerebral hemorrhage after fleeing to Busan with Hyein. Enduring these successive losses, Hyein came to believe endurance and loneliness were her lot, as ordained by her birth mother's suicide.

It was while she was displaced in Busan that Hyein heard on the wind that Byoung-gu was drinking his nights away. Though her eyes gleamed, she did not look for him. Through sheer will, Hyein restrained herself from taking any action and treaded time's water.

The winter passed and spring arrived. Hyein did not hear from Byoung-gu in the interval. She was heavily disappointed, as she had been convinced he would pay her a visit. She intuited that he could not find it in his heart to come see her when that same heart still longed for Sook-in. This was doubly aggrieving.

Then one day, she chanced upon him in the street. Around the bend in a Myeongdong bustling with evening traffic, Byoung-gu was pushing his way through the surging crowd, his face as vacant as a mask. Hyein turned on her heels and ducked into a grocer's in a deliberate act to avoid encounter. When she reemerged from the shop with a tin of tea, Byoung-gu was nowhere to be seen. Hyein was anguished that she'd foregone the very opportunity she'd longed for. Nonetheless, she knew that she would continue to act counter to her heart.

It was a clear day. Hyein gazed without interest at an advertising balloon afloat in the blue sky. Next to her, Myoungja, another tailor, was chattering away at a customer. Myoungja was an ideal assistant for the taciturn Hyein.

"In spring, fresh, bright colors are a must. Look: see how well they go together …"

Letting Myoungja's cheerful voice flow unheeded past her ears, Hyein took an envelope from her purse and opened it. It was a letter from Younghwa, who had gone to study painting in Paris. She wrote: *There's a forest called the Bourgogne outside Paris. On Sundays, they say couples visit in droves to frolic there. I went the other day, but I was alone and found it dull. So naturally I thought of you. Back then I thought that for stragglers in love like us, all that remained was a life of work. Why don't you come over to Paris, instead of staying stuck over there? I'm saying don't settle for being a designer just because you have a flair for it.*

Younghwa ended by saying how it choked her up to think of her mother. Hyein felt low as she folded the letter away. Her skin was fair and radiantly clear, and she looked true and simple in a light purple dress with white stripes.

Hyein knew why Younghwa referred to herself as a straggler in the life of love. But why she'd said "us" was harder to fathom— although Younghwa had insinuated as much several times before. Hyein had never spoken about her feelings for Byoung-gu to Younghwa. Not that they could be expressed in words in the first place. In any case, Hyein never asked Younghwa to explain herself or her insinuations, but she hadn't denied the implication either. In part because it occurred to her that perhaps Younghwa alone of all people *did* know her heart. Younghwa had once said to Hyein, "You'll never fully devote yourself to the business of love, Hyein, not with that pride of yours." The tone was light, but her eyes were serious.

"You have it the wrong way round—it's my inferiority complex that won't allow for romance," Hyein joked.

"Hyein, don't you hate your love rival? Or would hating her be an admission of defeat?"

Hyein had felt her heart drop. For there was no doubt that by love rival, Younghwa was referring to Sook-in.

The sky outside was still a clear blue. The ad balloon was no longer visible within the square of glass, swept away no doubt in the current of air. Myoungja was still jabbering with the customer. Hyein grabbed her purse and stood up. She meant to visit her aunt, Younghwa's mother.

It was dark by the time she stepped back out into the street after visiting her in Hyehwadong. Turning a corner in an alley, Hyein glimpsed the faint glow of a butcher's window. Reddish meat and a dead pig hung behind the glass. An ineffable terror rushed down her spine. There was no doubt: this was a mortuary.

Hyein walked out to Hyehwa Roundabout. She reached a tree on the side of the pavement and leaned against it. The dead passed in front of her eyes, one after the other. As did a countless number of cars and buses.

What horror, she thought. It is horrific when one thinks about it. Carnage condoned by social customs that rationalize the physiological appetite of humans— how is this any different from the cannibalism of cannibals? It is all custom. If custom dictates, even romance becomes mere mechanics.

Hyein was gripped by her own treachery. She thought again about Byoung-gu and Sook-in and herself. The problems were endless.

When and how she managed to grab a car escaped her; she was completely preoccupied by her thoughts.

She was about to step into the alley to her house when a quiet voice called out from behind. "Kang seonsaeng."

Hyein felt everything grow distant. She recognized Byong-gu's voice.

"Is this a bad time?"

Hyein managed, barely, to turn around. "No."

"I wanted to stop by as I was in the neighborhood." Byoung-gu's voice was inflected with drink.

"Oh? Come on in, then."

In the small Western-style home, the old woman and her daughter were waiting for Hyein to return. She had lived with them for many years now. The old woman glanced at Byoung-gu and acknowledged him in sour recognition.

Entering Hyein's room, Byoung-gu immediately lit up a cigarette and said, "It's as quiet as a nunnery here."

Setting a plate down as an ashtray, Hyein looked briefly insulted.

"Is the Hyehwadong house gone?" he asked, as if finally picking out a thread.

"No, it's still there. I've let it. It's a big house and having lost so many people there, I grew to dislike it."

Byoung-gu now had to search for another thread. He himself had lost Sook-in in that house.

"I've come to see you, yet I've nothing to say. What could I possibly have to say?" He laughed awkwardly.

It was a ridiculous comment. Not proper material for conversation.

Hyein felt the spare white walls of the bare room close in on her. Her face flamed. Byoung-gu's laughter, strange and discomfiting, hung in the air.

"That is our fate." Hyein managed to pluck her voice like a stuck thorn from her throat. Realizing the trite and sentimental nature of her comment, her face flushed again.

"I have a wife. I got married. Got a child as well, the poor woman. My wife, that is."

The Age of Doubt

"That's the alcohol talking." Hyein did not wish to listen to such things.

Byoung-gu tapped his cigarette over the plate. "This is a pretty bleak room."

His voice continued to hover in the air. Each comment was vague and unfocused, as if his mind were elsewhere.

"I guess it takes after the person living in it. Here, have some tea." Hyein offered the tea the old woman had brought in and tensed her lips into a semblance of her biting smile.

Byoung-gu held onto his cigarette even as he drank. A thick silence flowed between them.

Byoung-gu stubbed out his cigarette and got to his feet. "I should be on my way now."

Hyein stood and their eyes met. Hyein felt fear engulf her pupils. Her every emotion seemed to congregate there and throb sharply.

Byoung-gu turned away and opened the door. Hyein felt an overwhelming exhaustion. She felt depleted, like an intense flame that has burned itself out. She stood, mute and dumb, within her unalloyed self. She bowed but did not look again as he headed out of the house.

Somewhere, a dog was barking.

Hyein cradled her neck, leaned her head back, and closed her eyes.

Two weeks passed. Hyein was working again as dusk fell. As she slid a pair of scissors over the fabric, a strange feeling, an intuition that Byoung-gu was on his way to see her came over her. She looked up, her face flushed with anticipation, and sure enough, there was Byoung-gu entering the shop. Hyein was mystified by her intuition. Byoung-gu began showing up regularly in the evenings, when customers were less likely to be about, and each time, her keen sense never failed her. When he came, Hyein would leave what she was doing and follow him to a tea house. That was all. They talked about nothing of substance and what they did say was vague, unfocused.

One Saturday afternoon in early summer, Hyein was working on a bright red fabric that made her feel as dizzy as standing in sunlight. She turned for a moment to look outside. Byoung-gu opened the shop door, fishing out a pack of cigarettes from his suit pocket. As Hyein stood, he grinned at her in his boyish way. Hyein could have wept at this palpable extension of his mood, for she felt it so acutely. Nonetheless, her eyes remained wary.

"I wondered if we might have dinner together?"

Hyein stumbled into her chair instead of answering. She contemplated his smile. He had smiled like that at Sook-in once. Why was her vision clouded, what was this dizziness?

Hyein sent up her unfinished work to the factory and followed Byoung-gu out of the shop.

After a simple dinner at a nearby restaurant, Hyein once again followed as Byoung-gu led the way. They crossed the road not far from where a car accident had occurred, and Byoung-gu reached out to take Hyein's arm. She made it across the street and wriggled her arm out from his hand. She felt a prickling sensation behind her ears, right below the earlobes, as though someone had sprinkled salt there.

When they reached Y Department Store, Byoung-gu turned to look at Hyein. "Let's stop here for a bit." Hyein signaled acquiescence by not responding.

They entered the store at the basement level and Byoung-gu

began climbing the stairs. Her mind elsewhere, Hyein followed him. Then she stopped. She had assumed they were headed to a cafe, but it appeared not. She felt alarmed. Where was he headed? The rooftop? But it was night … She told herself her anxiety was unwarranted and resumed walking. It grew noisier. She realized he was bringing her to a dance hall. She had no experience of such places. Hyein panicked. But by now a waiter was bowing courteously and waiting for her to hand over her purse. "I don't want to!" Hyein blurted out, though what she'd meant to say was that she didn't know how to dance. Byoung-gu looked back nonchalantly at her flustered face and replied, "That's all right. We can just watch."

In the dimly lit hall, pairs of men and women were gliding about and swaying to the music. Hyein felt lightheaded. She found the scene nauseating and unpleasant. Reaching a corner seat, Byoung-gu invited Hyein to sit down, then waved at a waiter and ordered two drinks.

Hyein was on edge now. "What's the fun in strutting about like that? I find them pitiful in fact. Their fine dresses may as well be rags," she said in spite and anger.

"If you find it unpleasant that's your problem, Kang seonsaeng, it's not as if you can stop others from enjoying themselves."

This remark stunned Hyein. He was right, of course. She asked herself what had so enraged her. Was it her indignation at Byoung-gu for bringing her here in the first place? That was certainly part of it. But on further reflection, she had to concede that it likely had more to do with the frisson of excitement she'd felt and repressed.

Seeing her remain silent, Byoung-gu spoke in a gentler, jocular manner, as if regretting his earlier emphatic tone. "To think you have this glamorous job as a creator of fashion yet you don't know the first thing about dance …"

Hyein felt insulted and what he had said before about her home being a nunnery lodged itself, once again, like a heavy stone on her chest.

"A glamorous job doesn't require that one also have the emotions to match it."

"Why don't you enjoy it?" Byoung-gu stared at her from behind his spectacles.

"I could ask the same of you."

Byoung-gu looked away. With his eyes on the dancefloor, he said, "Back in the day I did dance, occasionally. But now, I mostly come to observe. It makes me forget some of the chaos …"

He trailed off, offered a Coke to Hyein, and sipped his whiskey. After a while he began to talk in a soft voice. As he spoke, the vague loose threads of their past conversations began to slowly come together to form a coherent strand.

The people moving in an embrace under the radiant lights, the fuss and commotion of jitterbug music—all felt remote to Hyein, as if it was happening somewhere far away from her. Only Byoung-gu's quiet words reached her and shook her like a storm. Byoung-gu was speaking of Sook-in. His drinking increased.

How much time passed was unclear, but at some point the hall suddenly grew clamorous. The people who had been entertaining themselves were bustling to leave. The music appeared to have stopped.

"Useless reminiscing on days long gone," Byoung-gu said. Hyein could only smile.

As they made their way downstairs, her head was filled with

The Age of Doubt

Byoung-gu's words. *If I'd crossed paths with them then, I'd have killed them both.* The lights splintered into fragments before her eyes, and Hyein lost her footing and staggered. Byoung-gu rushed in and grabbed her arm. Hyein looked at him to say thank you, but instead of his face, she saw the red fabric she'd been working on earlier that evening. It flapped in front of her eyes. The next thing she felt was fresh air on her cheeks—they must have made it outside. Her head cleared in the car.

At the entrance to her street, Byoung-gu got out first to see that she got out safely, then told the driver to wait for him while he walked her to her door.

After a few quiet steps, he said out of nowhere, "Do you know what it is to agonize about not knowing oneself?" Hyein didn't have the wherewithal to parse his words. Neither had anything to say.

When they reached the house, it was dark. As Hyein turned round to say goodbye, Byoung-gu abruptly embraced her. She felt the smell of alcohol drift over her face. Then his lips pressing down on hers. Hyein let her arms go slack. When he let go of her, her teeth gleamed in the dark as she brushed her hair back. She was laughing. The tears soaking the bridge of her nose, on the other hand, remained invisible.

"I see I'm a stand-in for Sook-in." Her voice was low. She turned away in a detached manner and pressed the doorbell. When the woman opened the door, Hyein bowed politely at Byoung-gu, quickly stepped over the threshold, and shut the door in his face. Hyein waved the woman away and made for her room. The white walls closed in on her. She crumpled to the floor. Sobs rocked her body. Irrepressible solitude and despair engulfed her.

"I can't bear it. I can't go on living here," Hyein muttered before sinking her head in her arms again.

This utterance led to the vague notion of setting out for someplace else, and before long the notion began to take on concrete shape. Younghwa's letters from Paris played a part in encouraging the impulse. Fortunately, Hyein owned the house as well as the shop; if she were to sell these off, she could afford to go someplace, say to Paris, and not struggle as far as money was concerned, at least until she was settled. In any case, she wanted to be where Byoung-gu wasn't.

Byoung-gu did not return after that night. Hyein found herself waiting for him, even as she told herself she would go live somewhere far removed from him. She worked late into the night to forget herself, to forget that she was waiting. Keeping her hands busy, she would push aside the temptation to dwell on him and occupy her thoughts with plans of departure.

It was nearly a month before she received a letter from Byoung-gu.

I apologize for my behavior. In the past month, I've tried to impose some order to and around my thoughts. But if I'm honest, I have to say I don't know myself. I want to say I love you. But reaching the conviction that I love you now, in this present—when I have in confusion and distrust as good as given up on myself, a self quite unable to bear itself upright let alone carry anything else—was extremely difficult. The world I once belonged to has crumbled away in the war. For me there is as yet no other world to substitute it. Sook-in's going north did form a part of that immense loss. I want to say I love you. But my feet remain without a foothold. In this uncertain reality, I am aware of how tiresome it is to think of love. I would like to tell you about my affection for you, fraught as it is with anxiety, and to ask for your forgiveness. I shall wait until 6 o'clock at the tearoom.

That was the entirety of the letter.

When Hyein arrived at the tearoom, Byoung-gu glanced up at her in agitation. Hyein sat down and faced him. Interlacing her hands over the table, she said, "I haven't come to hear you speak of your fraught affection for me. I've come to forgive you."

Byoung-gu looked at her for a moment as if taking in a deep breath.

"I see. Well, should I thank you then?" He smiled bitterly. "Am I not allowed to speak about my love, troubled as it is?"

"You wrote that you don't know yourself, but I know myself too well."

"Is that a rejection?"

Hyein didn't respond to this. Instead she said, "You do not consider what alternatives there might be to your current situation. In that case it seems best to not speak about anxieties and uncertainties."

"What alternatives?" Byoung-gu asked, nervously tapping his cigarette.

"A way to move past even a little from the present situation. I'd think denying or admitting our feelings isn't as hard as addressing the practicalities."

Byoung-gu appeared unable to speak. He drank his tea. When he finally opened his mouth after a long silence, it was to seemingly digress. "The practicalities include Sook-in, of course. I spoke about her to you the other night. That was a magnifying of my feelings toward you. I've come to terms now with the fact that Sook-in has followed another man. I've been thinking about the egoistical nature of love that prompts a person to follow another."

Hyein disagreed strongly. Certainly not, she thought, Sook-in didn't follow Bak out of egoistical love. All she said, however, was: "So have I."

Hyein looked down at her locked fingers and realized her words were entirely devoid of meaning. It didn't give her the least pleasure to hear Byoung-gu deny his attachment to Sook-in. Sook-in was well beyond the realm of confessions of love as well as any rivalry. Hyein felt no glory in her triumph. Instead, it felt craven.

The next day, Hyein began preparations for her departure to France. The house in Hyehwadong was bought by its tenants, other economies were more or less put in order, and the paper-work for travelling to France was filed. By the time these preparations were nearly finalized, they were well into autumn.

The night she received her visa, Hyein wrote to Younghwa: *I will be released from everything that surrounds me. I depart leaving everything behind, including the sky and the sunlight of this place. And the bodily scents that have seeped into my own body—I wish to shed them behind too. Paris is to be my new place of retreat. Perhaps in time I'll build an inner retreat out of that novelty.*

The following morning, Hyein stood in the quiet road in front of Joongangcheong, waiting for a car. Bright yellow gingko leaves littered the ground. The autumn sky was cold and clear. The neat rows of paving stones were bright with sunlight.

She raised her hand at each passing car. People borne away in each one. Hyein told herself that if the next car was occupied she would lose him forever, but if an empty car came to ferry her away she would not. So she stood trying to divine the future. Then she came to, feeling a shudder of shock go through her.

"No, no, cancel that. What a thing to do!" She shouted, rejecting her brief flirtation with prophesy. She was afraid now. Afraid to even glance at the passing cars. A taxi glided toward her. It was empty. Hyein felt her face burn. She jumped in and closed her eyes. The frisson of excitement she'd felt just moments ago seemed absurd. This didn't stop her eyes from watering though. The decision to leave had been made; the visa was in her bag. She only meant to say a final goodbye to him. Wasn't she travelling halfway across the world to a strange land after all, in a bid to avoid him? And on reflection, hadn't her every decision been one of a succession of actions at odds with her heart? Like two parallel rail tracks, when it came to Byoung-gu, what she felt and what she did would never come together.

Yellow leaves spiraled down outside the car window.

Byoung-gu greeted Hyein with a face riven by emotion.

Before the waitress brought their teas, Hyein said briskly, "I've got my visa."

Byoung-gu's eyes stirred. But the flicker died down quickly.

"How long will you be gone?"

Forever, Hyein answered in her mind even as she said, "Well, I'm not sure …"

Byoung-gu was silent for a long time.

"The peculiar position of not knowing myself while knowing you all too well …" He struggled to stifle his emotions, trying to assert himself, in however small a way, within his overwhelming anxiety.

"It is our fate." Hyein repeated the trite phrase, this time intentionally. Her inner voice said, Fate reunited us, but everything else has been my will.

Their tea arrived.

"To apprentice as a designer, then?" Byoung-gu asked, blowing out a smoke ring and watching it drift away.

"No, I want to go to school."

Byoung-gu looked inquiringly at her. Hyein looked quietly back at him. Holding back with her whole body the nostalgia for humanity that burned inside her.

"I'd like to study. To give words to something I've carried inside me, to explain it ... I mean to study."

The visa had settled in advance where her new retreat was to be.

Quiet music played in the tearoom.

Translated by Emily Yae Won
First published March 1958

The Era of Fantasy

It is impossible to recall the emotions you felt in the most godawful moments of your life, those where you can only shiver in fear, despair, and the assumption that your time has come and you have nothing left to do but die, or in the memories of days gone past where you were beside yourself with happiness or bone-crushingly sad or furious to the point where your veins were about to burst. It is not so much the inability to understand the reason why you felt so happy or sad or angry or scared at the time, as the fact that the very emotions themselves have drifted on, like mist, to a place beyond reach. That is why Minee instead held on to the most trifling memories in all their vividness. Apart from being vivid, these memories conjured up a host of stories and scenes, sinking Minee into a state of utter stupefaction.

Faced with certain surroundings or feeling overwhelmed by events unfolding in front of her eyes or even without being prompted by colors or sounds around her, Minee would travel to an imaginary place, crossing the hazy, dream-like realm of time. Here, everything was more clearly defined than in the present and yet nothing made sense. Then, marching over and across the past, Minee made her way back to the present day. And so, sprinting back and forth, she found herself searching for her hopefully brilliant future self.

Due to Minee's daydreams and memories, it happened more than once that her overly enthusiastic math teacher, waving his limbs so violently that his glasses fogged up, launched a piece of chalk at her to catch her attention, and she often caught herself walking past her destination without realizing.

At that very moment, she was not by the windowsill in her classroom, where her teacher's voice would sound distant. Nor was she wandering about the wide, empty-looking streets. She found herself in her room, the moonlight seeping in through the paper sliding doors, casting the space in a dim light, as she gazed up at the faded floral pattern on the ceiling. She shifted her focus, directing all her senses towards the old, dilapidated window, towards the world that seemed to be contained inside the glass, a flickering image though it was.

Equally as loudly as her math teacher when he boasted that his head is shaped like a symmetrical diamond—when in fact while he was in the thick of teaching he looked like a boiled octopus, his eyes nearly bulging through his glasses—Room 9 of Dorm 1 resounded with people snoring, sleep talking, grinding their teeth, wriggling … But the sounds reached Minee from far, very far away, disorderly like dust particles flitting this way and that when a single ray of sunlight makes them visible in an otherwise dark room, as if being heard when they can only be seen. And yet, from time to time she was able to distinguish the sound of weatherstrips flapping in the wind, of the wind crashing into a tree.

It was late spring, no, early summer, and the wind outside seemed rather wild.

At high tide, she watched the sea rushing in. In the blink of an eye, the water came up to her ankles and before she knew, it rose to her calves. Every time the sea lost its calm—colliding with the breakwaters and foaming up—a bulging wave unfurled itself, kissing the inky line left behind when the tide was last full. Along the coastal trail, covered in foam, a woman in an azure skirt made her way, carrying a white parasol. To Minee, watching from across the breakwaters, the white parasol looked like a butterfly and a seabird at the same time.

Minee's mother's hair, smeared with camellia oil, radiated freshness. Even her bun, held in place by one golden and one metallic-gray pin, glimmered. In her own words, it shone like a flowering wheat stalk.

"So you're the one who's so fond of my little Minee?" Mother said, as she drew an ornamented knife from a tasseled pouch and peeled an apple. "That's nice of you. Minee doesn't have any siblings, you see. She's lonely. Think of her as your little sister and be kind to her."

Ok Sunja pursed her thin lips and sat still, unsmiling.

Her nose was as sharp as a knife blade. Her eyes were narrow and fierce, and she had a long face with a protruding chin and prominent cheekbones, but a short forehead. Her fingers were long and slender, as was her entire body. And above all, her scanty yellowish hair. Pretending to be coy, Sunja kept her eyes downcast as she picked up a biscuit from the table, only slightly lifting her chin.

Ok Sunja was the daughter of the vice-principal at Minee's elementary school. This countryside school had six grades and, counting the principal, six teachers, but only a few girls per class. Ok Sunja was in Grade 5, Minee in Grade 4.

There were two tokens of extravagance around school, unbefitting its impoverished state. Just outside the teachers' room stood a small, informal Shinto shrine. It was anyone's guess whether or not the principal, a Japanese man, had formerly served as Shinto priest, but he always approached the shrine in an incredibly solemn way, spreading his arms wide before bringing his hands together in front of his chest and making peculiar sounds, and although he never wore any official Shinto attire, his body seemed so soaked in worship that he exuded more loftiness than the real priest in charge of the local Shinto rituals.

The second token was a bronze statue in front of the school gate, portraying a boy with a bundle of firewood on his back and a book in his hand. It was a youthful depiction of a man named Ninomiya Kinjirō, an industrious farmer and scholar the principal always referred to when he found it necessary to give the entire student body a moralizing lecture. Since many of the students came from poor farmers' families, the principal seemed to consider it his personal goal as an educator to imprint on the students' minds a historical figure who had attained herohood in the face of poverty. And so every time a student passed through the gate, be it morning or evening, they took off their hat and bowed to the statue.

The principal lived in a tile-roofed house, hedged in by a row of well-trimmed junipers. His two sons attended the Japanese school in town, and his charming wife was occasionally seen offering a selection of side dishes to Minee's homeroom teacher, an unmarried Japanese man who lived by himself in the night watchman's room. A short way up from the principal's residence, across a brooklet, stood a scattered array of mulberry trees as well as the clay wall surrounding Vice-principal Ok's thatch-roofed abode preventing his two darting chickens from escaping. Apart from these two buildings, not a single dwelling was to be found anywhere near the school. It was only after a lengthy walk, following a path downhill flanked by cherry trees towering so high overhead they seemed to form a tunnel, that a small shop selling lamp oil, confectionery, and a meager selection of school supplies would come into view and an occasional farm could be recognized by the sound of horses chewing fodder in their stables.

Much like his daughter Sunja, Vice-principal Ok looked feeble. His face, hidden behind his polished, silver-rimmed glasses, failed to show even the slightest bit of color regardless of the time of year, and his emaciated shoulders hunched forward. He even had the same gait as his daughter. Like Japanese women wearing geta, he pointed his feet inward as he struggled to make his way across the school grounds. His suits were always stained with grease due to his wife constantly being ill. In contrast to his thin and angular appearance, Vice-principal Ok was a taciturn and unassuming man. What with his wife suffering from an illness, Sunja, their eldest daughter, took care of the household chores and looked after her siblings at all times. Sometimes, when Sunja crouched on the ground behind her house, poking through a fire of pine needles to prepare dinner, Minee perched on their kitchen threshold and observed her. And while the rice was boiling, Sunja would take a calabash bowl outside and pick black mulberries for Minee. Minee absolutely loved mulberries. Once, Sunja gathered some French thread in the finest colors, a bundle the size of a child's ponytail, and wove them nicely together like the ponytail on a grass doll, as a gift for Minee. Even though Sunja took such a liking to Minee, she was hardly a well-behaved student. Given the way she cared for her ailing mother without a word of complaint while simultaneously looking after her siblings, it was hard to believe how big of a rascal she was in school. Not a day went by without her ending up in a fight. She would lay eyes on a victim and annoy them to death by waving her long, slender fingers in front of their face before taking a swing at them and fluttering her lips faster than an airplane propeller as she poured forth all the foul language she possibly knew, leaving her victim without the wherewithal to say anything in return, until a splatter of her spit landed on their face and they burst into tears. Crying their hearts out, they would moan:

"You … You think you're the boss because your f-f-father is a teacher? My father works for the government! Who even cares about teachers?"

"What! What! What! The government? The government, she says! The government! Your loser clerk of a father can't hold a candle to my father! He can't! He can't! He just can't!"

"Well, you can s-s-shout as much as you like, but you still live under a thatched roof with your poor family! W-w-we have tiles over our head! I know it all! I do!"

"What do you know! What do you know! What are you blabbing on about?"

"Where did you even get the money for all that thread? You stole it from your mom, didn't you?"

The Age of Doubt

"What? What? What? What makes you think I did? When did you ever see me stealing anything? Tell me! Go on, tell me!"

Sunja launched at her opponent, foaming at the mouth, grabbing her hair with one hand and scratching across her face with the other. Whatever happened, Sunja never lost a fight. But she was a loner, and whenever she got into a fight she fought with no one at her side. The one who actually held the reins at school was a girl in Grade 6 named Wonee, who was slightly older and had proved herself such a powerhouse that she even held sway over a grown-up, her homeroom teacher at that—but never once did she contend with Ok Sunja. There was one other girl in Grade 6 beside Wonee, but due to family circumstances the days she was absent outnumbered the ones she came in. Minee's class had six girls in total. The oldest among them was Namsu, the youngest daughter of an enormously tall man who ran the fruit shop in the local market. Namsu took after her father, as Minee only came up to her armpits when standing next to her. Apart from her extraordinary height, she spoke with the voice of a grown woman, being three years older than Minee. She was the only one among the girls who measured up to Sunja when it came to bickering, but unlike Sunja's nervous shrieks quivering through the air, she argued in a voice as hoarse as earthenware pots being smashed to smithereens—it was a remarkable cacophony. Namsu was worse at school than Minee, but apart from that she was better at everything. Thanks to her long, flat hands, she was in a league of her own when they played ojami, collecting bean bags from the floor.

"*Ohitotsu, ohitotsu, ossyara! Ofutatsu, ofutatsu, ossyara!*" the game began. "*Chīsana hashi watare! Ōkiina hashi watare!*" After the bean bags scattered to all sides, Namsu managed to collect them effortlessly, leaving none behind.

Namsu, who alternately wore her black and her orange jeogori blouse over a violet muslin skirt; Sanghee, whose family owned a number of enormous roof-tiled mansions fenced in by a high stone wall; and Minee—the three girls did everything together, clasping hands as they walked to and from school, as if they were siblings living apart. It never occurred to Minee that Sanghee, despite her whale-sized house, came from a wealthy family. Minee often saw her perched on the maru as she shared her breakfast with her dozen or so nephews and nieces, barley rice in a bowl of cold water and two slices of unseasoned daikon kimchi. Sanghee passed the winter with one black cotton jeogori, which bore comparison with the worn-out roof tiles on top of her house and whose originally white collar had gotten so smudged from her greasy hair that it was now indistinguishable from the rest of her black top. Her dark complexion always gave the impression she had just emerged from a chimney, and her long eyelids made her look like she was about to doze off.

Every day except Sunday, Namsu, Sanghee, and Minee shuffled along the wide, tree-lined road on their way to school, crossing the tunnel to the other side of the bay, their footsteps echoing in the wind. In the mornings, the road was sprinkled with children on their way to school. Pupils from the two prominent elementary schools in town, Japanese children from the school in the Japanese neighborhood on the edge of town, boys from the fishery school who looked like grown men—such were the crowds on the morning streets, each and everyone proudly wearing a uniform with the emblem of their respective school. The crest from Jaeil Elementary with its red ribbon fluttering in the wind looked particularly imposing, and when girls from Jaeil came across the three shabby-looking girls and eyed the books they hugged to their chests, they felt a rush of superiority at being able to look down on them.

Minee hated these morning walks.

Until very recently, Minee had attended an even more reputable school than Jaeil Elementary, a school in the big city. The schoolyard was spacious, the buildings were large, they had a piano, and, most importantly, classes were taught by gorgeous women. Her homeroom teacher had beautiful curly hair and lived in a pretty, chocolaty Western-style house with high, decorated windows. She was an outstanding music teacher and Minee loved her to bits. Once, during some kind of ceremony, the teacher stood on a platform to give instructions. Her face, tinged slightly red, looked as otherworldly as a nymph's, making Minee's heart swell up with pride to the point where her chest almost hurt. And now? All of her six teachers were men and only once a week some woman came in to teach girls from Grade 4 and above a sewing class, but her face was covered in liver spots, her belly was as bloated as a watermelon, and she heaved her shoulders up and down when she drew breath, which made for a pitiable sight. Minee's current homeroom teacher was an old, unmarried Japanese man who wore a black uniform with a standing collar. He was fat and his clothes were so tight around his body they could burst any minute, which luckily never happened. Nonetheless, he had to turn his entire body if he wanted to look the other way due to an extraordinary swelling in the nape of his neck. He lived by himself in the night watchman's room. The daughter of the local barkeeper, Yeonok, often cast him a disapproving look during class because, lonely as he was, he would often pay an evening visit to her mother's bar in search of the barmaid. It might have been a rumor, but even so the man seemed to be rather fond of one of his students, Jeongae, who dressed elegantly thanks to her widowed mother's sewing skills. When it was Jeongae's turn to read from her book or when her pretty eyes accidentally met his, his swollen neck would turn so red it could pass for purple, while his saggy eyebrows would droop even further, his narrow eyes grew even narrower, and his snaggletooth popped out in between his smiling lips, protruding like a boar's tusk. Be that as it may, he made an effort in teaching his students and rarely scolded or hit them. All the girls in Minee's class were two to three years older than her, and most of them were wise beyond their years. Only Seo Duri, Minee's elder by one year, behaved like a child. Her face was everything but pretty, and her unruly hair stuck out above her narrow forehead like the bristles of a broom. She did not brush her teeth very well, and, as a solution, she always had a piece of chewing gum in her mouth. When she was caught by the principal, he stuck her gum in the nape of her neck by way of punishment, which did nothing to change her habit. Her father was a wealthy farmer living in one of the houses by the breakwaters on the other side of the bay.

Beside the anguish Minee felt on the way to school, there were other hardships. From the moment she transferred to this school, the boys had picked on her. Simply because she wore a suit and dress shoes. Even when she saw no other option and replaced her dress shoes with white plain shoes, nothing changed. Innocent teasing turned into actual harm. Once, when she was about to go home, her shoes had disappeared from the shoe cabinet. She cried in the dusky hallway. It was Sunja who went out of her way and searched for Minee's shoes in every nook and cranny until she finally encountered them buried underneath a flower bed and washed off the dirt. Minee's name was often written on the bathroom wall, side by side with the name of a boy who lived in a Buddhist temple. Except the Buddhist boy, who wore his uniform properly and had a face as pretty as a girl's, all the boys were rascals who hitched up their hanbok pants and wiped their noses with their snot-stained sleeves, country bumpkins who liked to wear old rubber shoes or even ones made of straw. Although Minee soon resembled their appearance, replacing her white plain shoes with rubber shoes and her suit with a hanbok, they still picked on her.

"Ey, ey, ey, pretty girl! Ey, ey, ey, pretty girl!" the farm boys roared as they encircled her, intent on never stopping teasing her. In such moments, the one who stood up for Minee was Ok Sunja.

Minee's transfer to this school was a thoughtless mistake on her mother's part. First, Mother had suddenly decided to move to the countryside, as one of her siblings lived there. Mother's only concern was to live a life less lonely than before, close to her sibling, and so she made Minee transfer to this countryside school. They searched for a place of their own, but in the end Minee's father and grandmother suggested that they move back to town, which they did.

"You said your name was Sunja, right?" Mother asked when she finished peeling the apple.

"Yes, maaaa'am," Sunja said, dragging out her answer until it died of itself.

"Eat up and go play."

"Yeees, maaaa'am." Sunja furrowed her brow, pinching a slice of apple with her slender fingers.

Mother went outside. Suddenly, Minee found Sunja repulsive for reasons she did not understand. Her sharp nose looked crooked, and the setting sun seeping in through the window made her scanty yellowish hair look like corn silk one moment and like the disheveled tresses of a witch the next. The long, flat nape of her neck, laid bare because her hair was tied up exceedingly high, reminded Minee of a rice cake she once ate, which had brought her excruciating stomach cramps, and she fell into a terribly bad mood. As soon as Mother left the room, Sunja chattered away.

"That girl, Wonee, they say she's seeing a teacher. I saw it with my own eyes yesterday. I was on my way back from buying rice and I saw those two coming my way, you know? They went for a walk along the coast, I'm telling you."

As Minee remained silent, Sunja picked up more food from around the table and put it in her mouth.

"Can't you see how arrogant she is, you know, pretending to be so well-behaved? Her dad's a pissing fishmonger, no less. You know what would happen if she ran into him on the streets, say, with a rack of fish on his shoulders? He would call out to her, 'Wonee, hey, Wonee!' and she would turn red and act as if she didn't even know him."

All Minee could think of was how crooked Sunja's nose looked. How the back of her neck looked like the rice cake that had given her stomach cramps. It felt as if someone was chafing her chest with sandpaper. A wave of nausea, the same kind that had accompanied her stomach cramps, came over her. When Sunja saw Minee's face crinkle, she said:

"Tomorrow at school, I'll bring you a pretty gourd." When no reply came, she added: "I have this pair of twin rings, with beads and all. They're yours if you want."

The Age of Doubt

As Minee's indifference did not fade, Sunja, now irritated, added a red purse her uncle had once given her to the list of items she promised to Minee.

The following day, when Minee saw Sunja running towards her on the schoolyard, she scurried off. Debating where to hide, she ran into their empty classroom. She heard the children on the schoolyard whooping and hollering. Crouching underneath her chair, she felt her heart leap out of her chest. In the window, the willows swayed and danced in the wind.

After class, Minee went along with Seo Duri towards the annex building standing by the sea across the hill. As they passed the school garden, lush with sweet potato sprouts, Seo Duri asked:

"Why're you following me?"

"Uhm …" Minee shuffled, fumbling for a plausible answer.

"Aren't you going to Sunja's house today?"

"I don't know!" Minee shook her head without wanting to.

"Did you fight?"

"No."

They passed the vacant plot of land that belonged to the local government and was surrounded by a dark forest, barring every sliver of sunlight, after which they came up to a hill with pine trees. As they climbed the hill, Minee and Duri glanced at the pine tree stumps on the ground. Every now and then, Duri halted to pick something up and put it in her mouth. But every time she did so, Minee only managed to glance at her enviously from the corner of her eye, unable to discover what it was that she put in her mouth. The distance between Minee and Duri grew as the two little girls wandered along, staring at the patchwork of light created by the sunlight falling on the ground between the small lacquer trees. It was a good while later when Duri shouted:

"Lee Minee!"

"Uh, I'm here!" Minee's voice echoed from down below.

"Let's move on!"

"OK."

Minee walked over to Duri. Duri, chewing gum, asked:

"Found something?"

"No."

Minee stretched out her palms, stained with resin. A few pieces of yellowish, crystallized resin were in her hands.

"That's useless! Toss it."

Minee knew that the yellow ones gave off a terrible smell as soon as they broke apart when you put them in your mouth, but she thought it a shame to leave them behind. When Minee tossed them aside, Duri opened her hands. She held out more than a dozen crystal-like little balls, as small as mung beans and as white as pearls or granulated sugar. So it was resin she was chewing, not gum. She gave one to Minee for her to chew. Unwrapping the cloth around her books, Duri took out a red stick of crayon from her pencil case, tore off a strip as narrow as a match and gave it to Minee, then tore off an equally narrow strip for herself. The two little girls chewed the strips together with the resin gum. The gum turned a beautiful pink, growing soft and soggy in their mouths.

The annex was a wooden building standing lifelessly at the foot of the hill, adjacent to the coastal trail. It was used as a classroom for Grade 6.

"Let's peek in. Just for a moment."

They crept up to the window and stood high on their tippy-toes, craning their necks like turtles. Most of the boys were as tall as grown men. Wonee, who was sitting next to an empty chair because her neighbor was absent, stared intently at her book, her yellowish green jeogori the only pretty color amid the boys.

They had yet to finish class.

"Who's there!" the teacher shouted angrily, interrupting his stride between the desks while reading from his book with a pretentious accent.

Minee and Duri fled towards the breakwaters, towards the sea.

"Let's search for clams. Look! Do you see how far back the water has retreated?"

Duri placed her books on top of the breakwaters and walked across the rocks, overgrown with algae, down to the beach. Minee unwrapped the handkerchief from around her lunchbox and carried the empty box with her as she followed Duri.

Before long, more girls came running down the hill carrying their books. Grade 5 must have finished class. Of course, there was no sign of Ok Sunja. Even Namsu and Jeongae came down after cleaning the classroom, but Sunja must have gone home to prepare dinner. Perhaps, fixing her gaze on the schoolyard as she washed her rag by the brooklet, she was wondering where Minee was.

"I feel like eating oysters."

With that, Duri went over to a group of rocks largely submerged in the sea. But Minee did not even think of going there and continued to scoop up sand with empty clam shells.

The other girls were jumping rope on top of the breakwaters. Sometimes they played a round of ojami or hopscotch. At some point, Grade 6 finished class, cleaned their classroom, and, as if the wide-open coastal trail were exclusively reserved for girls, the boys and the teacher made for the hill, back towards the main building.

The desolate road without a single passerby, the annex looking all forlorn, the empty classroom, sunlight flickering in its window. On the other side of the bay, a thatched house and a stone wall with gourd vines creeping over them stood at the foot of a mountain, and people were coming and going.

Minee carried her aluminum lunchbox around and searched this way and that, eagerly turning over the sand, but she only managed to gather a few tiny shells, no larger than rice grains. Well, she also had some baby turban shells.

Then, Minee finally spotted a big one. Her heart started racing. But upon inspection, it was an empty shell, whose occupant had long died. Disappointed, she squatted down and looked at the sea. White froth clambered up the lighthouse. The sea crashed ruthlessly against the structure, but to anyone watching from afar, the foam must have looked as creamy as the head of a beer. A small boat passed by and the surge around the lighthouse quieted down.

"Minee-ya!"

Minee looked around to find Wonee's smiling face, light-skinned but covered in liver spots, reminding Minee of a much older woman.

"I found some."

In her outstretched hand she held two shells as big as erasers. The pattern on the outside was as grand as it was beautiful.

"Take them."

Ecstatic, Minee held out her lunchbox.

"Tee-hee, what's all this?" Wonee chuckled. Her white, regular teeth were truly pretty. "How can you see the small ones, but not the big ones? How does that work?"

"There weren't any," Minee said downcast, puzzled by the two large oysters Wonee put in her lunchbox.

"It's because you don't know how to spot a clam hole."

"I think I saw a few?"

"Some of them are empty, silly. Look, if you do this, the water goes all the way up, see?"

Wonee tapped on top of a clam hole with an abalone shell she must have found somewhere. On command, the water rose up. As if the animals inside were scared. Wonee dug out three or four big shells and walked away. Minee did exactly as Wonee had, but could not find a single big one.

What do I do wrong? Why am I so unlucky?

Not only Wonee, but everyone except Minee managed to collect shells without even getting their clothes messy, without cutting themselves on the edges. They needed only to set their minds to it and they would gather enough shellfish for a bowl of doenjang jjigae. Despite putting in more effort than anyone, Minee got her clothes drenched and dirty as soon as she set foot anywhere near the sea, and she always cut her feet open on an oyster shell. Once, she went to the mountains with her cousins to harvest chestnuts and got her feet stung by thorny plants, which led to some festering bruises causing her a lot of pain, and yet she was crazy about going to the mountains or the sea and plucking fruits or finding clams. Her mother was firmly against it, rebuking her for getting her clothes dirty and her feet cut only to bring home scraps that were hardly even edible, but Minee could not resist placing her clams or herbs or whatever else nature had to offer inside her lunchbox and bringing them home. Except for the school she went to, she much preferred her countryside life over the one she had in the city, but she was sad that her cousins and her peers gave her the cold shoulder. She envied them for doing well at everything. Rubber bands, ball games, skipping rope, ojami, marbles, they did it all. Especially when she watched them play with a rubber band, two of them standing upright, holding the band high in the air while others ran towards them shouting "Ee-ey!" as they kicked the band down with one leg at a time, Minee was taken aback, her mouth slightly agape. But if suggested that she join, Minee backed up with fear in her eyes. Despite not playing the game, Minee collected strings of rubber bands and treasured them. She believed that everyone had a special talent. Be it the marathon runner who breaks through the yellow tape to win the race, propelled by raucous music echoing through the stadium and a roaring volley of audience cheers rising up to the autumn sky, or the gifted singer whose awe-inspiring voice sweeps the stage in every role—Minee felt an incredibly strong, burning aspiration to be like them. In the face of such amazing talent, she felt that she was no match for her peers, a sentiment which possibly led to the deep sense of loneliness she carried with her. It made her feel perplexed and dejected and consumed with aspiration. Why did she keep hiding her feelings, not blending in with others, when she actually wanted to get along with them?

"Minee-ya!" Wonee called.

When had she arrived? The girls playing on top of the breakwaters had formed a circle and were singing a song. Duri had apparently gone up to join them at some point, fitting in perfectly.

"Did you and Sunja fight?" Wonee asked, posing the same question as Duri had.

Minee silently shook her head.

"That girl makes a whole fuss about her dad being a teacher, doesn't she?"

"…"

"Minee, if you keep following her around, you'll become a bully too. Get it?"

"…"

"Don't hang out with her. You're one of us now."

Wonee stretched out her hand and opened her palm, just like she had done before. Instead of resin, she held out a piece of real chewing gum, a pink one, poking its head out of its half-opened, oily wrapper.

"I don't want it."

"Come on, take it."

When Minee tried to walk away, Wonee grabbed her hand and placed the gum inside her palm. Then, as if Minee needed more reassurance, Wonee pressed her fingers into a fist and made her hold the gum.

"I don't want it!" Minee shouted, flustered, but she did not open her fist.

At high tide, she watched the sea rushing in. In the blink of an eye, the water came up to her ankles, and before she knew, it rose to her calves. Every time the sea lost its calm—colliding with the breakwaters and foaming up—a bulging wave unfurled itself, kissing the inky line left behind when the tide was last full. Along the coastal trail, covered in foam, a woman in an azure skirt made her way, carrying a white parasol. To Minee, watching from across the breakwaters, the white parasol looked like a butterfly and a seabird at the same time. Minee tossed the resin she was chewing into the sea, stealthily took off the oily wrapper from the gum in her hand, and put it in her mouth. Telling herself to put it back in the wrapper and hide it inside her pencil case before entering her house, lest her mother found out. Because her mother found chewing gum unseemly … And so, Minee betrayed Ok Sunja.

For a moment, Minee paused her travels. She heard someone walking in the hallway, dragging their slippers. Perhaps the dorm superintendent, an old spinster, had woken up and was making her rounds, in case any students had turned on their lamps underneath their quilts, secretly reading books. The footsteps grew distant, then whispers stirred the night air, sounding as if something banged against the walls, *thud thud thud*. Had the superintendent been on the prowl all the time? Minee was sure she heard her exchange whispers with the custodian. The sounds came from somewhere near the custodian's office, after all.

Minee's chest quivered violently. She knew something was about to happen. No, it already was happening. When the day dawned—Minee curled up from shame, worried that the sunlight would leave her no place to hide. The voices died out and the dormitory grew quiet again.

"Tamayama! What are you doing!"

"Yeeees, sir?"

The chemistry teacher, his hair trimmed short on all sides, shook his head in anger at Tamayama Junko's long, drooping answer.

"Stand up!"

"Yeees, sir."

Tamayama Junko got to her feet. But even being upright, she could hardly keep her body straight, swaying from side to side. Her scanty yellowish hair was stuck to the nape of her neck, making her look childish. She wore her hair loosely to one side in an attempt to give it some shape, without much success. Lifting her chin slightly, she kept her eyes downcast.

"What were you doing!"

"I was studying."

"Don't lie! You little troll!"

"It's true."

"Shut it! Show me what's underneath your textbook."

Tamayama Junko picked up the novel hidden underneath her textbook and wobbled over to the teacher's platform. Her skinny body and her uniform seemed to move independently from one another.

"You dimwit!"

The teacher grabbed the novel and hit Tamayama Junko on her head with it, thrice.

"Back to your seat! Blasted troll!"

Without a hint of shame, Tamayama Junko walked back to her seat, ever wobbling, biting the tip of her tongue. It meant nothing to her. She even enjoyed it. Except one time, when she got the history teacher so angry he all but choked. Almost as skinny as Tamayama Junko herself, he had a short face and his eyes bulged out like ping-pong balls. He was an avid supporter of Japanese imperialism, to the point where he would never let any other teacher support it more avidly. It was almost touching how, during that fateful history class, he got carried away as he rambled on about the underlying structures of the Japanese Empire and started to whine, "His Majesty, His Majesty!

Oh, oh …" Tamayama Junko made one simple mistake: she let a chuckle escape her lips. The man jumped to his feet, wiped his tears with a handkerchief, and stormed up to Tamayama. As he dragged her to the teacher's platform, he turned into some demonic spirit, then slammed her head against the wooden wall, kicked her and grabbed her by her hair, fuming with anger.

"You disloyal wrench! You traitor!" he yelled.

Everyone watched the dreadful act of violence unfold—the Japanese kids with the same anger in their eyes as the teacher, the Joseon kids with quite a different kind of anger. It was the teacher's first incident beating up a girl, and though she may have been the notorious Tamayama, it must have been her first time being so severely beaten up. With her face covered in bruises, she did not come to school for three days on end. Strangely enough, no one so much as mentioned the idea of expelling or suspending her.

After Vice-principal Ok transferred to a school on an island, Ok Sunja was never seen getting involved in a fight again.

One day in Grade 5, Minee was trimming the sweet potato vine in the school garden when she cut herself with the sickle. She wrapped a leaf around her bleeding finger and went back home to find her mother in surprise.

"What happened to your hand? It's bleeding!"

"I cut it."

"How!"

"With a sickle."

"A sickle?"

"We were in the school garden and I had to do the sweet potato vine …"

The Age of Doubt

"Hmm."

Mother applied a balm to Minee's hand and placed a bandage over her wound, then said she was going to visit the ajeossi from the chestnut grove and left. She came back late that night.

"We decided to have you transferred to the elementary school here."

"Mom!" Minee shouted in excitement.

"We discussed it and he says it's fine as long as we pay the contribution. He agreed to go and meet the Grade 5 homeroom teacher."

For someone who is as money-sensitive as Mother, this could hardly have been an easy decision. She kept pushing the problem of Minee's transfer to her father. Her father was so young he could have been Minee's older brother or Mother's younger brother. He no longer lived with them, as he had married a different woman with whom he had had another two daughters or so.

The next evening, Minee followed her mother to her grandfather's house. He was sitting on the maru with his tobacco pipe in his mouth, sticking out underneath his long mustache. Minee's grandmother, an old but charming woman, looked as if she had been snoozing for a while. The ajeossi, Mother's second cousin, must have just come home and was still wearing white dress pants with taut lines and a black serge school uniform top. His eyes smiled behind his thick-rimmed glasses. It looked like everything had gone according to plan.

"How did it go?" Mother asked.

The ajeossi walked out to the maru.

"Humph, well, yes, I had to buy her something, didn't I? Never bought a woman a present before, so I wasn't sure. I bought her some expensive sandals. She liked them."

"So she said it's okay?"

"You'll have to pay a small contribution, but otherwise yes, no problem."

Minee's grandfather, while emptying his pipe on top of a stepping stone, said that Minee had ended up getting hurt, because they had failed to hurry. Grandmother said all's well that ends well, bobbing her head.

"I don't want to say anything, but you might have done your daughter a disservice," the ajeossi said reproachfully. "She is clever enough for a decent school, but thanks to you she got stuck in a corner of the countryside. Isn't she in Grade 5 already?"

"Well, there's her father, so what can I ..." Mother said before bursting into tears. Minee's grandfather went into his room.

"They should hang that man, they really should. Treating his own family like they don't exist, how does that help anyone?" Minee's grandmother, now fully awake, heaped a load of cuss words on her father in an attempt to comfort Mother.

As soon as Mother stopped crying, the ajeossi started to talk about the Japanese "young lady" whom he had gone to meet on Minee's behalf. In a curious and pompous way. In fact, the ajeossi had failed his university entrance exam about three times. Despite the fact he had graduated from middle school with the most outstanding grades, the "academic devil" had interfered, as Minee's grandmother put it. While preparing for the exams with a towel wrapped around his head, he also taught evening classes at a private school. His short height being his only flaw, he had a handsome face and a good taste in clothes, just like Minee's grandfather, and although there was some criticism about his overly polite gestures or his gait, he was definitely "famous among the girls."

The Age of Doubt

"When Minee finishes school, send her to pharmaceutical college. Being a pharmacist is a woman's best occupation," the ajeossi said with no regard for Minee, who was always at the bottom of her class.

In the end, Minee's long-desired transfer came true. Shortly after Minee changed schools, Seo Duri, as if receiving a nudge, paid the contribution fee and transferred to Jaeil Elementary as well. The two little girls, wearing the uniforms they had only been able to behold with envious eyes, now went to school on the other side of the bay, from where they could see their old annex building standing lifelessly by the shore. Duri's house and all her family's land were on that side too. Following Duri's sister, they walked halfway up the mountain, where the fields seemed to form layers on top of one another. They looked down at the dazzlingly blue sea, a sailboat floating on its surface like a dreamy, sleeping swan, reflecting the golden sunlight—how poor and pitiable the annex looked against the backdrop of such beautiful scenery and how unrefined the children, who as always were playing with rubber bands on top of the breakwaters. Only a few days ago, Minee and Duri had been in their midst, tagging along, but that was nothing more than a distant memory now. Like sailors setting sail and reaching land, significance departed as swiftly as memory loss arrived.

The sunset dyed the sea deep red, while flocks of birds chased after schools of fish brought in by the tide. Minee and Duri were eating winter cherries they had plucked from the banks around the fields, singing songs they had learned in their new school as they let the wind guide them downhill. The annex on the other side of the bay looked all the more gloomy and pathetic. Over from that side, Minee had once gazed at an azure skirt and a white parasol, but now, standing on this side, all she saw was the desolate coastal trail, devoid of children, and the lonesome annex. Duri talked about her new friends. But from one moment to the next, Minee felt deflated. As if she was suddenly cornered by unfamiliar faces. Realizing she had nowhere to go and collect shellfish or dig up shepherd's purse, she saw hundreds of strange faces and double the number of eyes gather around her, scared to have lost her refuge. Or perhaps she finally felt happy to be where she was.

The Grade 5 Cherry Class homeroom teacher of her new school was a beautiful Japanese woman with thick eyelids and thin, dark eyebrows, seemingly penciled on her face. Despite her hasty character and her tendency to have an opinion about everything, Miss Haraki was the most gorgeous and outstanding of all female teachers at school. A tenacious go-getter, she had a strong temper and would never forgive herself if her class came second in any regard. She was as thorough in her insistence on eloquence as she was adamant about leaving the classroom spick and span at the end of the day, to the point where she banned socks altogether, even in winter. Be it academic pursuit or sports performance, she managed to spark the most original thoughts in her students.

When Minee first joined Miss Haraki's class (Duri enrolled in the co-ed Hawk Class), Miss Haraki asked her about the ajeossi several times. Whether she was truly interested in the ajeossi, as he seemed to suggest, or whether it was Minee whom she found charming, Miss Haraki frequently put Minee, a newcomer, in charge of making tea, which was normally a task for model students. Rather than joy, Minee felt fear at being placed above others. Perhaps because of the envious eyes directed at her or because Miss Haraki's choice seemed so misconceived that she could hardly accept it. Although she fervently wished to do better at school, praying for a miracle of sorts, she consistently remained in the bottom half of her class. She endlessly toiled to express herself cleverly and with flair, but what came out of her mouth could only be described as mumbling or stammering or incoherent gibberish that she did not intend at all. However much she tried to amuse her teachers or her classmates, her attempts only resulted in a deep blush, sending a fit of laughter across the room, which in turn almost brought her to tears. The only two honors she received was that she was once selected as one of two students to receive special arts instruction and once her writing was given a special mention. Nonetheless, Minee found it burdensome, almost suffocating, to be singled out by Miss Haraki. She feared Miss Haraki would start to hate her at some point. Until, after a while, Miss Haraki's interest in Minee ceased to exist. It happened when the bell rang and Miss Haraki entered the classroom. Minee coincidentally discovered a half-eaten cracker on the floor just beside her desk. Needless to say, it was not Minee who had dropped it. But, fearing a reprimand in case Miss Haraki were to notice, she instinctively picked it up and threw it out the window. Miss Haraki, who happened to be in a particularly bad mood that day, approached her with an angry look on her face.

"Minee! What was that?" she shouted.

"A c-c-cracker," Minee said, trembling from top to toe.

Without another word, Miss Haraki slapped Minee on the cheek. Miss Haraki's face was red like a radish, boiled with rage. It would take a long time before Minee managed to forget this shameful event, as if it were singed into the middle of her chest with a glowing iron.

At this point, Minee's lengthy travels came to a standstill, lingering on that shameful event. The night was deep and even the wind seemed to have dozed off, Minee being the only one wide awake. It was as though she felt blood dripping from the burn marks the iron had left behind.

What if the morning comes?

Minee wished for the night never to end; it was her sole desire. A desire that must have sprouted from the idea that she was bound to die. She had no hope, no doubts, nothing to wish for, the only thing she longed for was darkness. Darkness, not a sliver of sunlight trickling in.

It had been independent study hour at the dormitory, the second of the day. In the courtyard, surrounded by dormitory buildings on all sides, the orchids were covered in droplets of rain, shimmering in the light. In between the clovers, more droplets shimmered. A sudden shower had poured down before dinner. Now, the moon was floating in the sky. The sound of cautious footsteps reached Minee's ears.

"Rinoie-san, Mr. Majima is looking for you," the custodian said from outside her room.

Minee's face contorted. "What?"

"Hurry up, please. I said Mr. Majima is looking for you."

"Where do I find him? Should I go to the superintendent's office?"

"No, he's waiting by the front door."

As Minee rose, her legs wobbled. Apart from being Minee's homeroom teacher, Mr. Majima was also head of discipline. If he was looking for you, it almost certainly meant bad news. Minee's room senior and the other girls in her room knew as much.

They all looked at Minee with eyes that said, "What could it be?" Driven out by their stares, Minee left the room.

Mr. Majima was standing immediately outside the front door. On the other side of the glass window, Minee saw him in profile, his face partly hidden behind a field cap.

Minee took her shoes from the shoe cabinet and stepped outside. As the nearest streetlights stood all the way in front of the gates, only the moon shone light on Mr. Majima's face from behind bleak, speckled poplar leaves. The round shape of his face, his lips pressed firmly together, the visor of his cap sticking out, and his small eyes nearly invisible underneath its shade.

"Rinoie." His deep and low voice rang out.

"Yes, sir."

"Did you give Ogawa Naoko from Grade 8, Class 3 a letter earlier today?"

"…"

"Speak up! Did you?"

"Yes, sir."

Mr. Majima let a brief silence pass. The visor of his field cap inched forward. He seemed to look down at his feet. "And did you write it because someone asked you to?"

"No, sir."

"Hmm …" Mr. Majima's visor tilted further down. "Were you aware you were violating school regulations?"

"…"

"Did you know?! Or did you not?!"

"I knew, sir."

"Go inside."

Mr. Majima whipped his body around. The shadows of the trees were dancing on the ground as Mr. Majima strode off in between them. In Minee's eyes, Mr. Majima's thick legs, wrapped in gaiters, seemed to float up and down in the air.

The bell signaled the end of independent study, seemingly crushing Minee's skull as it rang. The bustling noise of children pouring out of their rooms, the noise of chatter. Minee, as if escaping, ran to the kitchen maid's lodging and sank down on the maru.

Part 2: The Punishment

Exhausted from lying awake all night, Minee finally fell asleep just before sunrise. She drifted into a shallow slumber, until the ear-piercing shriek of the morning bell bludgeoned her awake. Remembering how it once rang because of a nightly fire, the bell weighed down on Minee's chest like the groaning wind.

A twinkling star crashing into the thicket—how could she have dreamt so many dreams in such a short time? She could not bring any of them back to mind, let alone the one forewarning her of the day to come. Her head was so heavy that she struggled to keep her frail neck from collapsing. Her blood-shot eyes lay deep inside their sockets and, strangely, emitted light.

The dormitory building was tumultuous, like a train station at dawn. Sounds and movements stirred the air. Someone shouting from afar, people flocking to the washroom, the superintendent counting heads, friendly "good mornings," vigorous laughter, and the everlasting quarrel between the kitchen maid and the rest of the kitchen staff, bickering in the canteen. The cacophony created by these noises grew as loud as a battle cry one moment and as soft as a murmur the next, while the day got underway like the tide rolling in and drawing back. The very sunlight Minee dreaded so much would soon seep through the window.

Minee found herself kneeling in the middle of her room, having folded away her quilt with great difficulty. She was unsure when she had begun to feel left out of this morning commotion. She did not know why she was kneeling there, absent-mindedly, encircled by sounds and movements. The bell had long died out, but inside her head it continued to ring.

Minee's room senior, Aoki Shukuko, who was about to leave the room with a towel slung over her arm, turned to face her.

"Rinoie-san," she called.

Before dropping out, Minee had been classmates with Shukuko, but by the time she returned to school a year later, Shukuko had moved up to Grade 10. She was looking down at Minee, her face round and flat. As Minee turned her gaze up, her eyes reflected the ceiling light, looking even more dazzlingly crimson.

"You're sick, aren't you?" Shukuko asked, but Minee could only think about what Mr. Majima had said the night before and whether Shukuko was hinting at the same thing.

"How about I tell them you can't get out of bed, so you can take the day off?" she asked in a friendly voice.

Minee, her chest trembling, felt ashamed and trapped, as if Shukuko came up to her face, saying "Confess, confess!" Of course Shukuko was not the only one curious, the other girls in the room knew too. They knew something very bad must have happened, as they had seen Minee when, just before lights out, she had returned with an ashen face. The girls opened the cupboard, took out the broom and dustpan, and clanked them against each other as they waited for Minee's next words.

What if I pack my bags and run? Homebound!
What on earth happened? My letter, oh, my letter!
"What do you say? You look so pale …"

"I'm going to school."

"Are you sure?" Somewhat disappointed, Shukuko turned towards the other girls. "Hurry up and clean this place," she said, then left.

The others started to organize the room, discreetly trying to read Minee's face. With difficulty, Minee dragged her body from where she was kneeling to the window. The turquoise morning mist had slowly spread in all directions. On the far side of the green clover field, drenched in dew, ceiling lights shone through the doors to the rooms, which had been flung open in orderly succession, as girls walked out to the hallway, barefoot. Gradually, the lights lost their intensity, growing dim.

"Unni, if you're sick, just stay in. Your eyes are so red."

As if driven by those words, Minee grabbed her towel and left. Miss Miura, the dorm superintendent, was pacing up and down in front of her office. As her nickname, "Miss Chinless," suggested, there was no distinction between her jaw line and her neck. Her body was plump and even for a spinster she had an exceptionally cross temper. She said something to the custodian before going into her office and closing the door behind her. Minee hurried past the door. She was about to enter the washroom, which was not as crowded as before, when she heard her name.

"Rinoie-san," Shukuko called, as she wiped her face dry. "Let's talk."

She dragged Minee into the storeroom next to the toilets. Since the dormitory included a recreation room for the nurse, the storeroom was stocked with an organ, a sewing machine, and several piles of miscellaneous household items. It was pitch-black and smelled of mold.

"What happened last night?" Shukuko asked in a soft voice, wiping the last drops of water from her face. "Don't bottle it up, tell me."

"They probably found out I wrote someone a letter," Minee disclosed, swallowing the hatred she felt for her listener.

"A letter?" As if she'd imagined something far worse, all interest disappeared from Shukuko's round, flat face. "Who did you write it to?"

"Ogawa Naoko."

"What? You mean that Japanese kid from Grade 8?" This time, she was very surprised.

"Who says I can't write a letter to someone who's Japanese?" Minee shot at her viciously.

"Oh, oh, oh! A Japanese kid of all people … There's not a single Joseon girl in our school who's been in a S-relationship* with a Japanese kid. You're a weird one, you. So what did Mr. Majima say?"

"He asked me if I wrote the letter. Because I didn't write my name on it."

"Well, your handwriting gives it away anyway. That snake knows the way you write, doesn't he? But how did he find out? Do you think that bitch just handed it to him?"

Minee had kept a straight face out of hostility for Shukuko, but now her face turned bitter. "I don't know." She looked the other way. *My letter … My letter …* Tears welled up in her eyes.

* S-relationships (S관계), also called *Kurasu Esu* in Japanese, were romantic friendships between an older girl and a younger girl. For more information, see the commentary at the end of the collection.

She thought of the small azure sheet of paper with a pretty girl on it. She wondered whether it was right for that piece of paper, with all her dreams and feelings written on it, to be the object of such disdain and for her holy letter to be touched by tainted hands.

When the so-called "Greater East-Asian War" neared its end, this quiet, picturesque city with plenty of educational institutions, favorably located at the heart of fertile land and maintaining a high rate of consumption, suddenly faced a supply shortage. As shops started to run out of products, even sloppy, ink-blotted notebooks were hard to get, and an ordinary bar of soap became a precious commodity. Most students living in the dormitory came from respectable, small-town families who sent their daughters to school for them to grow into suitable marriage candidates, which meant that girls from Grade 9 and 10 developed the habit of asking their parents to remit them large sums of money, so they could accumulate items they might need in the future. This habit only worsened on account of the war and the supply shortage, to the point where shops were crowded with young girls every Sunday, even when there was almost nothing left to buy. Apart from cosmetics shops, they also flocked to the kimono seller, a place which had very little to do with the Joseon people, where they collected whatever they could find, including loosely woven imitation textile—they said they would use it as a blanket—as well as bowls, teacups, and plates, picking them up at random as long as they were free from cracks, while the tougher ones among them acquired light bulbs, straw slippers, and so on. Although Minee spent almost equally as much money as they did, she did not add a single item to her wicker suitcase throughout this fad. However, she did store a few university-style notebooks, which were impossible to get by then, safely in her desk drawer. From time to time, she found pleasure in writing poetry for her eyes only, and when her heart so desired she wrote something in her personal diary, as opposed to the one she turned in at school. As far as precious possessions went, her notebooks knew no equal. Above all, she treasured the small, azure one with the little girl on it. A few times she had meant to reorganize her poems in that most special notebook. But, it being only a single notebook, she had trouble deciding which poems to select and put off the task, using its first page to write a letter to Ogawa Naoko instead, only for her to hand it over to Mr. Majima? Really?

Minee bit her lip.

"And you gave the letter directly to Ogawa?" Shukuko's voice sounded distant.

"No."

"Then who did?"

"Tamayama-san."

"What? Our glamorous phantom?" A scornful grin appeared on Shukuko's face. "Jeez, you must've lost your mind. Wouldn't it make sense for her to steal the letter?"

"…"

"Someone must've given it to Mr. Majima, if it wasn't Ogawa herself."

"You don't mean she told on me, do you?"

Minee freed herself from the storeroom, went over to the washroom, and splashed water in her face for a long time. Her tears refused to stop flowing.

Avoiding the canteen by skipping breakfast, Minee went to school. When she walked through the gates, she noticed Tamayama Junko standing like a shadow beside the juniper in the corner next to the lecture hall. She waved to Minee. Furrowing her narrow brow, grinning. The moment Minee saw her, she felt humiliated. Ignoring Tamayama Junko, Minee rushed to her classroom with a blush on her face.

Inside the classroom, a group of Japanese kids from the village on the opposite side of the river huddled together. The principal's daughter, Mori Kazuko, with her wide mouth and prominent eyelids; Sakamoto Akiko, known among her friends by her warrior nickname "Sakamoto Ryuma," whose nose, mouth, limbs, and every other body part were so big and whose voice so deep that people wondered whether she was accidentally born into a man's body; and Suzuki Teru, with her beautiful white skin and her pretty red lips, whose family ran a boarding house and whom the rest of group, knowing she was keen to please them, used as their personal assistant. Beside them, a few more congregated, whispering. They all did well at school and yet were full of mischief. Since the principal's daughter was one of them, the teachers were lenient towards them and treated them with caution, but these trouble-makers were clever for their age, despite being self-absorbed and full of condescension. Willy-nilly, everyone was under their sway, given that they lived in the same Japanese village as the high-ranking government officials and academics. Ogawa Naoko also lived there, so perhaps she had been in a S-relationship with a member of this particular club. Perhaps they were secretly discussing Ogawa Naoko's letter at this very moment. But when Minee entered the classroom, none of them showed her any interest. They probably had yet to find out that Minee was behind it all.

As Minee put down her backpack, it felt as though her feet were unresponsive, as if they were stuck in a quagmire, and she panicked. She fled to the tool shed in the backyard and stood against the side of it. It was always shady and humid next to the shed, above which an old fig tree extended its branches, reaching beyond the school fence, towards the sun. Leaning against the tree, Minee looked up at the blue sky, alone.

If only it were to rain …

If it were to pour, they would call off the morning assembly, normally held on the schoolyard. That way, Minee would be spared from having to face Ogawa Naoko. But the late spring sky only seemed to quiver with heat. She felt every shake coming at her, physically, as if to mock her. The mockery and the shaking beat against Minee's chest in unison, violently battered her whole body like the morning bell had done earlier. A whirlwind of feverish agitation, seemingly driving her mad, urged Minee on. The initial chuckles of the club members from across the river, followed by roars of laughter as they doubled up—it sounded as if they were right beside her. Minee made a fist and punched the fig tree. But as her hand hit the sturdy bark of the tree, so too did Minee's heart hit upon despair.

"Rinoie-san!" It sounded like the voice of the devil. "Rinoie-san!"

Tamayama Junko ran up to her, crossing the wooden stepping panels in the gallery that connected the janitor's room to the main building. Her scanty hair fluttered up and down. It reminded Minee of fallen leaves being swept up by the wind.

"Do you even know how long I've been looking for you?" Tamayama Junko asked slowly, without panting, as if she was so skinny that the wind had simply carried her.

"Why would you!" Minee shot an angry look at Tamayama Junko.

"Why would I? I was afraid something terrible happened!" she said, her thin lips agape.

"It's none of your business!"

"Gosh, calm down."

"Can't I just drop out of school?"

"Drop out? Again?" She snickered, as if to ridicule Minee for being naive. "What you did was nothing serious. Some kids did something way worse, but they keep going to school as if nothing happened."

"Easy for you to say, isn't it?"

"Hey, so what if that snake-man called for you last night?"

"Who told you!"

"One of the girls from your room."

"And why do you care!"

"I'm partly responsible, aren't I? I mean, I made a mistake. I was rash."

Minee looked Tamayama Junko in the eyes.

"You know who did it? The black giant."

Minee was confused.

"Well, no matter how long I waited for Ogawa, she didn't come. You know, I waited and waited, until I had no other option but to give it to the black giant, see? I asked her to pass it on to Ogawa. I thought: 'It's just a note, not a letter, it'll be fine.' But that was a mistake."

Minee kept staring daggers at Tamayama Junko.

"I thought my job was done and went back to the dormitory. Then my next-door neighbor came over to my room. Now I just want to punch myself for not thinking about it earlier." She pretended to beat her own chest. "If I'd just given your letter to my neighbor, nothing would've happened. So, we were just talking about this and that, until suddenly she says that the black giant gave your letter to Miss Ueda, you know? I immediately felt a lump in my chest. According to my neighbor, the black giant is a nutcase. Everyone knows her for her foul temper, the worst of all the Japanese kids. Even the Japanese kids hate her, but when she's around, they don't even dare budge. She's really ugly and she has something against Ogawa, apparently. So yeah, this note of yours went straight into a tiger's cave, if you get what I mean?"

"Who's this black giant?" Minee felt her anger cool down.

"This really ugly Japanese girl. Her eyes are as big as an owl's and she looks dark and murky. She's called Hori."

"So you're saying Ogawa-san never even received my letter?"

"Exactly. Hori gave it to her homeroom teacher at the end of day assembly, which began only a second after I gave her the letter."

With that, the angry look on Minee's face vanished completely.

The relationship between Minee and Tamayama Junko was a strange one.

Three years earlier, Minee had ran into Ok Sunja for the first time since Sunja's family had moved to an island after Vice-principal Ok was transferred to a different school. That day, the schoolyard was crowded with examinees. Students gathered from all directions, inhaling crisp winter air as they fretfully grouped together in twos and threes. Minee and her classmates, enraptured by the idea of being older than others—as they were moving up to Grade 9—walked crisscross among the examinees. They had gone to play games in Dorm 2 and were on their way back to Dorm 1. When they were about to pass the school gates, Minee spotted Ok Sunja among the examinees, a name tag pinned on her chest. She was wearing a black skirt and jeogori. Even though she seemed to have no friends, she stood there without a hint of awkwardness, accompanied by Vice-principal Ok, his shoulders as ever hunching forward. Unable to calm his nerves, he took out a white handkerchief and wiped his nose. Minee instinctively moved away from them, until one of her classmates, unaware of the situation, grabbed her arm and dragged her back in Sunja's direction.

"Aigo, who do we have here?" Sunja said with a fumbling voice, as she noticed Minee and grabbed her by the hem of her skirt. "If this isn't Lee Minee?"

In the confusion of the moment, Minee, feeling increasingly ill at ease, bowed deeply to Vice-principal Ok, who failed to recognize her.

"It's Lee Minee. She was in your Grade 4 class in XX District," Sunja said, seeing the puzzled look on his face. "She used to come to our house too."

Vice-principal Ok nodded, but his face betrayed that he did not remember. He seemed to have aged since the last time Minee saw him, and he was clearly worried about Sunja's exam.

Ok Sunja went on to explain how she had been forced to stay home for a year because of her mother's illness and how she had applied for S Girls' High School in Seoul, without success. Unlike before, she spoke politely and had a cautious look in her eyes. Minee was able to quell her surprise and confusion, but the next thing she felt was a sense of complete disbelief. If Sunja had passed the entrance exam and was about to enroll at this school, it meant someone who used to be Minee's senior was now to become her junior, which was hard to comprehend, let alone accept as a potential reality. How many years had gone by? Already clouded by the spell of time, Minee now felt entangled by yet another spell. Dreams and reality straddled her mind, blurred her vision, and made her head spin in tiny circles, at the center of which fragments of time resurfaced, making her awkward state of mind draw near when the fragments distanced themselves and stand still when they seemed to be rolling around. When the fragments of time stood still, she felt a bitter pang of pain.

Ok Sunja's sluggish tone of voice deepened Minee's confusion and disbelief. She had to ask herself whether the Ok Sunja standing before her was the same Ok Sunja she knew, whose thinnish lips moved faster than an airplane propeller. Did her memories of Sunja—shapes, colors, images lingering in a distant corner of her mind—bear any relation to the girl she saw in front of her? She could not combine them, nor could she separate them. But when it occurred to her that she might as well ignore these strange things, her memories and the present alike, a sense of guilt creeped up on her. The same kind of guilt she had felt at the stormy breakwaters when she discarded her resin gum and secretly replaced it with real gum. However, her instinctive hatred, which she had had then as much as now, was couched in her guilt, and the more this rang true the deeper her guilt grew, until one day perhaps guilt and instincts would coexist, forever entrapped in an race with no end.

While giving half-hearted answers to a rambling Ok Sunja, Minee looked at Vice-principal Ok's silver-rimmed glasses from the corner of her eye as he took out his white handkerchief and wiped his nose so hard his philtrum turned red. Despite his not remembering her, it was Vice-principal Ok who embodied the fact that images of past and present were visibly connected, finally making Minee feel certain about the images in her mind.

Anyhow, Ok Sunja had passed the entrance exam. And thanks to her striking appearance, she immediately made a lasting impression as she entered the scene. Although Sunja never bowed to Minee when they ran into each other on the street, she was undeniably Minee's junior. For that reason, they did not like bumping into each other.

After the first term of Grade 8, Minee spent the summer in her hometown. Immediately after the end of term, incidents started occurring both at her family's house and at school. Despite being different in nature, the incidents came to a joint explosion around the start of the second term. Details will surface in the next chapter, but Minee, having an inborn tendency to make mistakes and harboring a deep sense of anger, stubborn as she was, ended up dropping out of school on her own accord. The incidents may have been the last straw, since she had felt the urge to suspend her education several times before, finding it difficult to adapt to life at her new school and abhorring the rules and regulations that such institutions represented. However, during her first year at home she hardly gained any peace of mind. Around that time, the ajeossi from the chestnut grove graduated from the very university he had failed to get into so many times, what with the academic devil—he had somehow got accepted and completed his degree. He initially promised that if he were to be assigned a post at the girls' school in K City that he had applied for, he would take Minee with him. But after graduating he received word that he was to take a position at a pharmaceutical company, forcing him to give up on his promise.

"What do you say? Why don't you go back to school, huh? If you go back to your old school, it'll be a simple procedure," the ajeossi placated Minee.

After returning to school, Minee noticed that her once kind-hearted friends now looked down on her from a pedestal of seniority. Her peers, who used to be her juniors, gave her strange looks. Only Ok Sunja was different. First she had been Minee's senior, then Minee had been hers, but now, being peers, the gulf that used to separate them seemed to have disappeared. The second and third term of Grade 8 went by without any interaction between them as they were in different classrooms. But when they moved up to Grade 9, they were assigned to the same classroom, and Ok Sunja came to occupy the seat right behind Minee, meaning they were bound to see more of each other, whether they liked it or not.

The moment Ok Sunja joined the school, she was labelled as a "blacklist student." Although she had never even come close to the most dangerous transgression of all, namely a romance between a girl and a boy—an extremely rare phenomenon within the walls of the girls' school, though not entirely non-existent either—school authorities kept Ok Sunja under surveillance as if she were capable of far more serious crimes, the reasons for which Minee failed to understand. Teachers treated her indifferently, as they would an abominable student, and showered her with profanities such as "blasted troll." Fellow students, unsurprisingly, made fun of her for being skinny, calling her "Pretty Willow" to her face but "Pretty Phantom" behind her, constantly scrutinizing her and always keeping her at arm's length. Admittedly, the rumors that shrouded her would have made anyone scrutinize her. Although she never went as far as having a romantic affair with a boy herself, she did act as the so-called "errand girl" of such contemptible love. With Ok Sunja's help, it turned out, a relationship above and beyond the romantic sprouted right underneath the eyes of school authorities, a S-relationship. Allegedly, she also sold food under the table to hungry dormitory dwellers and brought in lodgers to the boarding house. Although most students did not want anything to do with her, it did not stop them from consulting her if they had a crush on one of their juniors. On Sundays, a number of dormitory residents went to visit her, filling their stomachs with whatever food she sold. Once, Minee went along, but only once. Why did everyone keep someone like Ok Sunja, who served the convenience of others, at a distance? She was always by herself at school. Apart from giving out relationship advice, she had no one to talk to as a friend. She no longer fought, she never spoke ill of others, and she was good at keeping secrets. She did miss class on a regular basis, which often resulted in her being punished and having to kneel in the schoolyard. She moved her limbs extremely slowly and lazily, like a clown, evoking a contemptuous smile along with the kind of pity you can hardly laugh away. She never kept her diary, never took part in handicraft or sewing, and never did her homework. But everyone borrowed her books and some even asked her to solve their math problems. Surprisingly, she managed to maintain a mediocre score.

Then, the letter incident. It was cooked up two days earlier, on a Saturday afternoon. Could the moment that set everything in motion be called … an accident? After lunch, the students went out to the schoolyard, bar three or four who stayed behind in the classroom, chatting. Minee leant against the windowsill and looked at the world outside through a veil of blue canna lilies dancing in the wind. When Minee poked her head out the window, the flowers, waving up and down, brushed against her face. Most of the seniors were gathered in one corner of the schoolyard, talking, while the juniors occupied the middle, skipping rope, playing volleyball, and playing tag. The school-yard bathed in white sunlight, its border being indicated by the shade of the assembly hall and the junipers standing next to it.

Minee's eyes froze. Her gaze rested on a pair of baggy pants with a pattern of water drops—white water drops against a persimmon background. Given the sports t-shirt above it, the girl probably had PE class soon. She had a bright smile on her face. Having tucked her hair behind her ears because it was hot outside, her roundish forehead showed. Her smile disappeared behind a canna lily blocking Minee's view. She pushed the flow-er aside and the cute girl reappeared. Ogawa Naoko from Class 3 of Grade 7, next door to Minee's classroom. That girl was a bouquet of violets. Like the violets Minee wrote poems about, a small head on a small body. Every time she jumped up, her shiny, lustrous hair shook wildly.

Minee followed Naoko with her gaze. She seemed to be play-ing tag, suddenly whipping around and running off. She ran up to the juniper, halted, then turned around and smiled brightly. Her forehead looked particularly white in the shade. If someone chased after her, she ran a circle around the tree and dashed away.

In the following days, Minee kept looking for Naoko from afar, afraid to go near her. She always tried to spot Naoko's recognizable pants. When she came to school in the morning, she hid behind the old shoeshiner and looked for the pants with the water drops. When the whole school went outside for a drill, she looked for the pants with the water drops. Wherever they were, whatever happened, those pants caught her eye. Always from afar. She had never even heard Ogawa Naoko's voice.

When Minee had watched her from the windowsill, Ogawa Naoko disappeared from view only to reappear a moment later. Like a billiard ball scattering away from the rest after a hit, then bouncing off the sides of the table and returning to its place. No, like a star scattering across the sky, she disappeared and reappeared in front of Minee's eyes …

If Minee went home after class without seeing the pants with the water drops, she felt sad and empty inside. Such moments were like endless voids, where she felt lonely and obstinate, despising ordinary faces and disdaining worthless talk, unwilling to share her private world with anyone else.

"Ogawa Naoko. She's a pretty one, isn't she?" A sluggish voice startled Minee, who immediately stood up straight and backed away from the windowsill. Tamayama Junko laughed, as if she saw right through Minee's heart. "Isn't she?" she repeated.

"Duh!" Minee shot back angrily, as she turned her head and looked back at the schoolyard.

"You like her, don't you?"

Minee turned her head again. She gave Tamayama Junko a hateful stare. "So what if I do? Anything against it?"

"Who said I had something against it?"

Minee bent over a little, leant on her elbows, and let her chin rest on her hands.

"Would you dare to write her a letter?"

Minee said nothing.

"You wouldn't?" Tamayama Junko asked again.

A letter? A letter, she says? It never even crossed my mind.

Minee felt herself being dragged along. Entranced by Tamayama Junko's magic spell. To be sure, her enchantments were hard to resist.

"If she finds out you wrote her a letter, she'll definitely write you back."

Minee's eyes sparkled.

"I mean, you're pretty too."

Is it true? Would she write me back? Minee felt short of breath.

"You haven't been in a S-relationship yet, have you? One way or another, you'll have to have it with someone eventually."

While the water drops on Naoko's pants were alternately visible and invisible between the group of children, Tamayama Junko's tongue whispered sweetly in Minee's ear, like the devil. Like a sorcerer playing the flute. Gradually, the mysterious music approached Minee and shook her chest, turning her beautiful, fearful longing into hunger.

She'll write me back. Yes, she'll definitely write me back.

The noise from the schoolyard grew dim, overpowered by the mysterious flute music. Everyone outside ceased to move, with Naoko's pants in the middle of the tableau. The beautiful music, whatever it was, made Minee's heart overflow.

"Her dad teaches at a famer's school." A human voice pierced through the flute music. "She has a younger brother, but no sisters."

What? She has a brother? Just like other people?

Instantly, the colors of the tableau grew faint. The music receded. The schoolyard noises came to the forefront again, as the kids continued to run around in dizzying circles. Minee's fantasy of Ogawa Naoko had suffered a blow. The fact that she, like so many others, had a sibling, felt strange in a decidedly bad way. This violet was supposed to bloom alone, she could not be one of those miniscule mushrooms clustered in the shade of a rock.

"So, you write that letter, I'll make sure she gets it."

"You?" Minee perked up again.

"Yes, me."

"How?"

"Just leave it to me. Write something nice and bring it to me."

That Saturday night, the dormitory was astir as if it were a festive day. It was independent study hour, but not a single student was actually studying. The superintendents had the tradition of gathering in Dorm 3, which only housed Japanese students, and taking a bath while eating all kinds of food they brought. Naturally, no one was stupid enough to observe independent study hours in a dormitory without superintendents. Instead, the seniors did their make-up and roamed from room to room in hanboks only meant for nightdress, kicking up a fuss—a usual Saturday. Having been cooped up in a cage for a week, the children would regain their freedom at the break of dawn. Such was the night. Minee did not join the others, nose-deep in a poetry collection by Saijō Yaso. Not that she was reading. She was thinking.

The bell rang throughout the noisy dormitory announcing lights out, and indeed, one by one, the lights dimmed. Dreams of eating to one's heart's content, dreams of visiting one's mother's side of the family, dreams of finally being able to buy a long-desired item; everyone was fast asleep, dreaming a whole range of dreams. Except Minee.

The following day, Minee stayed behind in the dormitory when everyone else went to have fun outside. The dormitory, completely deserted, was dead silent. Being alone, Minee felt a mixture of ecstasy and terror run down the nape of her neck as she wrote and rewrote her letter. It was impossibly hard. After erasing everything she had written and starting over again several times, she took her azure notebook from her drawer and diligently copied the final version of her letter onto the first page. She put the sheet of paper in a white envelope and walked along the deserted hallway, listening to the echo of her footsteps. Having washed her face in the washroom, she looked at her reflection in the mirror and returned to her room. She grabbed her backpack, stuck the white envelope in between two books, and went out to the courtyard. Finding a spot between the dazzlingly green clovers, she stretched her legs and lay back. The sensation of the clovers touching her bare feet was refreshingly ticklish. She imagined the rectangular building around her—the canteen and the superintendent's washroom facing each other and two opposing sides with student rooms—as the fortress wall of a splendid palace, the clover courtyard representing its main quarters. Clouds drifted over Minee's head, casting a shadow over her. She vaguely heard the voice of the kitchen maid from the backyard, until, the next moment, she fell asleep.

That night, she finally slept deeply again.

Knowing it was not Ogawa Naoko who had handed her letter to the teachers, Minee felt much calmer. Although she was unable to shake off her fear, dreading every possible way in which she might be punished for violating the rules, her heartache largely subsided. Even the terror of her imminent punishment did not make her abandon the idea of Ogawa Naoko. What if Naoko witnessed her receiving the punishment, what if the others made fun of her and spread rumors that reached Naoko's ears …

The morning assembly went by without trouble. Apart from Tamayama Junko and Minee's room senior, no one seemed to take note of the enormous trauma Minee was lugging around.

Ogawa Naoko, the reason for it all, did not seem to be aware of it either. Maybe she thought it had all been Tamayama Junko's doing.

The first period began peacefully. Civics class, as dull as ever, somehow seemed to fly by, while recess, which always seemed way too short, lasted as long as a summer afternoon. The bell simply refused to ring.

Several times, Minee thought she heard someone push the door open, poke their head out and say, "Rinoie-san, teachers' office." It was wretched torture, reawakening the extreme agony of having been born into this world. Every time she heard the sound of the bell, indicating the end of a period, she wiped off the sweat from her forehead and shuddered. After her last class, she would be safe until the end of day assembly.

During the assembly, Mr. Majima entered the classroom as usual, inching slightly forward and lifting his eyes.

"All rise!" the row head ordered.

Everyone rose to their feet. Minee hoped for the life of her that she could hide behind the girl in front of her, but it turned out to be wishful thinking as her seat was in a diagonal line from the teacher's platform. There was no way to avoid Mr. Majima's gaze.

"Bow!"

Bending forward, Minee finally managed to breathe.

"Be seated!"

Everyone took their seats.

Hardly a second later, Mr. Majima's deep voice reverberated through the room: "It appears someone from a different class went outside last night! Here in Class 1 of Grade 9 there is no such student, is there?"

Mr. Majima fired a sharp glare at Tamayama Junko. His small eyes flickered terrifyingly. Tamayama Junko maintained her composure without even slightly shrinking back. But Minee, sitting right in front of her, grew as pale as paper. It was impossible that he was talking about Minee, for she had been inside all night. But it felt like he aimed his gaze directly at her.

"It seems this wasn't the first time, as I'm sure those of you who are lodging will know! If any of you believe that it is acceptable to go on nightly walks like a godforsaken owl, you're a disgrace! The minute we find out who did this, they're in for a severe punishment from the school authorities! Understood?!"

"Yes, sir."

"Your minds seem to lack discipline lately. This country is in crisis and I will not allow for any unwholesome mind or degenerate spirit to go unpunished! At this very moment, brave soldiers are dying heroic deaths on the battlefront! Enemy planes are flying in our sky! You may not be able to go to the battlefront, but you must never forget the tension of a wartime attitude! The day you do, the enemy will devour us! Understood?!"

"Yes, sir."

Mr. Majima rolled his small eyes, almost touching his brows with his pupils. He pressed together his lips, which in a similar way almost touched his nose. Minee wondered if he was going to say something else, but he remained motionless for a long time before opening his mouth again.

"Recently, there has been an increasing number of good-for-nothings who fail to keep a diary! Make sure to write an entry every day, don't ever miss one! That's it for now."

"All rise!"

"Bow!"

"Be seated!"

Mr. Majima's chubby body disappeared through the door. He did not tell Minee to see him in the teachers' office.

"Hey, Rinoie-san, he didn't say a word about it!" Tamayama Junko whispered under her breath. Mori Kazuko, the principal's daughter, glanced at them from the corner of her eye. Her eyes betrayed that she was curious about them and the letter for Ogawa Naoko.

The following day went by without anything happening. If Minee had to be punished sooner or later, she would rather get it over with immediately. It made no sense for this situation to go on forever. Then, on the third day towards the end of lunch hour, it finally happened.

"Rinoie-san, teachers' office," the row head said.

After the Japanese kids had spread the story far and wide from mouth to mouth, the letter incident must have come to the surface. As Minee got up silently and walked away, the Japanese kids cast a look of disdain at her, whereas the Joseon kids looked at her in surprise.

Passing through the hallway, Minee was reminded of the depressing hallway in the hospital where her mother had been operated on. Her fear ebbed away, until the only thing she felt was helplessness. When she entered the teachers' office, Miss Ueda, the music teacher who was also Ogawa Naoko's homeroom teacher, quickly picked up her music book and walked out with an awkward smile.

Minee walked up to Mr. Majima's desk. He did not look up, staring intently at what he was writing. The skin in the nape of his neck was losing its elasticity and a number of silver hairs poked their heads out of his shortly trimmed coiffure. In the window, Miss Ueda's plump figure passed by as she carried her music book to the music room. For a while, Mr. Majima kept writing, unflinching and without looking up, until his pen finally stopped moving.

"You clearly do not reflect on your behavior!"

Minee let her head hang.

"You haven't written a single diary entry for the last three days! If you had thought about your deeds, you would have written your reflections in your diary, am I right?" he said, still looking down. "Kneel!"

Mr. Majima, fuming, pointed at the floor beside his chair. Minee knelt. It was her first time having to do so. Before she had dropped out, she had repeatedly defied her then homeroom teacher, a music teacher who was later transferred, but she had never been punished like this. Surprisingly, a weight was lifted off her chest. She was glad to be punished behind Mr. Majima's desk, where passing-by teachers could not see her, because she knew some students were forced to stand in the middle of the teacher's office or in the hallway, holding photos marked with an X in red ink, as a punishment for bringing them to school. Inwardly, Minee thanked Mr. Majima.

After her last class, Minee went back to her classroom for the end of day assembly. But Mr. Majima did not show up. Minee, while thanking him again, felt how deep a wound her punishment had left behind. For now, she had survived hours of anxiety and fear and her teacher's burning rage, but in every corner of her skin, every joint of her body, she was acutely aware of the fact that the world was a place as desolate as a heap of ash. Trampled and befouled as she was, she headed towards somewhere gray, reminiscent of a dreary ghost town.

Part 3: Colors and Sounds

In reality, there was nothing on the other side of the paper sliding door, but in Minee's eyes a succession of silhouettes passed by. As she lay in bed, countless feet made their way through the hallway in front of her room, the echoes of which made her feel like she was in a high, round dome.

Minee had never seen any such thing.

In the cold light falling from the rail of the glass outer door on the hallway, she saw something different from the usual procession of people carrying their chopsticks and floor cushions to the canteen. The silhouettes seemed to wear perfectly ironed skirts, straightened out like sheets of paper having been placed underneath a mattress overnight. They had tied their hair with white ribbons that were only used during festivities. The girls were quietly shuffling towards the lecture hall, which a purple curtain had turned into a ceremonial venue, in the middle of which the sacrosanct Rising Sun flag hung.

"Mizuhara-san, did you do your homework?"

"Oh, shoot! I didn't know we had any. What do I do? Fox is going to go flip."

The voices of Masuyama Sadako and Mizuhara Fukuki, classmates of Minee. Sadako's high hairline and Fukuki's fuzzy curls flitted past side by side, disappearing out of sight in the blink of an eye, while their steps echoed through the hallway as they crossed the stepping panels, and an image of them meekly forming a line to enter the lecture hall lingered in Minee's mind.

Since the dormitory roof warded off the sun, the grass in the courtyard was still covered in dew, making the clovers glow bright green, while the sounds of footsteps and conversations traveled across from the other side.

The sounds, as sounds tend to do, trampled and pounded Minee's chest as they passed her by, whereas the images, as images tend to do, observed a solemn silence.

"Red cape! Blue cape!"

Swarming out of their classrooms, the students shrieked and squealed. They ran out to the schoolyard without putting on their shoes. Thousands of feet flooded out, galloping across the hallway, down the stairs.

"Red cape! Blue cape!"

The spooky phrase spread out at an alarming rate. Even faster than the words, the shouting gave rise to a succession of echoes, which in turn were swept up in the enigmatic cries: "Red cape! Blue cape! Red, blue! Cape, cape!" Hearts froze, the classroom windows shook, the ceiling spun, the chairs danced in circles, and, seen from above, dots as black as spider eggs swarmed about the schoolyard, while the early summer sun blasted its white rays.

Every last teacher came running out, as did the janitor and the students from Grade 6. Miss Min, homeroom teacher of Grade 1, who was wearing a black skirt and a white ramie summer jacket, with her bulging eyes and her salt-and-pepper topknot in disarray, spanked the children on their behinds and yelled her lungs out, as her face went from red to crimson. A good-looking Japanese teacher, who only had a few pockmarks and was wearing a white satin blouse with greenish yellow stripes reminiscent of a cookie wrapper, fervently blew her whistle, fluttering the bow of her blouse. Her shiny golden tooth showed repeatedly as she drew breath. The male teachers, not knowing what to do with themselves, smiled wryly.

"Aah! Aaaah—"

The echoes reached a climax, as if heralding the end of the world.

The ridiculous uproar was soon suppressed.

Who on earth had fabricated the story where a red-caped or blue-caped monster resided in the toilet, munching on innocent children? It was like so often with fires: cause unknown. A whirlwind sparking commotion.

The students returned to their classrooms. Rays of sunlight, like pieces of broken glass, continued to dance on the completely deserted schoolyard. Against the backdrop of the charcoal-colored wooden building, the windows, painted white, looked like the eyeballs of a dark stranger, while their lattice panels were motionless, creating a strangely dreamlike atmosphere.

"Butterfly, butterfly, fly this way! Blue butterfly, white butterfly!"

Someone in the Grade 1 classroom read out a Joseon language text, trying their best to articulate every word. The sound of a pump organ drifted by too. Empty seats, full seats, places crowded with noise, places wrapped in silence—as time went by, such things changed like a merry-go-round.

Minee, walking home by herself, crossed the stone bridge. When she passed underneath the hollow acacias, she picked up her pace. The tree stumps near the creek were covered in moss, and their reflection on the water surface made the creek look green. Leaving the forest, Minee reached a quiet backstreet where government officials resided. As the road widened, so did the breadth of sunlight, making visible the dust that had settled on the weeds by the roadside.

Minee continued to walk in the shade, sticking closely to

the walls. She saw traditional Japanese storehouses plastered with white limestone, a small garden patch where a juniper lay horizontally, its roots bound together with a rope, and a neatly aligned row of wooden houses, their paint having faded gray over the course of time. When she walked past a fenceless house, standing right by the roadside, she heard someone reading from a book. Behind the window, its blinds rolled up, a Japanese girl of around Minee's age sat in front of a desk with a bowl of red candies by her side. The girl stopped reading and rolled her eyes at Minee.

"Go back to your people!" the girl yelled.

Minee flinched. "Stupid fool!" she said in Japanese.

And she ran. A rush of fear came over her, because it seemed not as if the Japanese girl was chasing after her, but a Japanese policeman brandishing a long sword. When she looked back, the road was empty save the blinding sunlight. She thought about hurrying back home, asking her mother for one jeon and using that money to buy herself a white bean paste cookie. The sensation of the cookie slowly melting in her mouth, the slightly bitter taste of the blackened tip.

You know what, I'll buy myself some cotton candy.

Whenever the seller pressed the pedal, *click-clack*, the candy floss would gather on his skewer, like a pink cloud. Materializing out of thin air and floating up as if bound for the blue sky.

Where did I leave my jeogori?

Minee cocked her head. Last spring, shortly after she started Grade 1, she lost her ivory serge jeogori with her nametag and a handkerchief pinned to its chest, and she had immediately knew her mom was going to give her a good thrashing on the calves. That day, she did not receive a jeon. Instead, she had sobbed and sniveled underneath the spindle tree, wondering secretly whether her mother was a cruel stepmother like the one she knew from a folktale.

Did I lose my jeogori? How strange.

However much Minee racked her brains, she could not think of any place where she might have left her jeogori. She could hardly even recall whether she had taken it off before walking home. But she vividly remembered her mother's words from the day she had had her calves thrashed.

"Did you hang your mind on a tree somewhere, you little brat? You lost your jeogori, huh? Well, tomorrow you can walk to school naked!"

She did not get a single coin, and she could not buy herself cotton candy.

As she walked further down the road, carrying her backpack, she ran into an old sign, which said something about an office, written in ink. Through the half-open iron gate, a red brick house was vaguely visible, hidden behind a dense group of trees. The strips of its lattice windows were coated in white paint. The branches of the old cherry trees, through their almost black leaves, gave off a velvety, ashen glimmer. Minee saw their red fruit dangling here and there. Such charming little fruits. Despite knowing their bitterish taste, Minee felt mysteriously attracted to the fruit and forgot how she had wanted to run home and buy herself a white bean paste cookie with her mother's money, staring at the trees as if she had lost her mind. The change from red to purple, the smaller fruit gradually growing big. All inside Minee's heart. On the ground, there were winter cherries, squidgy and orange. With the spotty red pouch, which you had to tear open for the cherries to come out. During the festival of Tanabata, held on the seventh day of the seventh month, Japanese people crafted paper boats, loading them with winter cherries and other kinds of small fruit before sending them off onto sea. That night, the whole shoreline was awash with fireworks, full of light and the sound of geta, the lingering smell of gunpowder intermixing with that of the ocean. The paper boats with burning candles, small and thin like candy cigarettes, only traveled for a moment before sinking to the depths, but the colorful, noisy fireworks, the lights, the laughter, and the paper boats being sent to sea time and time again, did not stop as the night deepened. The paper boats carried the winter cherries. Minee would put her hands behind her back, taking in the enchanting shoreline, thinking of nothing but the winter cherries on the paper boats. Would they get eaten by a fish? By an octopus? Sometimes a different scene would drift into Minee's head.

On the night of Buddha's Birthday, monks in wonderfully embroidered robes along with thousands of devotees carrying lamps paraded through the city, including Minee's mother, wearing a light blue skirt and holding a rosary in her hand. Minee struggled to keep up with her mother, but when she grabbed the back of her skirt, Mother took her hand, saying she did not want it to stain. Minee remembered the crunching sound of her mother's skirt as she walked on. On the day of the Dragon King ritual, they sprinkled a mixture of rice and millet out on the sea, heaps and heaps of it, after which they set terrapins and turtles free. Buddha, as always, sat on top of his lotus flower. Minee thought about how intimidating Buddha's smile looked on the mural paintings of hell. The nutty taste of a seaweed side dish. And in the Buddhist sanctum, packed with people, the bustling noise: a chanting voice swelling up and dying down, someone tapping the wooden block.

"*Yo'isyo, yo'isyo!*"

Japanese young men shouldering a palanquin threaded their way through the streets. They all wore white clothes, their hair held together by a yellow headband. They lifted the palanquin high into the sky before bringing it back down and circling around. Hurrah! And again! In between, a demon ran towards the crowd, spreading its deep-red, fiery lips. Knowing full well that the demon was fake, just like a circus troupe's horse mask, the kids shrieked and ran around. Minee even cried. *Yo'isyo! Yo'isyo! Yo'isyo*—the palanquin went up and down and around.

The Joseon kids watched the spectacle while being shoved around in a country where they were unwelcome, like wanderers in their own hometown, their stage, their world.

Minee trudged back home. Shrugging off every last thought of cherry trees and winter cherries, instead concentrating on the coin she would get from her mother, which she would use to buy pink cotton candy, floating up towards the blue sky like a mist.

Red cape! Blue cape!

Whoa—cotton candy and the cape monster had merged into one.

"Red cape! Blue cape!" Minee shouted, as she ran down the empty backstreet, her pencil case clunking in her backpack.

Countless footsteps echoed through the hallway, making their way to the canteen, followed by noisy conversations. On this side of the courtyard, the hallway noise was like a dense cloud, a thick wad of cotton, while on the other side of the courtyard it was as thin as a bridal veil.

The Age of Doubt

"Why are you so loud? Can't you be quiet?" Chinless Miss Miura thundered, her voice piercing through the clouds of noise. Minee imagined her entering a wedding hall in her *hakama* skirt and *motsuki,* maintaining her solemn expression.

Whenever there was a festival, it was Miss Nakayama Humi who wore her ceremonial garb most elegantly. Miss Nakayama had a flat nose and a disproportionately big head, but for some reason everyone thought she dressed fashionably. When the now public H Girls' High School was still private, she was the only Japanese woman to be hired as a so-called "national language teacher." Amid all the Joseon teachers, who even by the standards of the time were highly educated, knowledgeable, and nationalistic, she inevitably became the target of ill will, not to mention the wave of contempt she received when they found out she had been born in the rural prefecture of Aomori and had just graduated from a women's university in Japan, unable to shake off her unrefined roots.

"She's made it, she really has. No more country girl, that woman," graduates would say, knowing about her past.

Given the number of years she had been working at the school, she was a veteran teacher, ranked high among the others and had a strong influence. But it was not because of her being a veteran or due to her rank that her influence was so strong. It was thanks to her character and her abilities or, to be precise, the authority in her eyes. When she gazed composedly with those eyes, beaming vivid energy, she made every student tremble. Her head was exceptionally large, her nose low, and her lips thin and small. Her hairline had the shape of a Japanese warrior's, high on both sides like a U, and she always wore her bangs down in an attempt to cover her forehead. Besides being short, her lower legs suffered from the beriberi disease, which had made them swell to tragic proportions, and whenever she accidentally banged her leg against a corner of the teacher's platform, the indentation in her leg took a long time to disappear. Despite having a yellow tinge, her skin was in fact beautiful. The hand she used to write her smooth, elegant characters on the blackboard was a pure work of art, possessing a queenly grace. Taking away her eyes and her skin and her hands, Miss Nakayama was essentially a hag. Nevertheless, her eyes did more than just conceal her shortcomings. They were never fooled, they were never fazed, and they never forgave—they always commanded. Miss Nakayama may have been unrefined in the past, but around the time Minee entered H Girls' High School it was rather difficult to imagine that had been the case. She possessed a magical sensibility for color, with which she mysteriously managed to remodel her unappealing physique. To conceal her piano legs, she wore a kimono almost every day, the hem of which cleaved the air, its dignity and sensual charm provoking a peculiar atmosphere. On National Culture Day, when the chrysanthemums bloomed beautifully, Miss Nakayama wore a black *montsuki* with a black, ironed *hakama*, and a dark cobalt *haori* hanging loosely around her shoulders, so that, even in the midst of beautiful women such as her slender-bodied colleagues, she was the sun among inferior lights. Rumor had it that she had taken up playwriting, refusing to rot away as a simple language teacher, but given her cold, serene, and overscrupulous character, it was unthinkable for her to be gifted with a sense of creativity. Miss Nakayama did not know how to be affectionate to her students, nor to her colleagues, and yet she loved like a little brother a novice language teacher who had missed out on the honor of being conscripted, perhaps because of his insufficient height. She loved him for his literary talent and pitied him for his gloomy state as he waited for his conscription letter, young and unmarried as he was.

In summer, during a school-wide drill, a man reminiscent of an old goat was seen under the shade of the willows. He turned out to be Miss Nakayama's father, minding a stroller while waiting for his daughter. After Miss Nakayama had married her sister's former husband—her sister had passed away—and had a baby with him, her once elegant skin had started to show liver spots, while her hair had grown faint with age. And as soon as she started to wear the national uniform instead of her impressive outfits, she completely lost her edge. She was well over thirty, after all. Still, the students were as afraid of her as ever, and even the teachers found her fearsome, not to say they were not also in awe of her. Realizing that her eyes were no longer commanding after losing her strange charm, she gradually started to mouth off, passionately venting her cross temper. Her mouth was as fiery as her eyes used to be and at least as malicious. Especially towards Joseon students. Hence, the students nicknamed her "The Fox."

The footsteps on the hallway died out. The breakfast preparations in the canteen seemed to have been completed and it grew quiet. Then:

Born in the land of the rising sun
Blessed with the crop of sweat
Immersed in divine benevolence
He provides us with sustenance …

They were reciting the words like a spell, as they always did before breakfast. Minee, lying in her room, pulled her arms out from underneath the covers and placed them on top. Much relieved, she felt a sense of peace and security land on her face. Breakfast would soon be over. Then, after everyone slouched around for a bit, the bell would announce the start of classes and the nearly eighty lodgers from Dorm 1 would leave the dormitory. An empty dormitory, how satisfying would that be. Time, like a pile of cookies to nibble on one at a time; or rather, space, abundant like a dozen new notebooks without a speck of ink.

Minee felt happy and stretched one arm towards the ceiling. She felt her blood flow down. Her fingers turned white, then green. She put her other arm up, parallel to the first. Again, her blood flowed down and her hand turned pale. She put her arms up and down, repeating this game a few times. Even if a storm were to rage outside, she was safe, like a hermit crab inside its house. A teeny-tiny hermit crab, protected by an impregnable fortress.

On her desk was a textbook on composition. It was some line from that textbook that she had used as her starting point, continuing to weave out her endless daydream. The book presented the story of Miura Tamaki, waving her handkerchief from aboard a passenger ship covered with colorful tape, on its way to foreign lands.

Minee seemed to take on Miura Tamaki's brilliant figure, and the number of her diamond rings grew from one to ten. Minee went to great pains reducing the list of names whom she should gift those diamonds—to her mother, her aunt, and friends.

Whenever she wandered around the infinitely wide world in her mind, time flew by. In the canteen, breakfast was ending with another recitation. Minee pulled her quilt over her head. Again the noise, the noise.

"Unni, please eat something," one of her juniors said, cautiously carrying a bowl of rice into her room.

"Come on, are you really heartbroken over something so meaningless? You're gonna get sick at this rate," the room senior said, grabbing her backpack. "If you knelt, that was all you needed to do. It's all over now, so why the long face?" With those words, she rekindled Minee's humiliation, as if lashing her with a whip and leaving red scars behind. The room senior left the room saying she was on duty.

"Hey, did you hear that monkey this morning?"

"*Netsu ga takai wa ne. Kyō wa gakkou yasunda hō ga iiwa*. You're burning up. It'd be better if you stayed home today." The juniors cackled as they imitated the glutton nurse, whom everyone despised.

"Ha, right, she was actually trying to do Miss Shimizu's voice."

"Hahaha … Doesn't she know ugly women are even uglier when they imitate beauties?"

As they joked around, the bell announced the start of class and the juniors took their backpacks and left.

At school, the bell kept ringing.

After the footsteps of the latecomers echoed through the hallway, the dormitory was deserted. In the back kitchen, the young kitchen maid sang a childish song as she stirred a pot, while the old maid, who always seemed to be annoyed at everything, pestered the young one.

Yesterday—the student platoon faced each other in two rows until someone said, "Turn around! Forward!" and one of the rows moved away from Minee, who was eyeing them from the shade underneath the willows, while the other row approached her. "Turn around! Forward!" Then, the receding row drew near, while the approaching row turned their backs and moved away. They looked like the Royal Guards she had seen in pictures— not students doing a drill. No, heavily armored soldiers. Robots without a dash of color in their eyes! Teachers' faces. Japanese girls' faces, fast approaching Minee, like balls of yarn, like a wave swallowing boats, on the verge of washing over Minee. The eyes of her friends. The smiling lips of Tamayama Junko. The smiling lips of her music teacher. The words that her room senior had said on her way out, echoing and reechoing, as sound and shape became one lump, charging at Minee.

When she stood up after kneeling in the teachers' office yesterday, Minee felt her feet floating in mid-air because of her cramps. Resting on air, she walked out. When she carried her backpack out of her classroom and looked for her shoes in the shoe cabinet, Minee felt something in her feet again.

My feet hurt.

When she walked out the school gates, the windows of the buildings standing on the opposite side of the narrow ditch had their mouths agape like fools. Walking along the path to the right for about fifty meters and reaching the crossroads, she saw the black woods on the far side stretching out from the school gates. As dusk drew near, the golden sun turned its back on the village, which stood on the edge of the woods. The red brick wall of the school, the hospital, the pharmacy, and the hardware store each stood on one corner of the crossroads. A familiar-looking doctor and nurse came out of the hospital carrying equipment for a patient visit. Inside the pharmacy was Minee's aunt, wife of the second eldest brother of the chestnut grove ajeossi. Minee rounded the corner of the school wall lightning fast. She felt a glare resting painfully on her back.

The Age of Doubt

She had followed her mom to visit the pharmacy ajeossi's family once when she took her entrance exam and once more when she started school, but for the last three, no, four years because she took a year off, she had never visited again. Even though she passed by the store every morning and evening. Even when she ran into members of the pharmacist's family by accident, she avoided their gaze at all costs and pretended she did not see them. In the end, that was the kind of stubbornness Minee had grown into. She had no reason to behave that way. The two times she had accompanied her mother to the pharmacy, the atmosphere had been gloomy and the relationship between the chestnut grove grandmother and her daughter-in-law had been far from healthy, so she knew the family members would not welcome her particularly warmly. When Minee returned to her old school, the chestnut grove ajeossi came along with her to take care of the formalities, but then Minee moved into the dormitory and never visited the pharmacist's family again. She never felt so inclined, postponing and procrastinating, and after a while it seemed like she had committed a crime, leading her to avoid them forever. The longer she avoided them, the faster she rounded the street corner and the more she got used to that state of affairs, the more unbreakable the wall of alienation grew. The wife of the pharmacist was a stunning beauty. Her eyebrows were as lush as they were shapely, and the edges of her eyelids were so long that Minee could hardly picture her eyes. She had a deep and low voice, like a man's, sounding like a gentle breeze. At some point, when Minee was taught counterespionage at school, the pharmacy ajeossi played the part of a spy who had slipped through the police cordon, leaving Minee baffled as she watched the spectacle from afar. The ajeossi had a sturdy build, while his face looked rough and crude despite his glasses, but judging from the chestnut grove grandmother, he was a hen-pecked husband.

When she came up to the dormitory gates, where the high-towering poplars were shimmering like the sun, middle school boys walked out, cutting tall figures with their knapsacks on their shoulders. Their faces tanned from a multi-day military drill, they glanced at the female students loitering around the gates from the corners of their eyes, like flatfish. The girls, who were all too interested in boys, giggled behind their backs.

Back in her room, Minee collapsed to the floor. Her body was boiling over.

She could vaguely hear the instructions from the principal, carried over by the wind. By the sounds of it, he was reciting the glorious military achievements of the Imperial Japanese Army, as listed in the General Headquarters' announcement.

His Honorable Majesty kindly treats the Joseon people as equals and has accepted them as his own people. Therefore, the Joseon people are urged to take part in the front line of the War and achieve the final victory, fulfilling the Japanese Empire's great cause of unifying the world.

Minee got up and rested her face on her desk. Through the window, the blue sky peeked into her room.

—*Shall I go home? Shall I drop everything and just go home?*

—*If you do, it'll be the second time. Can you really quit school twice? You only have to stick it out for another year and a half.*

—*I'd rather die than go to school. I think I'm going crazy.*

—*This time, when you go home, Mom won't want to live another second. You won't be able to wander about the streets anymore.*

—*I can run away.*

—Where to? Dad?

—No, never. Why would I go to someone who ignores me when we run into each other?

—Exactly. So, where else?

—Japan, maybe.

—What on earth are you planning to do there?

—I'll learn to be a dressmaker. And I'll paint.

—Stop talking nonsense. So many people are trying to get away from there, but you actually want to move there and die in a bombing?

—Ajeossi … He said he used to study, eating barley powder in cold water …

—But you hate studying?

—That's why I'll just paint.

—Still, you have to finish high school before you can go to art school.

—Ugh … I can't take it any longer.

—Everyone is trying to flee from Japan because of the war, so don't go around making stupid plans. If you walk away now, it'll be the second time you're quitting school. The second time, the second! And Mom will say: "Let's die already." You think you'll be able to walk around freely? It'll be the second time for God's sake.

At the depths of Minee's endless monologue was Ogawa Naoko's face. In order to escape her name, Minee ran away.

The way downhill from school was lonely. Japanese people lived on both sides of the trail, where sharp pebbles stabbed your foot if your shoe slipped off and where you could take a moment to watch the ships enter the harbor. Something from the past was still present in this Japanese village: a statue of a Joseon general called Beoksu. And when the villagers saw someone staring into the distance absent-mindedly, they said:

"Who are you? Beoksu?"

The village was called Yoshino in Japanese, while Joseon people called it Beoksu Grove.

Minee always saw this lonely general on her way to and from school. In the past, she had crossed the stone bridge to get to school, then she had crossed the tunnel underneath the bay, and now, to get to her third elementary school, she passed by the lonely Beoksu.

This general, carved from stone, was mute. Samson had lost his strength after his hair was cut, but this Joseon general had lost his mind, watching over a Japanese village.

A bit further down the road, there was a photo studio. There was also a tailor, a snack shop, and a bookshop. An old road, merging with the wider road, led up to the last remaining watchmaker. Taking the side street left from the wide road, there was the sea. Then there was a wharf where all the ships were hoisted and beached. On both sides of the road towards the wharf were so-called "high-end shops." Among the high-end shops run by the Japanese, the imposing, two-story Hwashin Department Store chain belonged to a Joseon owner yet was located in the foreigner district of their own country. Inside the shop, the interaction between Joseon civilization and the West was on display, quelling the sense of inferiority local gentlemen and gentlewomen felt. Surprisingly enough, as if it were tacitly agreed upon, it was impossible to find Japanese colors or Japanese shapes. Here, a dignified woman wearing a short skirt and dress shoes, her hair in Western style, came face to face with her gentlemanly and ladylike customers, against the backdrop of such brilliant civilization.

The Age of Doubt

Minee followed her mother into the department store.

"Welcome to our store," the dignified woman greeted them, bringing her hands together.

"My daughter is going off to high school soon, but they told her not to bring … Joseon clothes. So I'm looking for … a suit that she can take with her," her mother said, slightly proud.

"Ah, is that so? You must be over the moon, then. Which school are you going to?" the dignified woman asked Minee. As Minee hid behind her mother, her mother answered in her stead:

"She failed her entrance exam in Seoul, but she got into H Girls' High School."

"Ah, right. Seoul is too far away, anyway. You're better off here."

Minee's face grew as red as a radish. Every idiot knew that H Girls' High School—which under the slogan of "Equal Education for Japan and Joseon" had recently expanded to three classes per grade, transforming a mission school into a public school by doing away with their adherence to hanboks and old traditions—was at the bottom of the ladder. But even if the entrance exam was a piece of cake, it was doubtful whether Minee would get in unless they removed arithmetic from the list of exam subjects.

"This summer I'll send you a dress, but first we'll get you some spring clothes."

Mother selected a yellowish woolen dress, a light sweater, and a skirt, then took out a dazzlingly fresh ten-won bill she had been hiding somewhere deep inside her chest of drawers.

"What else do we need?" mother asked, looking back at Minee.

"A sewing kit …" Minee answered in a soft voice.

"If you're looking for sewing materials, you'll find them on the second floor," the saleswoman said.

Minee and her mom walked up the shiny staircase, the worn-out iron having turned yellow. Minee thought about the time when she had taken the escalator at the Hwashin Department Store in Seoul. She had gone up to Seoul to sit her entrance exam, but found herself unable to move away from the shining products and the hundreds of picture-perfect saleswomen in blue uniforms, not to mention the beautifully aligned display of French dolls. It was there that she and a friend had lost their way, to the point where the newspapers reported how two students from outside Seoul who were supposed to sit an exam had gone missing. The two teachers chaperoning more than ten students had to run frantically from this school to that and ended up being late to pick up Minee and her friend, who, well beyond the agreed time of departure, had began to wander the streets. When Minee and her friend somehow managed to find their way back, the two teachers, instead of giving them a threatening reprimand, were so happy to see them again that they had tears in their eyes. They had only been gone for three or four hours, but the newspapers had somehow got hold of the news. Not the way she had shivered during the admission interview, not the rejection letter she had received from her school, only the five happy days in Seoul had made a lasting impression on Minee.

Up on the second floor, Minee bought the celluloid sewing kit she had been hoping for, the one with the pink faces on its sleeve. The pin cushion of red silk with the white floral pattern, the miniature iron, they took everything home.

The bell … All at once, the lights of the dormitory, where Minee had just spent her first night, went on and from Room 1 she heard:

"*Ohayō gozaimasu*. Good morning."

The Age of Doubt

"*Ohayō.*"

The exchange was repeated eleven times before the superintendent reached Room 12.

"*Ohayō gozaimasu.*"

"*Ohayō.*"

The superintendent crossed the canteen and went over to the other side of the courtyard, dragging her slippers. The exact same phrases were repeated. Over and over again. Then the bell sounded, indicating work hours. *Kwang, kwang, kwang*! A strange room filled with strange faces, a peculiar sound heard for the first time. Minee looked down at the buttons of her pajamas, attached the Chinese way.

—*I only need a piece of cloth from the tailor and I'll fix it for you.*

A lady's voice had said.

—*She looks like a baby chick in raincoat.*

Her mother had replied.

—*She'll grow into it … Just fold the sleeves and legs and stitch them up inside. You know how it is with children. Before you know it, they've grown like weeds.*

—*Yeah, true. Time flies, things change, girls wear men's clothes …*

Looking at the buttons on her pajamas, Minee burst into tears.

Part 4: The Procession

Filled with a dozen or so faucets, whose plated gold was stained with rust, facing in opposite directions so as to divide the room in half, the washroom had a high ceiling compared to its width. Sounds drifted up and away, like vapor, before bouncing off the smooth surface of the ceiling and intermixing with entirely different sounds on their way back down, seemingly creating a conversation between departed spirits without the slightest resemblance to this world while evoking a gloomy, obscure tone. Behind the wall, tainted yellow by the rain leaking through, was the home economics classroom, where braziers, ovens, bowls, gas meters, and other household appliances were lined up as if it were an exhibition center, and through the open window on the far side of the room, a few dark green juniper trees, covered in dust, watched over the washroom, the sound of flowing water echoing off the walls. Behind the juniper trees, on the other side of a moss-covered wall, the creek sent its foul water away from school, and a dust-laden wind blew. Along the creek, through the scarcely frequented backstreets, the same wind blew. Perhaps the wind came from the orchard, whose pear trees were always covered in white dust. In the backstreets, there was a corner shop with a tinned iron sign saying TOBACCO despite never having tobacco in stock, where an old Japanese woman with a pair of reading glasses on her nose sat on the floor, bending forward as if trying to touch a tatami mat with her forehead, while a black cat with a little bell stretched its back, tired of life. Perhaps the Japanese Nichiren Buddhist, wearing a black robe and a conical rain hat, was passing by the house surrounded by the recognizable smell of rotting wood, the poor one-man-village, muttering:

"*Namu myōhō renge kyō*! Glory to the Dharma of the Lotus Sutra! *Namu myōhō renge kyō*!"

Every time Minee saw that Nichiren Buddhist monk, she thought of the convict she had met in front of the damp and stuffy law court deprived of sunlight by a gloomy old tree, hollow enough for a family of squirrels to live inside. The feeble-looking man, wearing a shroud dyed gray or indigo or, no, neither of those colors—it was anyone's guess what he had been charged with or what his face even looked like, hidden behind the basket-like hat he was made to wear as an officer with a large sword and large shoes pulled him along by a red rope, unless those were handcuffs tied around his pale, scrawny hands. Minee doubted whether there was anything in this world more frightening than him, sweating as she raced along the walls of the court. At sunset, when the sea howled and the waves came crashing in, she tended to be less scared.

"*Namu myōhō renge kyō. Namu myōhō renge kyō!*"

Nichiren himself, recorded in Japanese history books alongside his legendary divine wind, is said to have urged for war preparations like a madman, predicting a national catastrophe in the form of a foreign invasion. Now, one of his descendants, passing by the tobacco-less tobacco shop, prayed to Buddha. How was that supposed to make sense? Perhaps the black cat instinctively stretched itself every time the monk came near, muttering something.

The washroom was jam-packed with students drinking water. Before going out, they were expected to drink some water and use the toilet.

Minee washed her hands, then cupped them to catch the running water. When would it be her turn to use the half-crumpled aluminum cup? As all the faucets were running at the same time, the gentle trickle of water reminded her of the way yeot candy melted. As she drank from her cupped hands, someone held something out to her from the opposite side of the faucet.

"Here."

The aluminum cup. Minee's eyes bulged. The small lips facing her were bluish green, as if frightened. Those eyes, which seemed entirely black, those bangs drenched in sweat, and, as she flung her hair back, that forehead whiter than her cheek.

"Here," Ogawa Naoko repeated. She made her way through the group of students, parting them in two as she disappeared like a squirrel. Minee picked up the cup Naoko had left behind. Her own lips were losing color, turning bluish green as well. As the water from the cup traveled down her body, like thawed snow on a cold winter day, a shiver ran across her spine.

Here. Ogawa's soft voice was particularly distinct, as if the word she had uttered was stamped with leaden blocks in a print house, unmoving and certain.

"This is great! At least we won't have to study!"

"Come on, weather! Just give us some rain! Then we won't have to worry about any incoming airplanes, and we won't have to do air defense training. The day will just fly by."

"I don't like that. I'm sick of getting rained on. Do you want your black dye bleeding in the rain?"

"That's your problem. My head scarf doesn't change colors."

Minee pushed aside the sounds of people prattling, water flowing, echoes from the ceiling, and went out. The cloudless sky was partly hidden behind the trees. The leaves seemed to hold their breath, while at the same time violently shaking up and down, almost squirming. Minee felt a pang in her chest, as if something sharp was lodged inside. And while it banged against the inside of her chest, spinning around in circles, it occurred to her that she had heard noises bearing no relation to this world at all.

A few days earlier, when Minee ran into Ogawa Naoko in the

backyard, the latter had stopped in her tracks. Then, too, her lips had been bluish green, as if frightened. Minee had walked straight past her as if they were complete strangers, as if she had had nothing to do with the letter incident.

After leaving the washroom, Minee put her shoes in the shoe cabinet and slowly walked up the two stone steps leading to the corridor, as if counting "Ooone, twooo" in her head. Through the corridor window, the blue sky stretching out like a colorful tapestry was partially blocked from view by the roof of the night watchman's room.

Minee, like everyone else, put on a black cotton head scarf and wrapped her hands in black cotton cloth as she entered the classroom, then tightly secured a rope around her wrists. The classroom was rowdy, like a choir of frogs croaking by the embankment of a flooded paddy after a rainy day. But because of the joy Minee felt imagining herself walking along such an embankment, the noise sounded like a cacophony of frogs, bearing no connection whatsoever to herself. She stared at the diagonal shadow of the light brown desk on the teacher's platform, looking like sandalwood jutting out. She relived the feeling of her socks sliding across the wide, long hallway as she left the classroom after drawing on her own, the pleasant sensation of gliding along. The window frames shook in the wind, and the autumn trees shivered, bereft of their leaves. As the cold hit her, a warm liquid ran through her whole body, while the sensation of the slippery maru floor tickling the soles of her feet, free and lonely, made her heart overflow with happiness. She kept staring blankly at the spot where the shadow of the teacher's desk fell on the floor, shimmering like sandalwood.

After everyone got dressed, ready to leave for air defense

training, the classroom became all the more chaotic, as the students, in anticipation of new orders, split up into several groups, bursting into laughter and gesturing wildly, ending up in discussions and cursing the teachers, which made them look like a wriggling swarm of beetles or a daytime masquerade with nasty, inhumanly grim clowns. Laughter seemed to emerge from behind the lofty calligraphy of the frame hanging on the white wall, and in this girls' school, which used to be a mission school, the wall heater, which had long become a mere relic, remained in a corner of the classroom like a mailbox, the most foolish spectator of all. With her mouth agape and covered by wires, Minee skated through the hallway, gliding endlessly and shining like the sandalwood in the window frame, where dry branches were shaking and shivering in the wind. And again, and again. Her mind turned and stretched across her heart, as her excitement rose and fell.

"Rinoie-san, what happened to your hand?"

The voice was mushy, like uncongealed tofu. A tall man with pink lips shaped like a young moon laughed at her. She had been about to push open the window, her pinky finger wrapped in a bandage, but dropped her hand. Minee felt a shiver run across her skin and fled from the hallway into the classroom, her hair dancing around her face. Chasing after her, her music teacher (who was also her homeroom teacher) halted on the threshold of the classroom, smiling sweetly. As a mixture of fear and hatred instinctively came over her, Minee's eyes sparkled in flashes. Like the eyes of a girl who grew up among wild animals encountering a human for the first time. Her classmates, sitting in a row, were polishing the classroom floor by brushing it eagerly with a roundish stone. The sound of the stone rubbing against the wooden floor was as loud as the machinery of a sawmill. Their hair jumped forward as they moved their shoulders back and forth. Seemingly in tandem, the canna flowers outside swayed back and forth in the wind. Everything was wrapped in a natural silence.

"What a troublesome child." The mushy voice rang out again.

The students pretending to brush the floor while actually lazing around elbowed each other in the sides, cackling.

"Why did you run off without answering my question?"

He turned his body, skinny as a twig and measuring over six cheok. As soon as he faced the other way, the laughter of the students struck against his back. He cautiously looked over his shoulder. Then, the music teacher smiled brightly. The skin underneath his caterpillar-shaped eyebrows turned red like that of a young child, and in between the corners of his mouth, reaching from ear to ear, an smooth row of small white teeth was visible. Slowly turning his head and clasping his hands behind his back, he walked off, as if he were a stick inside his baggy national uniform.

Minee untied the bandage from her pinky finger and tossed it in the trash can. All the veins on her forehead were popping out. Taking off the bandage and throwing it away hardly did anything to soothe her hatred, as she softly bit her wounded finger, the source of her anger. The tingling, stinging sensation gave rise to even more hatred and fear.

"Today's round of tag ended earlier than expected," someone said, jumping up.

"Whoa!" Another explosion of laughter.

"Rinoie-san, what happened to your hand?" They imitated

the teacher. "What a troublesome child." And again: "Why did you run off without answering my question?"

They managed to mimic the way he pushed his glasses up his nose, but they did not come close to his mushy voice and his scrawny body. Still, the whole class thundered with laughter, clapping their hands. Free from supervision, they stopped working and repeatedly let themselves go, having fun. When even the goody two shoes joined in, abandoning their suffocating sense of responsibility, the unrestrained atmosphere seemed to border on some kind of festival, cheering Minee on.

Show him your hatred! Fight back! Put him to shame! We will lift you up to the sky and root for you! We don't want that living skeleton, let him crawl back to his grave!

Amid those cries, Minee's body trembled from the amount of hatred she felt for the music teacher as she skidded into a state of confusion, where her own face and her surroundings were unfamiliar to her, as if she were a fisherman inside a hunter's cottage, unable to communicate, unable to recognize herself.

Minee did not stand up to the music teacher in hopes of becoming her classmates' heroine. Her defense mechanisms being abnormally strong, she simply feared a looming disaster and lost control. Her imagination was eighty percent to blame; the wings of her creativity being endless and its tenor both depressing and mysterious. From a general point of view, there was nothing peculiar about thin lips grinning from ear to ear or a mushy voice crawling out of one's mouth. But the strength of a whole chord possibly surpassed the strength of a single string.

"Ugh, gross. Doesn't he look like someone you'd find in an Edogawa Ranpo novel?" a friend said, immersed in a detective novel. "That devilish smile of his, laughing with his mouth in the shape of a young moon. Eek, just thinking about it makes me shiver! I mean, his face … You should really be careful."

When she told her, in a very adult, sensual way, "Your lips are as fiery as an actress's," Minee envied the boldness embedded in those words, while she could not escape feeling some form of hatred. In the same way, when she heard the words, "You should really be careful," she inevitably felt hatred and her body started to tremble, evoking the illusion that her lower half had disappeared into the sewers. A deluge of laughter drowned Minee even deeper into the illusion.

Show him your hatred! Fight back! Put him to shame! We will lift you up to the sky and root for you! We don't want that living skeleton, let him crawl back to his grave!

They seemed to yell those words, as if it were a festival cheer, as if they were singing a sports chant, waving their flags, like mutes mounting a speaker's platform to deliver an address amid oceans of laughter.

Stop! Make it stop! I'll be hiding underground. I hate that living skeleton and I hate laughter! I hate it! I just want to be still. If only they could leave me alone.

School regulations were orderly like a baduk board. Everything was time-bound. Language period was time-bound, which meant Minee always ended up with a completely blank answer sheet, and the same was true of home economics, sewing class, even the arts and crafts hour that she liked—all confined by time.

The shining clean oven was fitted with a black wooden door handle. A flower-shaped aluminum pudding mold, a jangling set of measuring spoons, the smell of charcoal, the color of mayonnaise, all the tools of the home economics classroom were confined by time. During the two-hour class, neither the long nor the short arm of the clock gave in to magic tricks or dreams. All kinds of colorful pins were stuck in a red pin cushion. A line-cutter made from animals, a slightly curved iron, red and blue thread wound around a spool, colorful strips of cloth moving about, the sewing class ran on for two hours—

"I'm going to inspect your sewing materials today. If you don't have everything you need, you'll get a low grade."

"Today you'll draw a consolatory painting for the front line. Paint a woman, as pretty as possible," the arts teacher said, his lips curling up higher than his nose, showing a row of yellow, tobacco-stained teeth.

"This teacher's grades are peppery," the students whispered when they got the chance to talk amongst themselves.

"If you bring me some sugar, I'll make them sweet," the teacher said.

"Where are we supposed to find sugar? Buy it on the streets?"

The conversation not only showed mechanical sincerity but also a certain level of rudeness, so Minee applied all her energy trying to get carried away by the clear and authoritarian arrangement of time. The moment she ran out of energy, she sought out the adventure called "absence," fearfully awaiting what came next. That, in and of itself, was already too much for her, as she tried to shrug off the salvos of laughter, to punch through an even row of bright white teeth, mouth agape like a young moon.

I hate it! I hate it! I don't want to go to school anymore! I hate school! It's the worst! I can't stand that stupid bell!

The principal was a corpulent man with a healthy complexion. He had a walrus mustache and a set of bushy eyebrows. His khaki uniform looked more blue than the other teachers', making him stand out wherever he went. He went around blathering like a sly businessman, promising the school would become unique thanks to his "Equal Education for Japan and Joseon" scheme. To be sure, the school had been deeply reformed ever since he took office. Reformed and imbued with Japanese ideals. All the old teachers from when the school had been private were shoved out the door and replaced by Japanese teachers. Students were obliged to pay a contribution so the school could acquire a plot of land and expedite the construction of a new school building, mobilizing students for the labor force, all in the hopes of attaining "uniqueness" both in name and in reality and making the school a model case of "Equal Education for Japan and Joseon." At the same time, the principal tried to curry favor with the school authorities by publishing and promoting books about his views on education. Given the way he made students clean the school from top to bottom whenever high-ranking officials came for an inspection visit, the principal, with his rattail-sized sense of heroism, was more of a dictator trying to make the impossible possible than a stick-in-the-mud educator. Once, when the school's most beautiful student snuck into the theater in a hanbok, he blatantly took advantage of the fact that her father was a member of the provincial council:

"Fujimoto has such a pretty face, there's nothing we can do," he said, smiling dimly as he put her on disciplinary probation for a few days, a remarkably light punishment which was met with a favorable response. The way he presented the new music teacher to the students betrayed that he was not merely a stick-in-the-mud educator:

"Mr. Uehara is taller than Prime Minister Konoe. And he's a handsome man, as handsome as the actor Uehara Ken," the principal said, smiling his characteristic smile underneath his walrus mustache.

A roar of laughter went around the jam-packed lecture hall. The music teacher may well have been taller than Prime Minister Konoe. But to say he was as handsome as Ken Uehara was baseless flattery. Given he was a pianist, his unusually long fingers may have been a welcome gift from above, but otherwise he was a pain for the eyes: his head, with his hair close-cropped like a Buddhist monk's, was so small it reminded you of a snake's head; his extremely narrow eyes and his sharp nose; his light thin lips, which, in the words of the girl who avidly read detective novels, extended up towards his cheekbones like a young moon. When he was angry or happy or embarrassed, his pale face tended to turn bright red, not to mention the skin underneath his caterpillar-like eyebrows, which blushed the way children do out of shyness or surprise.

"Kaneyama! What are you doing?"

When he called out students who were not as pretty, his face was frigid. Even at their slightest mistake, he would fly into a fit of anger, raising his eyebrows and taking on a harsh tone of voice.

"Fujimoto-san, would you stand a bit more over to this side? Just a bit this way?"

When he positioned the students into a choir formation, he would bow like a servant to the pretty delinquent who had been put on probation for entering the theater. While his face, pale to the point of being transparent, was stern and unrelenting towards students he disliked, his expression melted like spring snow towards his favorites. In other words, it was blatant aestheticism on his part, especially considering how much of a pushover he was when admonishing the whole class. It was this aestheticism, not his terrible looks, that led the students to despise him. Although he was a Joseon teacher who could have secretly received support, potentially allowing him to become close to his students, there was no one they cursed more.

"Pa-paa, pa-pa-paa, pa—"

Once, during music class, when he spread his long fingers like a hand fan's ribs, tapping to the beat, not a single student was stupid enough to actually read from their music sheet and take part in his vocal exercises. Oceans of laughter, jeering, chairs shuffling around—music class always resulted in a din, until he picked one student who did not meet his aesthetic standards as a scapegoat and gave them a hard time. He would bristle up his eyebrows like moving caterpillars, shouting:

"Yasumoto! Come see me in the teachers' office after class!"

Even though the students wound him around their fingers, he managed to drag student after student to the teachers' office, punishing them by making them kneel.

Another time, he slapped Minee in the face. When she dropped a pebble from her hand and it started rolling across the classroom floor, he went for her cheek.

On the teacher's platform, where the light fell like sandalwood, the shadow of the teacher's desk still slanted vaguely.

As if walking along with someone, Minee went out to the schoolyard. Flocks of ravens! Gathered in the sunlight, the students looked like flocks of ravens pecking away at their feed. Dorms 2 and 3, the former of which was low, while the latter's two stories soared high, had their windows tightly shut. Minee felt tempted to stealthily escape and run away towards those empty dormitory buildings. They had the same attraction as forbidden substances.

The bell rang. The male teachers came out the door in their gaiters—they always wore gaiters. Their field caps covered their heads tightly, while the female teachers had their head scarfs on.

As if head scarfs will protect us? Minee thought. She drew a picture in her mind's eye, a picture of a firefighter struggling to climb up a rope ladder, as she followed her platoon. Now Minee stood on her assigned spot in the third row of the first platoon of the second company. The platoon leader's verbal commands, organizing the ranks, were as loud as the racket in a hardware store. The leader of the second company was the tallest girl in school. Her head scarf made her look taller than she already was. In fact, she was even taller than the teachers. When the giant music teacher had been around, the girl had been in Grade 7 and leader of the fourth company, Minee being in Grade 8. But now, both she and Minee were in Grade 9 and the music teacher had left, so there was no one taller than her anymore.

The principal stepped onto the speaking platform. Unlike his predecessor, the principal was short and lanky, his physique was meager. With his hair and beard around his chin turning silver, his scholarly appearance showed that he had dedicated his whole life to academia.

After mounting the platform, he delivered his address without any intonation or any gestures. Of course, he once again promised victory, and, earnestly urging everyone to believe him, he predicted the downfall of the Allies. Amidst the war consuming all of humanity, at least this elderly man would survive. But perhaps the remaining school employees of over forty years old and the bachelor language teacher nicknamed "The Dwarf" were trembling with fear every day, dreading the nightmare of receiving a red conscription notification card.

On the empty streets, especially the central streets without young men passing by, a long procession of students in black clothes made its way forward. There was no way to know whether Western monks had ever taken up arms, but the procession of Japanese monks carrying long *naginatas*—a kind of falchion— during the Genpai war, a period when Japan coped with nationwide civic unrest as a major power struggle unfolded, might have looked the same.

War made no sense, it was insanity. Fighting soldiers, civilians at the home front, even children and people who initially were just spectators like the Joseon people, went insane and continued to let insane deeds take place in front of their eyes as if there were nothing strange about it. For example, a bulletin board in some rural village indicated that inhabitants would only receive their ration of grains if they managed to memorize the *Kōkoku No Shinmin No Chikai*—the Japanization Oath. A woman who knew no Japanese, at a loss, said:

"Six pairs of Chikatabi shoes."

Even if a hilarious farce were staged right besides her, everyone would still laugh at the woman's illiteracy and find it completely normal to put up a notice saying one is only entitled to their grains if they are able to recite the Japanization Oath.

The strange and grimy black procession left the city area and continued on roads covered in layers of dust. The feet of many shapes and forms sticking out underneath those black ankle-length pants were covered in old western-style shoes and crumpled dress shoes, or bare in geta. They trod firmly, keeping with the rhythm. At the front of every platoon, a tall student walked with composure, shouldering duster-like tools made from torn rags and long hooks used to tear down burnt houses.

A girl with small eyes, a small nose, a small mouth, and many little pimples on her fat, tofu-like face, pouted her lower lip due to the weight of the tool she was shouldering. The tall students in front strode forward, while the short kids towards the back, carrying buckets made from old sailboats, were almost running in an attempt to keep up. To the back, students carrying khaki backpacks with the Red Cross logo on them were basically sprinting. Four companies, twelve platoons. At the very front, five people were in charge of protecting the school flag bearer, keeping their formation. The very last ones carried stretchers.

Minee wondered whether Ogawa Naoko might come running in pursuit.

"Hey, Rinoie-san," Mizuhara Fukuki whispered to Minee, her curly hair flopping forward. "Do you know why Emodo-san dropped out?"

"I don't know. Why?"

"Remember that time she went for a hospital checkup?"

"Yeah?"

"Turns out she has it."

"Has what?"

"Didn't you think she was a bit weird?"

"Well … She looked sweet."

"That's why it's so sad, so so sad. It's just terrible."

"…?"

Fukuki brought her lips even closer to Minee's ear, hovering right beside her. "She has it, the disease. You know, leprosy." She sounded like the devil whispering. "When she went for the hospital checkup, they found out."

"Really?" Out of fear that she, too, might have such a virus in her body, Minee half swallowed her voice.

"Really. You know she's from S Town right? Apparently, lots of people have it there, because the water is so good."

"No chit-chat, keep walking!" the PE teacher shouted as he passed them by. Fukuki quickly stuck her tongue out, shrugging her shoulders.

The black procession seemed to continue endlessly through the dust-covered streets. Minee recalled a movie about a leprosy patient called "Spring on an Islet." Harrowing scenes were moving closer and closer, one by one, towards a ghastly sorrow, or an even deeper fear.

S Town … Apparently, lots of people have it there, because the water is so good.

On the day Minee moved into the dormitory, she ate a half-moon-shaped *kamaboko* with blue and red lines on it and potatoes and beef and stock with sujebi—it was a whole meal. According to her seniors, they served a special menu to welcome the new arrivals. Minee's room was close to the canteen, housing a total of six girls. The room senior came from K City, not far from Minee's hometown. Her braided ponytail did not go well with her uniform. She was slightly chubby and although her deep-red lips made her look pretty, she had many spots on her face and her eyes were small. Since she was very soft-spoken, Minee sometimes struggled to understand what she meant. Then there was Hayeong—Japanese names were not required yet—who, although being in Grade 9, looked younger than girls from Grade 7, with her innocent angel-like smile, and Kim Hyeja, who had a pimply face with silver-rimmed glasses and was also in Grade 9.

The other three were new arrivals, two girls coming from the countryside and Minee from the coast. Yim Seonghee, hailing from H Town, had the looks of a genius, her eyebrows dark but slender as if they were neatly painted on her face. Her skin was tanned and resilient, and she wore a black cotton skirt and jeogori matching her big body in size, though she lacked a certain refinement. Ahn Du-im from S Town, from the very first day, kept saying:

"My father's bonkers. My grandfather's the one in charge of household spending. My mother secretly sent me away. My poor mother … I have many siblings too, but my father …"

She sobbed through her words, letting the tears flow. At the same time, whenever she laughed with her mouth open, her thick lips looked pale and her awfully white teeth looked blue, making a strange impression. Whether she was laughing or crying, her eyes were rather dim and seemed to lack focus. In fact, it was impossible to tell whether she was laughing or crying at any one time. Her face, while being youthful, was blackish, as if pigmented, and oily to the point of being unhealthy. She tied her short hair back with a rubber band but not properly so, leaving a few strands to flop out and hang in front of her eyes, strands which had no gloss and looked rather ashen. With sleeves reaching down to the backs of her hands, her unstarched black jeogori sagged and drooped around her body, as if she were dressed up as a ghost. Her voice had a life of its own, which meant that she was constantly mumbling or sobbing, even when she had nothing to say. And she always seemed to be on a wander; even when she walked fast, she did not seem to know where she was headed.

"Yes, Unni. Yes, Unni. I made a mistake, Unni," she would mumble if she got scolded by her seniors, taking on the attitude of a Chinese opium addict politely bowing to his superiors.

She looked more or less the same with or without a school uniform. Her mixture of crying and laughter, her wandering gait, all of it seemed to belong to someone upon whom the heavens had bestowed an eternal punishment, left forever to squirm in a bottomless pit of darkness. Minee was afraid of her. Rather than Yim Seonghee's subtle self-confidence, characteristic of someone who looks older than they are, Minee was afraid of Ahn Du-im's hollow eyes, darting every which way.

"My father's bonkers. My grandfather's the one in charge of household spending. He has a lot of money. But whether my mother will send over my tuition fee …"

Strangely enough, she did not look worried about the fact that her father had gone crazy. Instead, she happily told the news to whoever wanted to listen, while oddly mumbling and grumbling to herself. Once, while putting some other kid's gochujang on the lid of her lunchbox, she was caught by the superintendent. She was firmly reprimanded, given dormitory rules did not allow students to bring food from home, but all the while she kept complaining, sobbing about her father being bonkers. Taken aback by her sudden revelation, the superintendent showed compassion.

S Town … Apparently, lots of people have it there, because the water is so good.

Minee thought of Ahn Du-im from S Town. Provided she was still the same as ever, she must be marching in the front row, being Minee's senior. Once, a rumor spread among students that she had gone out of her mind, but she never violated any school rules and made it through without any incidents, maintaining her mediocre grades, which was hardly a reason for her to get picked on, meaning the rumor must have sprouted simply because people thought she was weird. But the rumor never reached the school authorities, since none of the teachers showed her any attention—when she was in class she seemed to be elsewhere and when she was absent she seemed to be there—which might have been the reason she never ran into trouble.

The dust-covered streets came to an end. When the procession crossed the dyke with the entangled bundles of dried grass and reached the riverside, they were joined by a khaki procession arriving from various directions. An elegant stream of middle schoolers, teacher-trainees, youths, and adolescents suddenly flowed towards the girls, giving a ridiculous, awkward, and distorted atmosphere. But at a loud command, they halted and reorganized themselves. As if to inform the god of war that human resources were as ever abundant, the group formed a battle array, then silence fell over them. A grave and somewhat solemn silence, as if a ceremony was about to commence, in anticipation of the big air defense drill. And yet, Minee felt how bamboo stalks were swirling around in the distance, propelled by the thin wind on the banks of the river. A vague line was drawn, like on a runny watercolor painting, across the river reflecting white sunlight and the riverbanks lush with green. The morning sun was far from kind, it was hazy and the wind was rough, but with their head scarfs on, the bamboo sticks in their hands, and their tender bodies armed with air defense weapons, an uncomfortable sweat broke from their pores. An air-raid siren was soon to go off. Followed by another. Someone would yell that an imaginary building had been bombed. Quickly, the troops would line up next to the river and use their buckets to scoop out water, passing them on to the person behind them as the mechanical motion repeated itself on down the line. Girls with hooks would tear down a non-existent burning building while the injured—fallen according to script—were lifted onto stretchers and carried away by the first-aid team according to emergency procedure. And when they shouted that a constant rain of bombs was falling, the buckets would be replaced with bags of sand, rapidly changing hands. After this grand, hectic mess, they might even hold a ceremony to commend the best-performing battalion of the demonstration.

Finally, the air defense drill began. On the wide sandbank without any shelter, underneath the naked, eerily quiet sky without an airplane to be seen, Minee passed on her bucket to the person behind her, and the next, going on endlessly, while thinking of the aluminum cup.

Maybe, at this very moment, Naoko was practicing how to stop a wound from bleeding in the sanitation room. Minee passed on her bucket, thinking to herself. Then, like the blackened cloud hanging over the opposite riverbank, something loomed over her heart. She felt her damaged sense of pride sting as she spotted Tamayama Junko in the row facing her, swaying her upper body as she passed on bucket after bucket.

I didn't send her a telegram that time.

It had been her second act of betrayal.

At that time, Unni was wearing high heels, even though she was pregnant. Given how swollen her belly was, the heels of her pumps looked even thinner. Her husband had an unremarkable face with a plump nose. He was hardly any taller than his wife when she wore heels, him being average in height and her being tall for a woman. They both looked rustic and unkempt, but at the same time virtuous, making Minee feel a cruel wind blowing past, regardless of whether it blew from her side or from theirs. For some reason, it felt both peppery and ice cold.

"As soon as the results are out, send us a telegram," Unni said, standing next to her husband's baby sister, who looked just like him. The small kid with a bob cut had an examinee badge pinned to her chest, but she showed no trace of the usual nervousness from sitting an exam. She was looking the other way as if she could not care less whether she had passed or failed.

Unni gave Minee two bundles of dried seaweed, a hundred sheets each, bound together by a white paper strap, and left. How could Minee feel so alienated, seeing her for the first time since she had graduated, having been apart for two years without the exchange of a single letter? Minee parted from her unni without the slightest bit of grief. Perhaps it was an extremely businesslike thing to do.

Was it because of the child inside her belly, because the heels of her pumps looked extra thin compared to her round belly, or because her plump-nosed husband was standing next to her? No, perhaps it was because Minee's dreams for the future had been thwarted? When Minee walked out the school gates, she felt certain that a bright, beautiful sky and a nature-filled earth would await her from that day onwards. She had never imagined her unni this way, pregnant and freckled.

A few days after Minee moved into the dormitory, the room senior from K Island, not far from Minee's hometown, handed her a letter. "You better write back," she said, laughing.

Not long before, a Grade 7 student had been tormented by a group of Grade 10 students, lined up on the schoolyard, because the girl who according to popular taste was considered the prettiest of the year's new arrivals had been dutiful enough to hand in a letter she had received from one particular Grade 10 student. Being all in one class, the Grade 10 students still felt a kind of independence from when the school had been private, and managed to form a strong alliance. Thanks to their mysterious power, even the Japanese teachers, who had success-fully ousted all the Joseon teachers, were frightened by them, treating Grades 9 and 10 rather amiably. The school authorities turned a blind eye; they did not force the seniors to kneel as a punishment when they found out that they had given a letter to their junior or a group of seniors had bullied one particular student. At that moment, Japan's position had yet to become dire, and in front of the students such terms as "wartime atti-tude" and "weapons of the heart" were hardly used. At any rate, knowing only the name of the sender, Minee wrote a reply. For every night during evening assembly, she was reminded of the fact that she was to obey her dormitory seniors to the point where her eardrums started to hurt. Minee found out that the person who had sent her a letter, unlike the room senior with her braided ponytail, wore her hair in a long bob and had big eyes with long shaking eyelids—she was beautiful. By the looks of her, she was an excellent student with her heart in the right place. After lights out, she would often come to Minee's room and sit in the windowsill, talking with the room senior until late at night, while Minee, holding her breath as she hid under-neath her blanket, eavesdropped on their conversation. Minee was shy and, to put it more precisely, scared. Using the room senior as her go-between, the girl sent Minee sports clothes and a summer uniform she had made herself, and she bought her a purple backpack. Whenever they crossed paths in the hallway, she smiled sweetly at Minee. On Mondays, when they assembled in the lecture hall, the girl went in first along with the rest of Grade 10, scanning the room for Minee as Grade 7 came in last. If their eyes met, Minee quickly turned her gaze away. When Minee went home for the holidays, she gave her mother evasive answers, saying "someone" had made clothes for her and bought her a backpack. She also said she should probably give something back. When she returned to the dormitory, she gifted the girl a doll.

It must have been autumn. Around the time when the joint sports competition of all the province's middle schools was held in P City. A disturbance broke out when the Japanese referees awarded a Japanese school the first prize in spite of the fact that a Joseon school had quite clearly won. That night, the situation escalated to the point where Joseon students stormed a referee's house and ransacked it, which led to the local law enforcement frantically breaking them apart, so as not to repeat the same mistake as with the Gwangju Student Independence Movement. Even after all the competitors had returned to their respective homes, the police found it necessary to keep them under close watch. Around this time, the unni, who had taken part in some track and field event, was repeatedly summoned to the police station. For the first time, Minee felt chest pains because of the girl as well as a dreamlike longing and a sense of pride. The girl was row head in school, and from the second term onwards she was building leader in the dormitory. Minee felt vaguely proud about that too, but her virtue and honesty failed to frighten her juniors since she lacked mystery and character.

Unni's sister-in-law did not pass the entrance exam. Therefore, Minee did not send her unni a telegram. The fact that she did not keep her promise to send her a telegram from time to time gave rise to guilt. Although it was largely due to her heart growing feeble, then tightening.

I didn't send her a telegram that time.

Surprisingly, the wish for a sudden shower was fulfilled. The black clouds which had gathered over the riverbank rushed forward at a rapid speed, as if flying, and heavy raindrops started to fall. In spite of the students' unwavering display of war spirit, the streaks of rain became thicker and thicker, until they were forced to cease operations, it being a mock battle, after all.

The reserves in the rear, drenched in rain, rearranged themselves as they continued to get rained on, then marched off in formation.

When they reached the orchard, which the rain had infused with fresh luster, the rain eased down to a drizzle. Despite the sky hanging low.

I would rather die than do any of this! Minee shouted inwardly, watching Tamayama Junko swing her arms as she walked, looking even more skinny behind the hem of her head scarf. She tried not to be optimistic about the way Ogawa Naoko had expressed her complicated feelings. She wanted to believe that it was nothing but sympathy, she wanted to close her eyes for the sake of her trampled self-esteem. Even though her heart's eye would never close, she was determined not to show Ogawa any more interest whatsoever. She knew better than anyone how pitiable and repulsive it was to be attached to ideals that would never be attained, let alone to act on such an ideal. She saw it in the relationship between her parents; it was the reason she hated her mother. She hated her father too, but only because she pitied her mother and because he was a despicable man.

—*Not being able to love is a greater misfortune than not being loved*—

Minee mulled over these words that she had once overheard for what they were worth. Love, friendship, affection—Minee reckoned she knew what it felt like not to receive any of those things. To what extent was her instinctive hatred, apart from being a misfortune, also a solitary crusade?

"Wow! Look! Isn't that Yoshino-san?"

"Whoa! It's Yoshino-san!"

"Yes, it's true!"

Suddenly the whole procession was astir. Everyone halted and shouted something.

"What are you doing!" a teacher yelled despite knowing the answer full well, waving his hands to spur the students on.

A village lay on the other side of the levee. It had tile-roofed houses with a high stone wall surrounding them. A girl in a deep-blue skirt leant against the stone wall, not moving a finger, her face hidden behind an umbrella. She must be crying. Perhaps, after the procession had passed her by and the streets were completely empty again, she would still be crying. The house on top of the reinforced stones being a gisaeng school, everyone had heard that Yoshino-san, who ran errands in the girls' school, was undergoing training to become a courtesan.

The hem of her skirt, drenched in rain—all the students walking on the wet road extended their undying sympathy towards her, whispering endlessly about her without the teachers hearing.

Translated by Mattho Mandersloot
First published 1966

The Sickness No Medicine Can Fix

Yongi was smoking, crouched in the yard thick with fumes from the mosquito fire. A breeze filtered through the loose weave of his hemp work clothes, but far from cooling him off, the muggy air only made him hotter. The thick smoke rising from the mosquito fire caught in his throat and made him cough, but he kept on sucking at his pipe. Having been bent over in the rice field all day weeding, his back was stiff and his limbs ached. But Yongi's exhaustion was far more tolerable than the effort it was taking to control his urge to run to the tavern at the fork in the road on the way to the town marketplace.

Who knows whether she might change her mind? Yongi thinks, *All sorts of men frequent that tavern, surely a few will be better looking than me, and there will be travelling salesmen with fine fortune and men without a woman at home already. What have I ever done for Wolsun anyway …? I bet there are plenty of fellas going around with an eye on her.*

Feeling anxious, like there was a great weight pressing down on his chest, Yongi stood abruptly and then sank back down again. He tapped the tobacco ash out of his pipe, refilled and lit it. No matter how stifling, how unbearable these feelings were, there was nothing Yongi could do. Maybe he could steal away with Wolsun, off deep into the mountains, without even the mice or birds knowing, and survive cultivating a slash and burn plot … he could think of no other way for them to be together.

Since the night of the players' performance, Yongi had gone to Wolsun in the middle of the night a few times over. And now he was sure he couldn't live without her. The feel of her silky soft skin and her deep scent always smoldered around him, and this was the only thing that made him certain he was alive. About ten years before, when Wolsun left the village following a man from faraway, Yongi hid behind a heap of barley straw and watched her back as she went. Something hot streamed from his eyes, but he had long since thrown away any hope of being with her. As he turned away, he repeated to himself, "Have a good life, wherever you go."

After leaving that way, Wolsun returned to the village and opened a tavern at the fork in the road on the way to the town marketplace. For more than a year, Yongi had been satisfied just being able to see Wolsun's face when he came and went on market days, and he never had the thought that he couldn't live without her. When they were young, Yongi was unable to do anything to stop the mudang's daughter leaving with a stranger because he could not go against his mother's will. Although Wolsun returned, by then he had already married Jungnim-daek with the six formal wedding rites, so all he could do was gaze at her as he passed by. Only ever looking from a distance, it seemed as though his feelings for the woman he'd loved might have been nothing. But since slipping away from among the onlookers on the night of the players' performance and making love with her, the carnal desire ignited in Yongi was taking him to an endlessly mysterious and powerful place. He had been lazy and spiritless, but was now industrious. His face that had constantly worn a weak smirk, like a spectator always feeling out of place, changed too. Both joy and suffering clung to him, and he could feel now and then that he was truly living his own life, no longer looking on from the sidelines.

"Hey Yongi!" came a call from beyond the fence where white gourd flowers were blooming, and then Chilsung stepped into the yard. With moonlight streaming down from behind him, Chilsung's topknot looked huge and black.

"You not going to Yeongpal's tonight?"

"Did he butcher a dog?"

"Sure did."

"It's a long time since I had some meat," Yongi said, tapping out his pipe and tucking it into his waist tie as he stood up.

"My missus hasn't come home yet," Chilsung said, peeking into the main room, "looks like yours is still out too."

"No different whether she comes or not …"

"They must be done with the day's work …"

"They'll be huddled 'round flapping their lips."

"Is your jealous wife still acting up?"

Yongi didn't respond.

"Just because her man went to bed with someone else," Chilsung spat on the ground, "she's way out of line."

A few days earlier Chilsung had to pull the two of them apart after Jungnim-daek lunged at Yongi brandishing a kitchen knife, screaming at him to go ahead and kill her.

"It's because you're too soft on her," Chilsung went on. "You've got to go at her like beating a dog for a summer feast. If it were me, I'd fix up her manners alright. That's the thing with women, if they go three days without a beating they turn into vixens."

"What's there to hit? She's such a tiny thing." Yongi wasn't about to join in with deriding his wife, "Anyway, if they butchered a dog there'll be something to drink too."

"No way they'd butcher a dog if they didn't have some drink ready."

Tall, slender Yongi and rounded, stocky Chilsung: together the two men headed out through Yongi's gate made of sticks. With the moonlight shining from ahead, two shadows stretched long behind them. As they walked along the rice paddy embankment, a chorus of frogs cried in the flooded field.

At the house of Duman's family, the women of the village had eaten their fill of a salty supper, with green chilis, doenjang soup, and salted fish stew, then washed it down with steaming scorched rice tea. Some of them had gone home already, and those who remained sat out on a straw mat in the yard, cooling their sweat and chatting. The women had worked all day beating out hemp fibers in the processing hut by the river, in a communal labor sharing arrangement for Duman's family, and had eaten both lunch and dinner at their home.

The women's talk circled around how the daughter-in-law of the Jinsa Choi household, Byeoldangassi, ran off with the farmhand Gucheon, and the encounter Jungnim-daek had with the pair on her way back from staying with her parents following a quarrel with her husband. The women had been over the story time and again, but it was an event that wouldn't leave their minds, so idle talk always clung to that thread and knew no stopping.

"It's all predestined by fate," said Turtle's mother, who always put everything down to fate. "If they ended up running off like that, how bad it must have been. Why, if one of them had died and the lovesick spirit stuck to someone, it would surely kill them too."

"That's true, come to think of it. When I was young, I saw an exorcism being done for someone possessed by a lovesick spirit, up atop lonely lover's rock," Imi's mother said, scratching at her scalp tickled by sweat.

"If it doesn't budge however many rites the mudang does, don't they throw the person possessed by the lovesick spirit off the edge?" Jungnim-daek asked.

At this another woman chimed in, "Well, who would want to go on living like that? They're better off dead. You know what they say, when a lovesick spirit possesses a woman it coils around her neck like a snake. When she goes to comb her hair, the spirit drops on the floor, and when she puts her hair up it coils itself under her chin again. Aigo!" she shudders, "Just the thought of it gives me the heebie-jeebies."

"The spirit must like it when the woman gets all dolled up," someone added.

The women huddled close together, terrified, as if at any moment a long thin snake might slither out from the dancing shadow of the persimmon tree swaying in the moonlight.

"They say that underwear stained with blood chases spirits away. And peach trees summon them. That's why you never see a peach tree within a perimeter fence, but a long time ago in some village there was a man called Ahn Beomsik …"

"That's all just the blabbering of mudangs," someone else cuts in, "and the thing about peach trees attracting spirits has been around since forever."

After talk of mudangs comes up, the women's minds turn to Wolsun, the mudang's daughter who opened a tavern in the town.

"Aren't you getting carried away being all high and mighty, Jungnim-daek? All husbands stray, it's only natural, and it's not like Mr. Yi is deserting you because of it."

Since Turtle's mother's household had fallen from the ranks of scholarly gentlemen a few generations back, it was ambiguous whether they were yangban or commoners, and they were so wretchedly poor that she couldn't refuse an offer of work helping out another family like a yangban lady should, but she still had her pride, and so she maintained good manners as she chided.

Jungnim-daek lost her temper and retorted, "Your heart is as wide as the sea and the sky, ma'am. How wonderful that must be. You toil all alone to scrape together money for your husband's drinking and gambling and still treat him as the divine head of the household. Well, it's beyond me."

"That's exactly what I'm saying. Your situation is far better than mine. Mr. Yi keeps up with all his work, and does he illtreat you because he has someone else? Quite the opposite, these days he's even more hardworking than before."

"What would happen if he did otherwise? You have to keep working when you've got jack else. All he has is that one nothing special d—. It's as ludicrous as trotting off on a sightseeing tour with nothing but a measly stick. He's no yangban like you ma'am, he's a commoner. It's stupid to think he could bring a concubine into our tiny house," Jungnim-daek had a fire of loathing in her eyes as she lashed out at Turtle's mother using vulgar language.

"Alright, that's enough. Give it a rest. If you keep acting up and one of them dies, the lovesick spirit could stick to you, and what will you do then? You should think of the way things are as better than dying at least."

"They have to express their desires," someone agreed enthusiastically with Turtle's mother. "If they don't, they'll get sick and go to an early grave." It seemed she found Jungnim-daek's cunning way with words and headstrong attitude loathsome.

"What a thing to say!" Jungnim-daek exploded. "If there's unfulfilled desire and resentment it's all mine, that nasty pair certainly have no sorrow or regrets!"

"Talking like that will never do," Turtle's mother gave a bitter laugh.

"If anyone dies it'll be me. I'll die because my blood dries up. Th-that's right! I'll become a spirit and stick around for a thousand, ten thousand years!" Jungnim-daek's eyes brimmed with tears.

"Goodness me, what's all this about? You're still so green, so small-hearted. What use are you with a mind as narrow as a minnow's entrails? Menfolk can't keep it up forever, and once it's over that's the end of it. You're his wife by formal process, you're safe enough, there's no need to go on about living and dying … Would you ever have time to think about such things if you dedicated yourself to keeping house? Your cotton field is thick with weeds, Jungnim-daek. Keep your head down with the weeding and don't say any more. We all know Mr. Yi's nature. He's not the kind of man who would neglect his family."

Without responding, Jungnim-daek found her sandals and put them on. "I'm off," she said, swept out of the stick gate, and was away.

Jungnim-daek walked along the embankment between two

rice fields. The moon followed her, reflected in the paddy water. A good amount of rain had fallen just a few days before, but the frogs were crying in a loud chorus as though calling for more.

He might look good, but what do they know! Wild apricots are pretty but they're too bitter to eat. What's so great about being a formally-married wife? He thinks of nothing but that woman and all I get is an empty shell. Without even one child to call my own, what pleasure am I supposed to get from weeding the fields and spinning and weaving? It's me they should be feeling sorry for!

Jungnim-daek felt the urge to run at Yongi scratching and punching. If only he were there before her. Such fits of rage rose up in her from time to time, even when she was sitting doing nothing, and since Turtle's mother's attempt to soothe her had touched that nerve, she was all riled-up and feeling wronged, so there was no way she could listen.

When she entered through the stick gate the house was completely empty. The mosquito fire had died down too. Jungnim-daek hastily slid open the bedroom door and groped around where the moonlight shone in. She dashed over to the outhouse.

"You in there?"

He was out. The only sound came from bugs crying in the corners of the yard.

"He's gone again. Of course! It's time for the final showdown. Even if it leaves one of us dead." Jungnim-daek hurried to the shed and seized the sickle. It flashed in the moonlight. "Why should I die? I won't go alone if I do!"

She flung down the sickle, raised her hemp skirt and tied it up sturdily with the tie, then dashed out as though in flight. She ran the ten li into town, passing through the endless spread of fields belonging to the Jinsa Choi household. The moon, reflected on the paddy water, followed along behind her faster than before, and the frogs clamored in a frenzy.

When Jungnim-daek reached the tavern at the fork in the road, not even a lone dog loitered in the street, and the low roof of the unlit building towered over her petite frame. She tried for a long time to get her breath back, but it was no use. It felt as though her pounding heart would explode, and with her mouth dry as paper, her lips trembled in a pout.

"Look here," her voice caught in her throat. "Look here!" She struck the front gate to make a louder noise. "Look here!" She rapped on the gate with her fist over and over. "Aren't you going to open up!"

"Who's there? It's the middle of the night." It was Wolsun's voice.

"Open the door! You bitch!"

There came a "Wait, what …?" and lantern light shone out from a gap in the gate. "Please, tell me who you are," having drawn near the gate, the voice was trembling.

"It's me, from Songhwa-ri!"

Wolsun stayed silent.

"Open up already!"

"Why are you being like this? Please come back in the morning."

"What? Stop your whining and open this gate before I smash it to pieces! I ran here through the night, there's no way I'm turning back now."

As soon as she heard the sound of the wooden bar being slid aside, Jungnim-daek darted in through the gate. As she climbed up onto the maru, she shouted into the room, "Let's end all this tonight—we only die once and today is the day!" The door rattled open. "Huh?"

There was no sign of Yongi.

"Where's he gone!"

"Who?" said Wolsun, who was standing blankly holding a lantern as though she were drained of all spirit.

"Oh, so this bitch is playing innocent? I mean my husband! Who else!"

"He didn't come here."

"Didn't come?" Jungnim-daek repeated, suddenly sounding worn out, then, like she had done at home, she groped around inside the room, ran over to the outhouse, and looked into the kitchen. "He really didn't come?"

"He didn't come."

Jungnim-daek crumpled to the ground. Perhaps with an ominous feeling about what the woman might do next, Wolsun placed her lantern far away at the end of the maru and pressed down on her chest with her right hand as though to still the throbbing beneath her white undershirt. In the hazy lantern light Wolsun's face wrinkled up as if she were about to cry, and then, nervous, became expressionless as though she was wearing a mask.

After a little while, Jungnim-daek seemed to come to her senses and got up. Coming to her senses, however, meant that her rage had found a clear target in Wolsun.

"You bitch!" She pounced and ripped right through Wolsun's undershirt.

"Wh-why are you doing this?"

"You really don't know? You bitch!"

Without giving Wolsun a moment to take in that her undershirt was ripped, or pull up her skirt that was coming down, Jungnim-daek went at her again, grabbing and twisting her hair.

"P-please, let go of me and we can talk."

"I won't! My rage wouldn't be calmed even if I took out your liver and ate it. Do you think I'm in a state to leave you unharmed? If you're better than me, let's see just how much. Let's find exactly what you've got that melts men's insides!"

She knocked Wolsun down, punched at her and tore her clothes to shreds, going crazy. If Wolsun had fought back, she wouldn't have suffered so much, but she merely curled up and wept.

"You bitch! You bitch! Will you not surrender even now? A bitch like you will be the end of every man you meet! You have to be killed, killed I say."

But Jungnim-daek's rage was already subsiding. No matter how much she hit Wolsun she didn't react, so the fight felt bland, and was even becoming embarrassing. As the strength fell away from her punches, Jungnim-daek thought, *Where did that man go then*? and was inwardly looking for a chance to make sense of the violence she was meting out to Wolsun.

"I-I won't meet him again, n-never again."

Wolsun had been repeating the same thing over and over for some time, while trying desperately to escape Jungnim-daek's grip, and as Jungnim-daek's rage subsided the words finally reached her ears.

"Is that so? I heard those words with these ears of mine. Alright you bitch! If you summon my man again even after all this, know that I'll see you to an early grave."

Jungnim-daek let go of Wolsun and straightened her clothes. After that, she made a few more half-hearted threats before going out into the night. The empty marketplace was visible a little way off. Still now, not even a lone dog hung about on the road.

A chill wind from the cooled-off fields dried Jungnim-daek's sweaty neck as she hurried along the path back to the village. But her heart didn't feel refreshed. She was the one who had done the hitting, but rather than feeling like she had vented her anger, on the contrary, she felt only miserable, as though she were returning having lost a fight.

"Oh my cursed fate! If only I had a child, I wouldn't be in such a sorry state. Aigo, woe is me."

Passing along the paths of the fields owned by the Jinsa Choi household that stretched on and on, she bawled and grumbled in turn.

Yongi went out to the town on market days, and Jungnim-daek would be so impatient every time that she didn't know what to do with herself, but she didn't get mad. The tavern would be busy on market days, she had reasoned, and he had companions with him, what could he possibly do? It was when Yongi started not coming home at night that Jungnim-daek's rampaging began. Because Wolsun's irises had a yellowish tint, she'd say that she had dog eyes, that they were the eyes of someone who would catch and devour men by the dozen. But although Jungnim-daek tried hard to find fault with Wolsun's appearance, dissecting her with twisted eyes, her smooth skin and greedless, benign disposition meant she never appeared particularly detestable. The reason Jungnim-daek cried and grumbled so as she hurried along the night road was the despair that came from thinking Wolsun was infinitely better than her, even though she was a mudang's daughter.

Summer nights are short. The first cock was already crowing as Jungnim-daek arrived home.

The Age of Doubt

"Huh?"

The gate made of sticks was open, just as she had left it.

"What's going on here?"

Yongi wasn't there, not in the outhouse or the shed or the kitchen. He wasn't just not there, there was no trace of him having come back after she left. She burned up at the thought that she had been fooled, but she had already run like crazy the twenty li there and back and used all her strength yelling and beating Wolsun, and not only that, she had worked all day in the hemp processing hut, so hard that her sweat soaked through her hemp underskirt. Her whole body was like a loose wisp of cotton, and she couldn't move. She hadn't noticed until she got back, but she must have sprained her left elbow while striking Wolsun, because it ached.

Yongi strode into the house as the day dawned milky white. Seeing Jungnim-daek sat crossed-legged on the maru he asked, "Did you boil the cattle feed?"

Jungnim-daek only glared at Yongi so hard her eyes bulged.

"What's with you?"

She didn't say anything.

"Those symptoms of crazy sickness coming out again?"

Yongi was heading towards the cowshed when Jungnim-daek threw herself at him from behind and grabbed his waistband, "Kill me and go to live with that bitch Wolsun!"

"Not this again. From first light," he shoved her away, not bothering to engage.

"Ack, ouch, ow!" Grasping her sprained arm with her other hand, Jungnim-daek sunk to the ground. "Aah. Ow!"

"Stop fussing over nothing. What, do you think I went into town?"

"Aah! Ouch! Aigoo, my arm!"

Realizing by the way she cried out that she couldn't only be fussing, Yongi asked, "What happened to your arm?"

"My arm? My arm isn't enough. Break my legs too, so I can't walk, then you can go to town as you please …" she began to rant then cried out in pain again.

Yongi bent down to rub Jungnim-daek's arm for her, and she cried out, "You're giving me the affliction and then the cure! Ah! Ouch!"

"What is all this? From the crack of dawn. Are you in mourning at a graveside or something? What's this woman wailing about? Give it here. You must have sprained it."

Jungnim-daek thought, if Yongi had just come from Wolsun's, there's no way he wouldn't know about what had happened. But she couldn't sense any sign at all that he knew.

"Look here."

"What?" he replied while massaging her arm.

With the morning fog clearing around them, Yongi's eyes were bloodshot bright red and Jungnim-daek's eyes were no different.

"Aah, ouch … Where did you go last night? You wanted to see me die of worry?"

"That's enough, enough now." With an exasperated tone, he stood up, shoving her away.

"Did I not ask you where you went?"

Heading towards the cowshed he stopped and turned, "I went over to Yeongpal's, what's it to you?" And then softening his tone a little, "I heard he butchered a dog, so I went and had a couple of drinks."

"So having a couple of drinks kept you out all night long?"

"It was hot so I went and slept in the village pavilion with Chilsung."

Jungnim-daek left it at that.

*

The yard outside the annex to the main house was shaded by trees. There, Bongsun's mother, the nanny, was perched on a low wooden bench picking out seeds from watermelon before feeding it to Seohui, Jinsa Choi's granddaughter. With her hair back in two braids to keep her cool, Seohui pecked like a baby swallow at the morsels of watermelon being held out to her. Heat rash spots stuck out on her slightly high forehead.

"You'll have to stop eating now. It would be terrible if you got a tummy ache."

Bongsun's mother put the dish of watermelon aside and lifted the back hem of her finely-woven summer blouse that was stuck to her skin with sweat, to fan in some air.

"Gosh, this weather, it's steaming hot."

Most people naturally lost weight in the summer, but Bongsun's mother was the opposite, when summer came her body would swell.

Stick-thin Mr. Kim's wife would say with jealousy, "Your pale skin is like the flesh of a gourd. They say that all widows are plump, but really, how is it you can gain weight in midsummer when everyone else is wasting away?"

Bongsun's mother twisted her arm behind her and aimed her fan towards Seohui to send the breeze her way, then looked over at Gilsang, who was sprinkling water on the yard.

"Come here, Gilsang."

"Yes!" he answered in high spirits, and ran over with the water scoop still in his hand.

"What wonderful thing has you beaming so?"

Gilsang merely grinned, unable to respond.

"Go into the village for me, to Mr. Yi. Ask him to stop by when he has the chance."

"You mean Uncle Yongi, don't you?"

"That's right. When's the next market day again?"

"It's the day after tomorrow."

"The day after tomorrow? I see. Since today is the fifth day of the month … Well then go and tell him and be right back."

"Yes ma'am."

As Gilsang stepped out of the front gate, the nanny's daughter Bongsun ran after him.

"Where you going?"

"I'm going to Uncle Yongi's."

"Why you going there?"

"On an errand for your mom."

"I'm going with you."

Bongsun had her hair out of the way in two braids too, and with slender calves and sandals worn without socks showing below her skirt that had gotten short, she looked lanky, as though she'd just had a growth spurt.

The two children headed down towards the village. In the baking heat of the middle of the day, an ox tied up beneath a tree stopped grazing, and let out a long *moo* as it watched them pass by. The sky was deep blue, from the distant horizon to high above the children's heads. As though mesmerized by a kite with a broken string flying away, Gilsang walked with his chin lifted way up high, giving no thought to his feet.

The Age of Doubt

"Hey Gilsang."

"What?"

"They say Gwinyeo must have a spirit stuck to her."

"Huh?"

"Well, you know they said before that Gucheon went off to the mountain every night?"

Gilsang didn't respond.

"Well, that was because he had a spirit stuck to him too. And now Gwinyeo keeps going off up the mountain."

"She says she's going to bathe."

"Every day? Who bathes every day?"

"'Cos it's hot."

"That's not it," Bongsun persisted, perhaps because she hated the maid Gwinyeo who lived in the same servants' quarters. "It's actually because she's got a spirit stuck to her. I heard it. The old maid Gannan told me. She goes to the mountain because the spirit calls her."

When the children got to Yongi's house, Jungnim-daek was sweating away in the midday heat pounding barley in the mortar to remove the husks, having neglected to do it before dawn.

"What d'you come here for?" she asked gruffly. Her eyes looked sunken and her hair was disheveled so she looked an utter mess.

"Is uncle not here?" Gilsang asked.

"Why? He's out in the fields!"

At her ill temper, although he didn't know the reason for it, Gilsang hesitated before answering, "She said would he stop by when he gets a chance."

"Who?"

"My mom," Bongsun chimed in.

Knowing that Bongsun's mother and Wolsun had a close relationship, Jungnim-daek responded fiercely, not caring what language she used around children, "For what? To give him a prize? To shower him with praise for becoming the main squeeze of that shaman bitch's daughter?"

With the thought, *That's right, on the night of the players' performance it was those rascals who begged Yongi to take them into town and that's why he went*, she hated them like a thorn in her eye.

"Humph! They're all peas in a pod, what whisperings has she got for him that she wants him coming and going?"

After sweeping the barley grains back into the mortar, she struck its side with the rice paddle. Just then, Yongi came in, probably looking for some lunch.

"What are you two doing here?"

The kids breathed a sigh of relief.

"Well, what is it?"

"She says to come over when you get a chance."

"Who?"

"Bongsun's mom."

"Really? What for?"

Jungnim-daek seemed to have no intention of preparing lunch. It was lucky the barley had been soaked, otherwise it would have been ground to dust, so violent was her battering of the mortar.

"Will you have lunch before you go?"

Yongi bent down and lowered his pant legs that had been gathered up.

A little later, Yongi stopped by to see Bongsun's mother.

"What did you want to see me for?"

"Are you going into town this market day?"

"Well, I don't know," he said as though wandering forlorn in his thoughts.

"If you were going, I wanted to ask you to deliver something to Wolsun."

In an instant, vitality rose to Yongi's face, "What is it?"

"I made her two ramie blouses, and I thought you might take them to her for me."

"I'll go," Yongi said, his face now beaming.

The next day when Yongi went out to cut stalks to lay between the rice plants, he noticed that the sickle wasn't cutting cleanly. When he examined it, he found the blade a total mess.

As Yongi mumbled to himself, "This needs sharpening," thoughts of Wolsun filled his head. For some reason Wolsun had been avoiding him. Every time he went to see her, she made obvious excuses, saying that she was sick or had to go out to see to something. However, it wasn't in Yongi's nature to force himself on Wolsun when she turned him away. At such times, his inability to do anything to help her because of his own situation pained him, so when they parted he would stagger along, chewing on his despair that shrouded the sun and darkened his vision. Eventually, Yongi stopped speaking. Staying in the fields all day long and passing the night in the village pavilion, it seemed Jungnim-daek's grumblings didn't reach him at all.

"Living like this will send a woman crazy. Crazy I tell you!"— before she knew it these words lived on Jungnim-daek's lips. "It'd be better if he died and was gone, then I could just get on with things. He'll be the death of me, I'm wasting away."

Previously Yongi's words had upset her, but at least he would say something. Occasionally he would even look at her with pity in his eyes and try to soothe her, but now that they slept separately too, Jungnim-daek couldn't even take in her husband's earthy scent.

Yongi thought, *Tomorrow is market day, so it would be better to go today, before it gets busy*. But his sudden urge to set off right away was held back by the thought, *Could she have found someone else?*

There was no way. Wolsun always treated him so warmly and was single-minded in her devotion. He couldn't believe it and he tried not to believe it, but the thought that, just maybe, it could be true, would agonize him from time to time. If he had only known that Jungnim-daek had assaulted Wolsun so violently. Jungnim-daek had told most of the women in the village, but the womenfolk avoided talk of extra marital affairs around their husbands, even if the straying man was someone they barely knew. They didn't want their men getting any ideas. Imi's mother had no affection for her husband, however, and she had a particular interest in Yongi, so she must have brought it up at some point. Chilsung could have tipped Yongi off, but he was busy with his farm work, and Yongi hadn't seen him for some time, so any talk of what happened passed by forgotten.

Yongi dumped his empty carrying frame in the shed and made preparations to go into town. Having left the house a mess, Jungnim-daek was out, most likely off in the village. Yongi washed his face and changed his clothes then collected up the sickle and some other tools and went out.

"But isn't market day tomorrow?" Bongsun's mother said when she looked up from her sewing and saw Yongi.

"Some of my tools need seeing to, so I thought, on my way to get them sharpened at the smithy I might stop by ..."

"Oh, I see." Bongsun's mother asked nothing more, and as she took a cloth bundle out of her cabinet and gave it to him, she said, "Tell her to come and visit. It's high season for chamoe and watermelon, she can bathe in the cool mountain stream too. I know she must be busy living her life, but how could she never come to see us?"

"I'm sure she just doesn't want to put you to any trouble."

"Trouble, what trouble? There's more than enough to eat, and she can sleep here with me. The lady of the house asks after her too—Wolsun's mother used to come to the house often when she was alive, so she must think of her from time to time."

Leaving the compound of the Jinsa Choi household, Yongi headed straight into town. As the town got closer and closer, he gradually became more anxious; his thoughts swung wildly between wanting to turn back to the village and wanting to arrive at the tavern as soon as possible.

A lifetime is no more than a moment … With this thought Yongi's mind was flooded with conviction: he must snatch Wolsun away and take off with her. *Didn't Gucheon run away with his master's wife? Surely my missus would get by fine without me.*

But the words of his mother before she passed away stuck like a fishbone in his throat.

"I won't have you marrying a mudang's daughter, even over my dead body. It'd be our downfall. It doesn't end with you, you know. The sickness would run deep in the bones of generations to come. How dare you consider taking a girl with a mudang mother to be part of our family! You know they go around doing petty ceremonies for everyone and anyone—even the lowest of the low."

When he'd married Jungnim-daek but still felt nothing for

her, his mother had said, "It will never do to mistreat the formal wife found for you. Women are whatever their men make them. You can teach her what she doesn't know."

The forge was in an alley on the outskirts of the town, before reaching the tavern. Since it wasn't yet market day, the place was quiet.

"Long time no see," Mr. Park, the blacksmith, greeted Yongi.

"Do you have a lot to do?"

"Not really."

"Then could you give these tools some attention?"

"Of course. How is it this year?"

"What do you mean?"

"You know, the season."

"There's no guarantee of that until I take the sickle out into the rice field."

"True enough. No knowing what sudden change the sky might bring," Mr. Park gave a low laugh, blowing tobacco smoke out through his sparse whiskers.

"There's somewhere I have to go, so I'll be off, but please see to those while I'm gone."

Yongi picked up the bundle and headed towards Wolsun's tavern.

"Huh?"

The gate to the tavern was locked up.

"Could she have fallen ill?"

He tried shaking the locked gate but it barely moved. It wouldn't do that if only the bar was slid across, but the gate didn't budge. Bending over to take a closer look, Yongi found that it had been nailed shut.

Fearing the worst, he called out, "Wolsun! Wolsun!"

The Age of Doubt

There was little chance anyone would be inside a gate nailed shut, or that he would hear a response.

"Wolsun!" he yelled with a sound that was half groan and half cry, but he could see no one on the quiet street.

Despair, as though a veil of darkness covered his eyes. Yongi turned towards the street, vision blurring. He felt like his consciousness was contracting and expanding.

"Has she taken a trip somewhere?" he mumbled, "Or gone to the temple, perhaps?"

He noticed an old peddler woman approaching from a way off, carrying a small basket of knickknacks on her head. A familiar face that showed up every market day—on other days the old woman went around the more well-to-do homes hawking her wares.

"Halmae," Yongi called out, feeling like he was clutching at straw.

"What's the matter?"

"Do you know the owner of this tavern? A woman called Wo-Wolsun."

"Well, I know her by sight."

"Th-then, you don't happen to know where she went?"

"Uh well … from what I heard, didn't they say she went off after a Gangwon ginseng trader?"

"A what?"

"I think I heard she eloped with a ginseng trader from Gangwon Province."

"A ginseng trader?"

The old woman with droopy eyelids watched attentively as Yongi's face drained of all color.

"It's true, isn't it?"

"Well, whether it's true or not, that's what everyone's saying. Why, did she owe you money?"

Although she talked of money, the old peddler woman was well-versed in the ways of the world, and there was a cold smile in her eyes that seemed to say, *You muddle-headed man, forget the girl who left you behind, just forget her*. Her watery eyes had seen it all before.

"Oh, no. Unpaid debts … no there's nothing like that," Yongi said, attempting a forced smile that merely contorted his face.

The old woman set down her basket of wares and perched on a rock at the roadside.

"Aha. That woman deserted you."

"N-no," trying to hold back tears, Yongi's throat seemed to close as he spoke. "It's not that either."

"You don't fool me. A grown man's eyes are brimming with tears and you say it's not that?"

The old woman smiled again, cruelly, like a crow that pecks and pokes at the sadness of others. As if getting to observe others' sadness was her compensation for aging and misfortune.

"Love is a foul thing, isn't it? It'd be best to forget her. Memories fade as time goes by anyway. You live a life and all that stands before you in the end is a burial ground. Getting all worked up about these things is the stuff of youth. I had a heyday of my own, you know. With my once pretty face I spent years in a gisaeng house, crying my fare share, and it was because of that foul thing called love that I ended up like this. The heart can't be tied down with a rope, can it? Forgetting is the only medicine, and once you're old, it all means nothing anyway. It's riches you need if you don't want to suffer, a woman is no use at all."

Since she was settling down to have a smoke, it seemed the

old woman's lecture was just getting started. Yongi, who had been staring vacantly at her, came back to his senses.

"No, Halmae. Th-that's not it," he said and hurried away.

Staggering along, he felt as though his legs would give way, bringing him to the ground.

Wicked woman, wicked girl!

Arriving with difficulty at the blacksmith's, Yongi said, "All done?"

Mr. Park was hammering one of the tools then put it back into the forge and said, "I'll have to give it one more go."

As the iron was heating to a glowing red in the fire, Mr. Park took out his tobacco pouch.

"What's up with your face? You're as white as if you'd had food poisoning. Are you sick? Or did someone steal some money or something from you?"

"Right … I've been robbed."

Yongi said whatever came out, crouching in the dirt and staring out at the road. At the foot of the mountain, he could see the figure of the old woman carrying her basket of wares towards a village. There was a cloud of dust rising from the road.

"How much?"

"A hundred nyang."

"That's crazy talk. A hundred nyang isn't the kind of sum to be spoken of like that."

"If you had to put a price on it, it'd be more than a thousand, more than ten thousand nyang."

Whatever Mr. Park said next never reached his ears—Yongi's gaze was fixed on the patch of road that billowed dust.

On leaving the blacksmith's, carrying the repaired tools tied with twine, Yongi went to the tavern a little closer to the marketplace. Since it wasn't market day, the tavern was quiet too, with only two idlers stretched out on the maru. Yongi drank the cup poured for him by the hostess in one go, like he'd been dying of thirst, but when he called out for another, the hostess was busy conversing with one of the prostrate idlers.

"She had a pretty face. Quite a common type, though, I suppose. She went off with a really old one this time, so who knows how they'll get on. She was inattentive and not much fun ... she couldn't steal our regulars, but it feels sort of bittersweet now that she's gone."

They must have been talking about Wolsun.

"Well, I had my eye on her, but I guess it's true what they say, there are those who run and those who fly above them," the idler, still lying down, looked up and laughed.

"Hurry up and give me a drink!"

Finishing his second drink in one go too, Yongi threw a coin down on the drink tray and left. When he got to the turn-off to the village, Dori, a servant of the Jinsa Choi household, was walking along leading a donkey by its bridle.

"You came out to fix some tools?" Dori called to Yongi.

"Yeah," Yongi said, then lifted his head and saw an old man with a long beard smiling at him from atop the donkey. "How do you do, sir?" Yongi automatically gave a low bow.

It was Doctor Mun, who practiced in the town.

"You've been well, I trust?"

"Yes, sir."

When Yongi was little and his mother frequented the Jinsa Choi household, Doctor Mun would lovingly make medicine for him when he had stomach troubles or cracked his head falling down a hill.

Looking out at the fields from atop the donkey, the old man said, "What will the harvest be like this year?"

"That's out of our hands now."

"Out of our hands, you say."

"It's been almost the same for a few years running, so we can't complain if it doesn't go well for a year." Although unintended, Yongi's tone was uncaring.

"It had better not be a lean year. The people will need to have enough not to starve at least," Doctor Mun seemed to be chiding him.

Dori chimed in, "They surely will, sir. We need enough not to starve. Being ignorant, all we have to worry about is the weather and whether we'll go hungry, but the king must be too burdened to sleep."

They walked in silence for a time, then, having heard talk of the events here and there as he went about his work, Dori began to speak, "No matter how you look at it, it seems the world is turning the wrong way round. What kind of place must the royal palace have become for the queen to be dragged out of there and murdered?"

Doctor Mun's barely opened eyes bulged and then thinned again.

Dori went on, "Even though such a thing happened, they fail to get rid of those Japanese imperialists, and now they're stronger than ever, running amok in Seoul. Ha, you know, if everyone stood up to them firmly enough, they wouldn't be able to gain a foothold."

"Oblivious to the maggots hatching in their side," Doctor Mun muttered under his breath.

"Those bastards should be killed. They'll receive divine punishment that's for sure. How could they do such an unimaginable thing?" Dori had his fists clenched tight, getting all riled up on his own.

"It's all because of the topography."

"Pardon, sir? The topography?"

"I mean the position at which the land of Joseon sits. The people are shrewd but … well, I suppose that shrewdness kept it intact all this time, at least."

Doctor Mun looked up at the sky, his long beard fluttering in the dusty wind. Yongi walked silently, as though he were alone, without companions.

When they entered the village, Yongi said, "Hey Dori."

Dori looked at him.

"Bongsun's mother gave this to me, but I wasn't able to deliver it."

He held out the bundle wrapped up in cloth.

"What is it?"

"If you take it to her, she'll know. Go and tell her: the gate was locked and wherever she's gone off to, she's not there." Then to Doctor Mun, Yongi said, "Well, sir, please take care," in respectful farewell, and turned and headed towards his home.

Arriving home, Yongi put the tools in the shed and went into the room. Jungnim-daek's grating voice boomed all around, but Yongi ignored her and simply hung up his clothes then collapsed onto the bedding.

*

With her hair all messy as though she hadn't combed it yet and her short, crumpled hemp skirt hitched up high, Jungnim-daek looked disheveled. Stepping through the stick gate at Duman's family's house, she said, "Is Duman's father here?"

Duman's mother was scolding the children as they ate breakfast on the maru, "Eat up nicely. Have you lost your chin? How can you get so much down you?" When she saw Jungnim-daek, she said, "Come on in. What is it, so early in the morning?" Treating her kindly, as always.

"Is it breakfast time already?"

"We try to eat while it's still cool. If breakfast runs late, the whole day falls into disarray."

Boksil, who'd had her muzzle rammed into her bowl lapping up scorched rice porridge, barked once and then rammed her muzzle back into her bowl. The yard was swept clean, and from the cowshed came the sound of fodder being chewed. Duman's father, sitting a little way off at his own meal table, belatedly asked, "What is it?"

"I was wondering if you'll be going to market today."

"I'd better. Have you had breakfast?"

"What's the use in breakfast? I'm so furious I could die."

"Sounds like you fought again," said Duman's mother. "Seon dear, would you go to the kitchen and fetch a spoon?"

Their daughter put down the loaded spoon she was about to eat and went to the kitchen.

Jungnim-daek said, "Oh. No, no. I mustn't stay."

"Have a bite with us. The rice came out just right."

"My nerves won't let me, and whether he eats it or not, I'll have to prepare some breakfast."

Having brought out a spoon, Seon says, "Auntie, please have some food."

"No, I won't. I have to make breakfast at home."

Duman's mother stopped offering and asked, "Is there something you need from the market?"

"I need some medicine made up …"

"Medicine for what?"

"For my husband, if you can call him that. He's been laid up for days on end and doesn't move a muscle."

Duman's parents say nothing.

"He won't say where or how he's hurting so badly, and he's refusing to eat or drink. It's so frustrating I can barely keep going."

"A burly man like that, what could it be?" said Duman's father.

"That's exactly what's so frustrating! He would never usually be on his back, and there's a mountain of work to be done in the fields and in the house. I really am at my wit's end."

"Since it's summer, couldn't it be dysentery or something like that?" Duman's father offered.

"No. It's not that. I mean, whatever it is, it'd be nice if he'd eat even some thin gruel … that's why I'd like to ask you go to Mun's pharmacy and explain the situation and have a course of medicine made up. I'm sorry to trouble you, but would you mind helping me out while you're at the market?"

"Well, that's easy enough to do, but it's only proper for the afflicted person to go and have their pulse examined for diagnosis, to make the medicine up right."

"Whoever said it wasn't? Though I tell him to go into town till I'm blue in the face, he doesn't bother to give any kind of answer. Since he doesn't speak a word, I'm boiling over. It really is like my innards are being turned inside out trying to put up with it. Whether he's sick because he can't see that woman he so longs to see, or because he can't stand the sight of me, I'm starting to lose interest in living at all. I just want it to be over."

The Age of Doubt

The couple offered no response.

"Having to boil the cattle feed and weed the fields and keep house all on my own … my insides are seething. How can I possibly get everything done?"

The couple said nothing to this either. Then, "Have a spoonful of rice, won't you," Duman's mother insisted again, as though trying to change the subject.

"Oh, no," Jungnim-daek declined as though intending to continue.

Having set his meal table aside, Duman's father glanced disapprovingly at Jungnim-daek as he drank a bowl of scorched-rice tea. Both husband and wife never said anything people wouldn't like to hear, so outwardly they acted glad enough to see her, but inwardly they weren't all that pleased by Jungnim-daek's visit. She blabbered away, not picking up on their mood, but unusually, she didn't stay long.

Placing a few brass coins wrapped in mulberry bark paper on the edge of the maru, Jungnim-daek said, "Well then, sorry to put you to the trouble, Duman's father but …"

Having returned home, crashing and clanging about, Jungnim-daek managed to get the rice pot on the stove and light the fire.

"Even seeing him healthy makes me so mad I could die, but now there's mountains of work to do and a big muscly man is on his back in the corner of the room lying flat like a splinter of firewood," she grumbled as she prodded at the fire with a wooden poker. "How much can a person take? What am I weeding the rice field and the dry field and weaving for anyway? There has to be some joy in sight to get excited about doing work. Do I have a child of my own crawling into my arms? Does my husband think of me with pity? He's even gotten sick from thinking of another woman day and night. Humph, that's right, he must be sick because he can't see that bitch."

The rice boils. And with it, Jungnim-daek's heart boils too. With Yongi sick, Jungnim-daek had been controlling her temper, but when her thoughts reached the conclusion that he must be sick over Wolsun, no matter how unwell he might be, she lost any patience she once had.

"Eugh! Look at me, I put the rice on without placing some doenjang on top," Jungnim-daek took the earthenware soup pot and rushed out to the big sauce jars. Just about to lift the lid of the doenjang jar, she stopped. "Oh, you're up."

Yongi was sitting out on the maru.

"Are you feeling a bit better now?"

Dull eyes stared back at Jungnim-daek, without a word.

"You're well enough to sit outside now then?"

Yongi said nothing.

"Will you eat some rice gruel at least?"

Still nothing.

"Come on, you have to say something. I can't live in a world where we don't talk."

Still nothing.

"I went and gave some money to Duman's dad and asked him to get some medicine made. Duman's dad agreed that it would be better if the sick person went and had their pulse read before making the medicine. Oh please, say anything."

"There's no medicine for this."

His first response in days. Having been on the verge of getting ill herself because she couldn't vent her frustrations, those words set Jungnim-daek off.

"Well then, what will it take to make it better?"

Yongi said nothing.

"Will it get better if we fetch a mudang and perform rites?"

Still nothing.

"Will it get better if we go to the temple and pray?"

Still nothing.

"What about if we do an exorcism for lovesick spirits on lonely lover's rock?"

Yongi just sat there, silent.

"Humm, then it must be a sickness caused by not being able to meet the bitch you're longing to see. That must mean that if you go off to town and bring her back with you, you'd get better."

"That's enough! If you keep jabbering, I'll pull the house posts out of the ground!"

Yongi's face had become ashen, being so long out of the sun, but now it grew red, and a thick vein protruded on his forehead.

"Humph, just the mention of that bitch and you start talking. No need to bring her here, just go, leave, get out of here! Go and never come back. I won't stop you," she yelled, forgetting that she'd come to the sauce jars to get doenjang, uncaring whether or not the rice on the stove turned to soot.

"You just try speaking of her one more time, see what I'll do! I'll start a fire in this house and burn the whole place down!"

Jungnim-daek flung the earthenware pot down on the lid of the jar and ran up to Yongi thrusting her finger, "What did you just say! Why shouldn't I talk about that bitch! Is she the daughter of the Great Jade Emperor? Is she the daughter of the king? Why shouldn't I talk about a bitch who's as filthy as wastewater in the drain, a filthy bitch who goes with anyone like a dung fly, a bitch possessed by an evil spirit who goes around eating men's livers!"

Having looked like she had the vigor to pounce on her ailing husband and tear him to pieces, foaming at the mouth like someone possessed by an evil spirit, Jungnim-daek then gave up and plonked herself down on the floor, both legs sticking out, and burst into tears, "Aigo, aigo! My cursed fate!"

With all the veins on his face swollen and looking as though they would burst, Yongi shuddered—his complexion so reddened it had become purple.

"I should have killed her and killed myself too. Aigo, aigo! I'm so furious, so resentful! I went all the way there, how could I come back without sending her to an early grave! This foolish weakling woman! Hapless, tactless woman! It's this woman who should die, this woman," Jungnim-daek beat her fist against her chest. "Aigo! I believed the words dripping from the end of her tongue and was deceived. To think that I just plodded back home, what a spineless woman I am! I'd be better off believing the words of a ghost. Aigo, I'm so vexed, I'm so bitter! Would I be this bitter if I'd at least broken one of that bitch's legs before I came back?"

Trembling violently, Yongi sprang up, "You! You, went there!"

"I went! Why! Did I go somewhere I can't! I grabbed that bitch by the hair and pummeled her like you beat a dog for meat! Do you pity her? Is she that precious? Right, you must feel so much pity for your precious love! You pity her while giving less regard to your own wife than a spot of eye gunk!"

All color drained from Yongi's face. He turned white like paper. He got down from the maru and went up close to Jungnim-daek. The look he gave her put a stop to the barrage coming out of her mouth. In one swoop, Yongi grabbed her by the hair.

"Aigoo—!"

Jungnim-daek was aghast, it was the first time she'd experienced anything like this. But Yongi couldn't bring himself to strike her in the end. He threw her down, out of his way.

"Aigoo! I'm dying!"

"You monstrous woman!" he yelled, then found his straw sandals and shot out through the stick gate.

The sunlight was sparkling in the air like drops of water. Visible in the distance, there were market-goers here and there on the road into town. Cowherds who had left their oxen on the embankment by the river were kicking and splashing and enjoying the summer.

That's what it was, that's what it was! Yongi staggers along with no thought for where he's headed.

Imi's mother approached, carrying a water jar on her head, pleased to see him. "I heard you were sick, you do look pretty rough."

Having sweated a lot in the extreme heat, the woman's face looked bright and fresh, like it had just been washed. As though Yongi had not seen or heard her, he failed to get out of the way on the narrow path, and ended up butting straight into her.

"Aigo!" After a wobble she quickly righted herself, so she didn't fall, but the water in the jar spilled and got on her clothes and wet her face. "Dear me, did you take me for a ghost?" she called in anger, but Yongi was already a way off and continuing on his way, without looking back. "Humph, he really has gotten strange. Looks like he must have fallen hard. Jungnim-daek's raging makes sense after all."

Imi's mother's chest smarted a little. Although she was spoken for, she had entertained idle fantasies about Yongi, so instead of her usual sense of superiority towards Jungnim-daek, she now struggled to contain a feeling of jealousy towards

Wolsun. For once she found herself siding with Jungnim-daek who was pouting all the time.

Going wherever his feet took him, Yongi had climbed up to the mountain where the shrine was and continued further and further into the forest. He went straight past the path that turned off towards the Samsin shrine and went up deep into the mountains. He heard water and birds, with an occasional bird-song that cut across all other sounds. The sky, visible in scraps between the leaves, was milky.

Deep inside the mountain valley, Yongi spotted a wide, round clearing and lay down. The fragrant, earthy scent of rotting leaves in the moist air reached his nose. And then his whole body felt weak, and he felt he was sinking into the earth. All around was pain and darkness. But in the dark, there was a single glimmering strand, a kind of grief that kept him anchored to the world.

The poor thing!

Wolsun, who had to turn her back on her hometown and leave twice over. Whoever she went off with, be it a ginseng trader from Gangwon or a rich old man, it was not worth quibbling over now.

Where could she have gone? Where did you go? Even if it's over a thousand li away, if I only knew where you were, I'd go. Poor thing.

Her face with the small satisfied smile, soft arms that embraced him; growing weak with the delusion that Wolsun was right beside him, Yongi began to shudder.

Wicked woman! Why couldn't she tell me. Wicked thing. How could she forget me even if she leaves?

But Yongi was to blame for all the tears that Wolsun must have cried as she turned her back on her hometown and left, not once but twice. It was all because of him.

The Age of Doubt

"Yongi, I won't become a mudang even if it kills me. Even if you get married and live without me, I'll never become a mudang."

Wolsun had given a smile, endearing and yet forlorn. When Wolsun's mother convened with the spirits, she would sing the song to summon the souls of the dead confidently at the top of her voice, then all of a sudden turn plaintive, and seem to be using her very last breath. Wolsun's mother acted tough like a man, opposing the contempt directed against her as a shaman, but Wolsun was not like her at all. She spoke sparingly and had no talent when it came to words, so her rare expression of intent was made with great difficulty. But, in the yard behind the Samsin shrine, Yongi had failed, in the end, to say, "Lets run away and live together."

"I'm getting married. Apparently, the groom's a peddler. I think they said he's twenty years older than me. And he's got a pockmarked face."

Leaning against the barley straw piled up by the watermill, Yongi had listened to those words in silence.

"What does it matter where I go? It means nothing to me."

He couldn't see her in the dark, but when she had said those words, tears would have been welled up in Wolsun's eyes.

"My mom said it's better than going to a young man and being mistreated because I'm a mudang's daughter. Since he's old and has a pockmarked face, he won't throw me out at least. What does it matter where I go? It means nothing to me."

What would have gone through Yongi's mind then if Wolsun had instead said, "They say he's handsome and rich and will give me a life of luxury"? He might have urged her to run away with him. Even if he'd end up being unable to go through with running off and leaving his mother behind, at least in that moment he might have said it.

Of course, there was no way of knowing what kind of man this Gangwon ginseng trader she had run off with this time was. Whether he was old and pockmarked, whether he only had one good eye or one good leg.

"What does it matter where I go? It means nothing to me." Wolsun's words that he had heard ten years earlier kept circling in Yongi's ears. They wouldn't stop.

The poor thing, what did she ever do to be born with such bad fortune? It's not your fault! You never did anything wrong.

If she couldn't be with Yongi, it wouldn't have mattered to Wolsun if the man was one-eyed or only had one good leg. It was her lot in life to obey without complaint.

After more than half a day passed, Yongi came down from deep in the mountains. When he was a little way past the path that turned towards the Samsin shrine, he collapsed beneath an alder tree, exhausted. Mountain ants swarmed all over him, but he had lost even the energy to brush them off and was just about managing to sit up, with his back against the tree trunk, when he heard the clear and bright voice of a girl.

"Bongsun's mom! There are wild raspberries over there, won't you pick some for me?"

"Yes, why not. But you must stay where you are, miss. It's all mossy and you could slip. How terrible it would be if you fell. Bongsun, you hold tight to little miss's arm for Mommy."

The latter voice was Bongsun's mother's. Although he heard them, Yongi was unable to stand. Even as he thought, *I must go down, I must go down, I shouldn't be here like this*. It looked to him now as though the sky between the leaves had turned blue, and the forest and rocks and the sound of the mountain stream and cicadas that surrounded him all seemed to reach his ears together, then grow distant and draw near again and grow distant, over and over.

Bongsun's mother had bathed the children in the mountain stream and washed her own hair too. When she spotted Yongi on her way down the mountain, she was not a little startled. "Wait, what are you doing here, Mr. Yi?"

"I was feeling a bit poorly … I came out to get some air."

"Oh, that's why you look so haggard. Whatever's the matter?"

Yongi said nothing.

"Why didn't you go to Doctor Mun to have some medicine made?"

"It'll gradually get better, with time."

"Your face is a real sight."

Yongi said nothing.

"Come to think of it, Dori brought me those summer blouses a while back, he said you couldn't meet Wolsun."

"Yes."

Seohui was devouring the wild raspberries placed on a leaf for her. While eating her share of berries too, Bongsun listened in to the grown ups' conversation. Freshly bathed, the children looked refreshingly clean and bright.

"Where do they say she went?"

"She's gone for good."

"For good?"

"Without a trace …"

Bongsun's mother's eyes widened.

"She nailed the tavern shut and left for good."

Yongi became choked up. Bongsun's mother surmised what must be going on and kept quiet. And she realized why Yongi came up deep into the mountains and why he was sick. Although she didn't know about their recent affair, Bongsun's mother knew their history. Everyone in the village knew, and of course Jungnim-daek did too.

But then, feeling wronged, she said, "So Wolsun went off without saying a word to any of us. Because of the affection she had for her deceased mother, the lady of the house even gave her the money to set up her tavern. How could she leave without saying goodbye?"

"She wouldn't have gone if she was in a position to be saying farewells."

"What position?"

Yongi said nothing.

"Where do they say she went?"

"They say she went off with a ginseng peddler from Gangwon Province, but who knows?"

"That doesn't sound like her …"

"It's all my fault." Tears glistened in Yongi's eyes.

"Who are you talking about, Mommy? Is it Auntie Wolsun?" Bongsun, who was extremely fond of Wolsun, pricked up her ears and asked.

"Not now dear," she avoided the question, and while turning away from the sight of Yongi, she said, "It really is unfortunate. If she was born in the right place … she wouldn't have to live like that. Come to think of it, how bad must it have been that she left without a word? Such a well-mannered and warm-hearted woman. It must be fate, but … be that as it may, what good is it for you to be here like this, Mr. Yi?" she said, as though feeling anxious.

"I keep meaning to get up and go … but I can't seem to lift my feet."

The Age of Doubt

"The ways of the world never go as we wish them. If she's gone, she's gone, but you mustn't be here like this, Mr. Yi. It was never meant to be … If you really can't walk, I'll go down and get someone to come up and fetch you."

Sending the children out ahead, Bongsun's mother made her way down to the village.

A little later when Dori came up on Bongsun's mother's orders, Yongi was passed out under a tree. He had starved for days on end, but it was the shock of Wolsun leaving that had hit him hardest.

"What in the world! Mr. Yi! Mr. Yi!"

Terrified, thinking he must be dead, Dori shook Yongi violently, and only then did he manage to open his eyes.

"Don't … don't shake me so. I don't have any energy, that's all."

"Humph, you gave me such a fright. What did you come up here for? Now then, come up onto my back."

Dori pulled one of Yongi's arms over his shoulder and heaved him onto his sturdy, muscular back. Yongi was tall and Dori was short, but he was a strong man, Dori made it back down to the village without too much trouble.

"I'd better go and get the doctor. Even healthy people get weak come midsummer, what were you thinking going up into the mountains?"

"Don't worry," Yongi said, all light gone from his eyes. "My insides are still intact, I'll be all right if I have something to eat."

When they got close to the house, Yongi mumbled, "Why would I come back here? Is there no place for me in the world but here?"

Dori said, "What was that?"

"I said it's a funny sight: a man who left after hitting his wife being carried back home."

Yongi's usual way of speaking had returned, but his lips were contorted into what looked like a smile of deep grief.

Jungnim-daek was lying down with the door wide open, and her loose hair spread out in disarray. The empty earthenware pot was still on the lid of the big sauce jar, untouched.

"Look here!"

Pretending not to have heard Dori call her, Jungnim-daek made no move to sit up.

"Look here, something terrible happened!"

"What's happened has happened, terrible or not. Don't bother me with it."

Pretending she was just rolling over in her sleep, Jungnim-daek peeked outside. When she saw Yongi being carried in, she couldn't hide a look of bewilderment, but she just lay there.

"Hurry and get up. Your husband collapsed on the mountainside. Hurry up and put out bedding so I can lie him down."

Having figured out from Yongi's words that they must have had a fight, Dori deliberately made a fuss. Unable to win out, Jungnim-daek sat up and gathered her untied hair together to tie it back.

"You should have left him to become a wandering ghost. Why would you carry him all the way here?"

"That's a bit much, isn't it? With someone in this kind of state, it's no time to talk like that." And with a grunt, Dori put Yongi down on the maru, then pulled down the end of his sleeve to wipe the sweat from his forehead.

Yongi's body had returned home, if little else.

Translated by Sophie Bowman
First published November 1968

Commentary

1

The Korean War (1950-1953) was a tragedy for every single Korean person on the peninsula, and as a result, Korean literature in the ensuing period was haunted by the memories of this war. However, through the stories of Pak Kyongni (1926-2008), we can see that she did not just view the war as a shocking, bloody event that ended with the armistice. The civil war which claimed the lives of around three million civilians was surely horrifying; but what was even more grueling to Pak was a postwar life which dragged one down to misery.

War broke out soon after Pak got married in Incheon and began a short-lived teaching career in Yeonan. After the outbreak of the war, her husband died in the wake of being charged with pro-Communist activities and her son lost his life in an accident. In her memoir, Pak emphasized that if she had been happy with her life, she would never have become a writer, and there is no doubt that this remark points to her heartbreaking experience of losing both her husband and son during this period. While much Korean fiction after the war interpreted the event as a right-left ideological confrontation or explored its raison D'être, Pak presented postwar life as an issue of "survival," where one had to overcome adversities or as an arena of fate where one's life lay at the unfathomable mercy of God. Pak deftly captured the persistent shame and humiliation that a proud woman had to endure in order to make a living after the war. Shuddering at her fate, Pak struggled to survive under horrific conditions.

During the postwar period, Pak wrote more than thirty short stories including "The Age of Doubt" (1957), and twenty-five full-volume books such as *The Daughters of Kim's Pharmacy* (1962), *Pasi* (1964), and *The Market and Battlefield* (1964). In fact, Pak's works of this period should receive as much attention and respect as her masterpiece, *Toji* (1969-1994). As a postwar woman writer, Pak palpably revealed her private life and sarcastic aspects of her personality in these short stories and then plunged into the trajectory of her country's long history and the lives of the grassroots. Many stories in this collection possess special significance as rare and precious accounts of a woman writer's sharp perspective of the most turbulent time in Korean history—the period from Japanese colonization to the end of the Korean War. Unlike most war narratives that dig into the horrible realities of the battlefield and failing humanity, Pak's postwar stories take a more multifaceted view, depicting the survivors' tenacious, brutal realities.

It is noteworthy that these short stories—based on her own experiences—always feature ethically overscrupulous female leads with a split in their ego. The more their world reeks of a reckless materialism, the deeper they sink down into solitude. They refuse to compromise with base materialism; instead, they suffer internal conflict and social marginalization, just as Pak herself endured. On the other hand, Pak's characters are also steeped in love, aflame with their pathos, and helplessly vacillate with no solutions available. Whereas *Toji* illustrates a world of spite where life tenaciously goes on, Pak's postwar stories in this collection clearly demonstrate a sharp insight and volition against philistinism.

2.

Pak Kyongni officially debuted as a writer with her short story "Calculations" for the literary magazine *Hyundai Munhak* in 1955, followed by "Black is Black, White is White" in 1956. In her first debut story "Calculations," Hwe-in, the female protagonist, heads to Seoul Station to see off her friend, Jeong-ah. Previously, Hwe-in expressed her intention to break her engagement, and Jeong-ah came to Seoul to talk her out of it. What matters most, however, is Hwe-in's bitter sense of betrayal and anger against her ex-fiancé Gyeong-gu. Despite the illness of Hwe-in's mother and their dire economic situation, Gyeong-gu thoughtlessly blurted out to other people his regrets about the engagement. Such weakness and irresponsibility is something that Hwe-in cannot reconcile with. Jeong-ah tries to dissuade Hwe-in on behalf of Gyeong-gu by reprimanding her for being unrealistically ideal. She urges Hwe-in to face reality, not abstract concepts. Yet Hwe-in reasons that if falsehood and selfishness is the essence of human society, then the concept of romance will naturally become extinct. If the reality is only this, she self-deprecatingly says, "she's not even an idealist." Pursuing such psychological idealism is a repeated theme throughout all of Pak's work. It is not difficult to predict that a woman who remains single or breaks an engagement will be embroiled in groundless scandals while striving to make a living after the war. Nonetheless, if a marriage were only a practical means to weigh profit and loss, Hwe-in is determined to turn it down. What underlies her intention is none other than a romanticism that views courtship as the fruit of pure love. This romantic element shown in Pak's debut story not only develops into the melodramatic features of her many upcoming novels, but is also closely intertwined with her world view that "pure" love is in constant conflict with the social system.

Hwe-in announces "things don't seem so shaky anymore" and breaks her engagement. Instead of keeping Hwe-in's sublime idealism intact, however, Pak shows how easily such idealism can be shattered into pieces against the solid wall of reality. Every time men do her little favors, Hwe-in bristles and obsessively "calculates" their favors into some kind of debt she has to repay as soon as possible. She is both too scrupulous to owe anyone any debt and anxious about any likelihood that the men might take her debt the wrong way. At the beginning of the story, Hwe-in happens to let a student pay her tram ticket. Feeling indebted to him, she tries to return it by getting him a train ticket at Seoul Station. However, the ending is tragic: she forgets to retrieve her precious change of seventy hwan, gets her thick envelope of money stolen, and is called a trickster by the student and his friend. Hwe-in's pristine and proud character and her precarious idealism evaporate in the face of a cold reality in which all kinds of dirty tricks are deployed. As Hwe-in's "calculation" terribly fails, her face turns pale. The future of this idealist—a woman who breaks her engagement, dreaming of a perfect love—doesn't seem so bright.

Nonetheless, the ending does not necessarily imply only despair; rather, it is more Pak's conscious attempt to gain a sense of balance and refrain herself from disproportionately leaning toward idealism. The conversation between Hwe-in and Jeong-ah situated in the middle of the story seems to reveal one person's split ego. Jeong-ah's impulse to hug Hwe-in like a comforting big sister, or her description of Hwe-in as simultaneously "an unwavering empress" and "an utterly defeated woman" shows her deep sympathy for Hwe-in's non-negotiable idealism. A sharp conflict deepens between a materialistic lifestyle that acknowledges weakness and ugliness, and a psychological idealism that never compromises with any falseness in life.

While a woman's plan to leave her fiancé is aborted by worldly reality in "Calculations," "Retreat" features a woman leaving her love to start over in a bigger world. Kang Hyein, the female protagonist, is the owner of Mimosa, a tailor shop in Myeongdong. One late night, she comes across Kim Byoung-gu when he drunkenly breaks her shop window. In fact, this is their second meeting: Byoung-gu used to date Sook-in, Hyein's half-sister. With their polarized personality traits, the two sisters are like each other's split ego. Sook-in, a medical student, is nothing if not logical, while Hyein, a home management major, loves literature. Despite Hyein's attachment to Byoung-gu, she suppresses her feelings out of guilt that "she and Sook-in had inherited the unhappy fates of their mothers and were snared in an orbit around one man." Yet, Sook-in, as a devoted communist, leaves Byoung-gu for another man who comes from North Korea. Hyein doesn't conclude that Sook-in chose ideology over love; instead, Hyein likens Sook-in to Alexandra Kollontai's Genia from *The Loves of Three Generations*. Kollontai's book triggered a heated real-life argument about the combination of the socialist movement and free love in colonized Joseon, and therefore many contemporaneous readers of "Retreat" would have perceived Sook-in as a more human, relatable character. Later, we come across the character Kihoon in the novel *The Market and Battlefield*, a communist who breaks the false shell of ideology, craving a decent human life—a character Pak undoubtedly developed based on Sook-in.

It is also interesting to note that while ideologies are mostly embodied by male characters in Korean postwar novels, it is the opposite in "Retreat." In spite of her love for Byoung-gu, Sook-in chooses her principles. Byoung-gu lets himself go, helplessly floundering amid his regrets about Sook-in. Watching him, Hyein finds it impossible to keep loving him, despite their apparent destiny based on their accidental encounters. As many literary critics point out, there is a crucial scene where Hyein realizes the horrible artificiality of social customs in front of the animal carcass at the butcher shop. The overwhelming red color symbolizes the social system that is used to justify slaughtering people at war. And the color red is frequently associated with Byoung-gu. Hyein's vague fear that social institutions could even mechanize the feeling of love materializes through Byoung-gu's dissipated lifestyle and untrustworthy words and behavior. Two weeks later, when Hyein is working on some red fabric at her tailor shop, Byoung-gu visits her. He takes her to a basement dance hall in a department store, letting her witness the vanity of pleasure. That day, Hyein realizes that she is only a substitute for Kang Sook-in and decides to turn her back on him. The moment she gives up on Byoung-gu, who is still dealing with the war's scars through distrust and decadence, it opens up an opportunity for Hyein to study in Paris, and the blue sky and the forests of Bourgogne unfold in front of her eyes. Throughout the story, Byoung-gu symbolizes dark space and time by mostly appearing at night and attending the underground dance hall. On the other hand, Hyein sees the immense possibility of the future as she decides to escape from Korea. What is most important is Hyein's will-power to break away from her fate and her determination to find a new path in her life: "Fate reunited us, but everything else has been my will." At this watershed moment, her fate—the pain of unaccomplished love toward Byoung-gu and jealousy of her half-sister Sook-in—transforms into willpower. The driving force behind this is her cousin Younghwa, whose husband was executed by the communists. Hyein and Younghwa both lost their family to ideology, but their tragedy is resolved in a highly intellectual way—studying abroad. In other words, Hyein's sup-posed fate becomes loosened by another woman who shares the same tragedy.

Pak's earliest short stories feature unmarried female charac-ters who are frustrated by love. Not only do they fail to meet de-cent, lovable men, but also their world is deemed to be "vulgar" or scarred by the war. Ironically, these women seem more com-plete when they finally acknowledge their solitude and decide to leave the men behind. Pride does not allow them to entrust their life to just anyone. Wherever their proud faces turn, their split ego is staring back at them. They deeply understand each other and undauntedly set out to seek their dignity, accepting the split ego like their own shadow. This is how Pak engraves a single woman's proud, yet solitary face into postwar literature.

3

Pak's other early stories—including "Black is Black, White is White," "The Age of Doubt," and "The Age of Darkness"—present a consistent account of war widows. These women each suffer through multiple hardships such as losing their husbands to the war, losing their only, young sons in accidents, and financially struggling to support their mothers and daughters. It is obvious that the characters are partly based on Pak's own experiences, and this is why Pak's postwar stories are viewed as a desperate embodiment of her world, rather than the reflection of an empty ideology.

"Black is Black, White is White" is about Hye-sook, who was widowed by the Korean War five years previously and has to support her mother and daughter by herself. Focusing alternately on Principal Jang and Hye-sook, the story illustrates how a corrupt society can easily peg women as promiscuous. Yet, this sophisticated narrative structure also provides some leeway for readers to make active inferences and judgment. Set in a Chinese restaurant, the story begins with Principal Jang having a covert rendezvous with Hwang Geum-soon, his former student and a married woman. Even though he is an educator, Principal Jang is described as a shameless pig "with his oily, porcine neck," who has committed countless adulteries and misappropriated school funds with the bookkeeper, Mr. Hyeon. While waiting for Geum-soon to come back from her errand, Principal Jang overhears a woman's muffled sobs and a man's voice urging her to have an abortion as there is no way he is going to marry her.

Against this backdrop, Hye-sook appears in stark contrast with the shameless, greasy Principal Jang: "Hye-sook pressed her shins together until her bones hurt." Since her husband's death, Hye-sook has "lived from hand to mouth in sorrow each day" but never dropped her uptight personality—instead of compromising on unfair, offensive terms, "she is the sort who spits on the ground and walks away without a second thought." Then, two people visit Hye-sook one after another: Yeong-min and Mr. Hyeon. The reader realizes that Yeong-min is the woman Principal Jang overheard when she bursts out crying and confesses to Hye-sook that she wants to give up on life because of her capricious lover leaving her. Before Yeong-min leaves, she exchanges her coat with Hye-sook's. Soon, Mr. Hyeon arrives and ogles Hye-sook. The fact that Hye-sook previously asked him for a job catches up with her, and he takes advantage of her dire situation. Mr. Hyeon, another greasy face, seems to relish the awkward silence between them, while Hye-sook feels like she is "a little foal brought to an altar for slaughter." Despite Hye-sook's attempt to bring up the memory of her deceased husband, Mr. Hyeon blatantly leers at her. A sense of humiliation and defeat sweeps over Hye-sook. Like this, both Yeong-min and Hye-sook are constantly exposed to the inquiring male gaze, whether inside or outside their own home, and the scene where they exchange their coats foreshadows their ominous future.

The next day, Hye-sook leaves home for a job interview in her green coat. The moment Principal Jang recognizes the coat, tension escalates, and the anticipated tragic consequence materializes; based on the color of Hye-sook's coat and scarf, Principal Jang convinces himself that Hye-sook must be the pregnant woman abandoned by her lover in the Chinese restaurant. He stares at her critically, flat out despising her. Despite Hye-sook's near-obsession with integrity, who refuses to owe even a penny to her closest friend, she is stigmatized as a promiscuous woman, ironically by Principal Jang who himself is having an affair with his old student. Incapable of telling Yeong-min apart from Hye-sook, Principal Jang's sexual double standards make him rush to his moral judgment about Hye-sook. Confused, Hye-sook can only endure the awful humiliation, illustrating the adversities a postwar widow faces in order to stand on her own two feet.

Geum-soon's pregnancy, Yeong-min's pregnancy, and the false accusation of Hye-sook's pregnancy each reveal the infertility of the 1950s, the postwar period when a woman's pregnancy was regarded as the symbol of misfortune and moral degradation. Although a woman may have struggled to carve out an independent life in the contemporary social structure, the structure itself had been already dominated, contorted, and twisted by the caste of corrupted, predatory men. Although many literary works tend to personify this postwar period with morally corrupt woman, Pak offers a fresh perspective to this gender issue. "Black is Black, White is White" asks whether women's sexual sins, presumed to be prevalent in the postwar period, even existed in reality, or whether these sins were merely reckless expansion of unsubstantiated prejudices against women. Pak further elucidates the origin of the era's infertility, which is the moral deprivation of men who are deeply engrossed in their selfish, individualistic way of life.

"The Age of Darkness" was written on the day Pak said a final goodbye to her son at the crematorium. The protagonist Soon-young studied literature at college, but since she lost her husband during the war, she ran a small store, barely able to support her old mother, ten-year-old daughter, and eight-year-old son. One gloomy rainy day, a distant relative takes her children to a nearby mountain and an accident occurs. Myungsoo hurts his head from a fall and soon lapses into unconsciousness. Soonyoung rushes to the hospital and only trauma awaits her. While Myungsoo fights a life-and-death battle, Soonyoung is completely consumed with the guilt and shame of not being able to save him. In the end, the family fails to fetch the blood needed for the surgery in time and Myungsoo dies. Soonyoung finds her mother's constant worry about money, even in the face of Myungsoo's imminent death, utterly repulsive. However, Soonyoung's abhorrence toward her mother reflects her own searing self-loathing: she failed to save her son because of financial incompetence, "ran away because she was afraid of watching her son die," and considered herself a mom who "dumped" her child away. All of her thoughts reveal the miserable conditions and helpless poverty of a postwar widow, the sole breadwinner for the household.

The content of "The Age of Darkness" is equally devoted to the vivid description of the postwar medical system, which had fallen into the hands of the greedy and corrupt. While Myungsoo lies unconscious, the hospital does not even attempt to secure blood, nor take an X-ray; they only perform a perfunctory procedure on him. Postwar hospitals are not a place where lives are saved, but rather bewildering mazes where "it isn't even clear if someone is keeping watch or doing anything at all, if there is even any sort of line of command." In front of a young boy breathing his dying breath, the hospital staff remain deplorably aloof; their giggling and chattering is frivolous and dissolute. They claim that the hospital has no blood on hand, but signs of illegal blood transactions are everywhere. Soonyoung's female neighbor comments that if people want blood, they need to bribe the hospital staff: "You know, we can't trust hospitals or doctors at all. […] For the poor, the place is a living hell, not a hospital." Her accusation epitomizes how inefficient and corrupt the postwar healthcare system was: what determines life or death was only money.

Whereas "The Age of Darkness" is about the heart-wrenching experience of a mother losing her son at a hospital, "The Age of Doubt" portrays a mother desperately resorting to Christianity and Buddhism to commemorate her deceased son, one month after his death. The story begins with Jinyoung's husband witnessing the death of a young communist soldier, before his own death on the eve of UN forces recapturing Seoul from the North Korean army in late September, 1950. Like Pak's many other works, the story focuses on corruption, snobbery, and the prevalent distrust in the postwar period. Hospitals are still an outrageous place where they manipulate injection dosages and sell empty ampoules, but this story pays more attention to religion, which has lost both divinity and human dignity.

One day, Jinyoung follows her Galwoldong ajumoni to a chapel. Her Galwoldong ajumoni is a wife of Jinyoung's distant relative, who was once embroiled in a fraudulent gye, a traditional private fund. In the "holy" chapel, Jinyoung feels ashamed and guilty about her cold logic and lack of solemnity. She tries to believe in God but her attempt fails miserably when she is reminded of "the weathered hats of street performers being passed around onlookers for coins" at the sight of the church donation pouch. Later, Jinyoung learns that Christianity was used to provide a guarantee on a debt when her Galwoldong ajumoni was defrauded out of a fortune. Buddhism is not much different; the religion has been instrumentalized for economic gain. The Buddhist nun who stops by Jinyoung's home doesn't bother to listen how the boy died; instead, her only interest lies in cashing in her rice alms. On Baekjung Day, when lay Buddhists visit the temple and offer special dishes for the deceased, the level of commemoration is determined by the amount of their donation. Upset by the practice, Jinyoung and her mother turn to leave, even without retrieving their humble food offering. A monk sees them off saying, "Do you think a monk could eat otherwise?" This reflects the cold reality of religion, which in the story had become more calculative than anything else in the world. Therefore, Jinyoung's plan to religiously console the soul of Munsu, who met a premature death during brain surgery, fails dismally. No longer does she seek salvation from outside, and she explicitly likens her and her family to animals deprived of any human dignity. Despite the fact that her son died "like some calf in a slaughterhouse," Jinyoung and her mother continue to struggle to survive like "jellyfish floating on the ocean's currents," or "a worm stretched out under direct sunlight." Jinyoung is deeply disgusted with their pathetic life.

As the story reaches its climax, things take an unexpected turn. After dreaming of the dead communist boy soldier, Jinyoung rushes to the temple where Munsu's portrait is enshrined, and burns it. She decides to stop mourning her son through Christianity, Buddhism, or any other kind of religion, and confront reality on her own.

Jinyoung escapes religious delusions by burning Munsu's portrait, and at the same time, she readily accepts the fact that her life still matters, and newly recognizes herself as a living creature with a tenacious nature, rather than a pitiful postwar widow who has lost both her husband and son. In this way, Jinyoung manages to reach a calm, tranquil state of mind. Given the fact that Pak wrote "The Age of Darkness" earlier than "The Age of Doubt"—although the former was published a year later than the latter—"The Age of Darkness" reads more like an extremely tense, heartbreaking, and devastating account of reportage, rather than a fictional story. A few scenes stand out amid undiluted sorrow: whenever Soonyoung looks out the window, she finds the dead Myungsoo standing outside; the swaying shadow of a tree gives her the illusion of a carriage that will carry her son to heaven. Although her heart overflows with grief, Soonyoung still tries to raise her head and look out the window. And a further developed version of Soonyoung can be found in "The Age of Doubt," when Jinyoung finally rediscovers her life with fresh eyes.

Unlike single women in Pak's works, who eventually pursue their freedom and future by determinedly leaving any lingering shame or attachment behind, postwar widows find themselves mourning in interminable sorrow and misery. Even when Jinyoung embraces her tenacious life on her way down the snowy hill, she still wavers between a feeling of resignation to her fate and an excruciating struggle for survival. Nevertheless, we can find a glimmer of hope in her footsteps when she opts to put her feet on the ground instead of trying to overcome her sorrow through religion. Likewise, Pak's other widows are never described as weak: they refuse to depend on anyone and perfectly understand their physicality and despair. Right after the serial publication of "The Age of Darkness" from June to July 1958, Pak continued to serialize a children's story, *The Milky Way*, from June 1958 to April 1959. In this story, the son, Kyeongsu, suffers from a concussion after slipping on a rock on the beach. Although he ends up losing his eyesight, he miraculously survives. The story reflects Pak's heartbreakingly desperate hope that her own son could survive. To Pak, her son's death is a never-resolved tragedy, but both "The Age of Darkness" and "The Age of Doubt" offer a glimpse of her determination and imperturbability to keep a distance from her own sorrow. While war narratives tend to revolve around soldiers, Pak's works focus on the burden of female breadwinners and the miserable deaths of their loved ones. Having endured this dark period, Pak's stories are the most vivid and intense works of the postwar period in Korean literature.

4.

Pak once revealed her special attachment to "The Era of Fantasy," a story based on her own childhood and school days. She said the story resonates with the true nature of life, describing it as "fantastical, yet unclothed; of the original nakedness, without self-flattery." The story centers on Minee, the development of an intense pathos beyond friendship, and the keen sensitivities of an adolescent girl who feels suppressed at school under the Japanese occupation. Unique for Pak's work, it uses stream of consciousness, revolving around the two key themes of Minee's special feelings for a Japanese student girl, Ogawa Naoko, and Minee's shame and denial of this feeling.

The major event starts when Minee takes a fancy to Naoko and sends a letter asking her to be in a "S-relationship" with her, also known at the time as being "S sisters." The term, "S sister" first appeared in the colonization era and refers to an intense sorority. The homosexual desire in this kind of relationship was regarded as temporarily beneficial for emotional development, or even as a safeguard to prevent girls from being tempted by boys. However, things get out of control when Minee's letter falls into the hands of Mr. Majima, a discipline teacher. He sternly warns everyone that he "will not allow for any unwholesome mind or degenerate spirit to go unpunished." The dorm leader also criticizes Minee by pointing out, "There's not a single Joseon girl in our school who's been in a S-relationship with a Japanese girl." However, none of this concerns Minee, who only cares for Naoko's response. Wondering what she will think of her, Minee's mind goes through an emotional roller coaster of ecstasy, fear, and shame. The pure love and fervent feelings toward Naoko invalidate the confrontation between good and evil, or Korea and Japan. The fourth part of the story confirms this point more clearly. The moment Minee realizes that Naoko was the one who gave her an aluminum cup at the water fountain, she feels pure happiness: "[…] like thawed snow on a cold winter, a shiver ran across her spine." In fact, her passionate feelings for Naoko were no different from those she felt as a freshman for "S Unni," a Korean senior. Her unni, literally "older sister," had a long bob hairstyle and trembling big eyes with long eyelashes. Whenever Minee heard the unni and the dorm leader talking deep into the night, leaning against the window, Minee's heart raced wildly. Even though Minee was shy and afraid, she exchanged gifts with the unni. When a Japanese referee blew calls against unni during the school-wide sports day, Minee explicitly expressed her feelings: "For the first time, Minee felt chest pains because of the girl as well as a dreamlike longing and a sense of pride." Like this, the way the female student reflects on her homosexual intimacy faithfully follows the rules of romantic love.

The Age of Doubt

Throughout the story, anti-Japanese and anti-imperialist sentiments are evident, as displayed in the episode in which Ok Sunja was beaten up by the history teacher who always praised the Japanese Emperor. However, hostility and fear are mostly directed toward the Japanese male teachers, the main agents of discipline and regulations. On the other hand, the Japanese female teachers are illustrated as being sophisticated and peculiarly aesthetical. Even when these teachers exert violence, the students blame themselves for failing to win them over. Among women, the national boundary becomes blurred. Minee finds Sunja instinctively repulsive and guilty, as this Korean girl acted as a sort of "errand girl" for "contemptible love," but Minee likens Naoko, a younger Japanese student, to "a bouquet of violets" and profusely expresses infinite love for her. One of the fantastical images repeatedly shown in the story is a woman in a sea-blue skirt walking with a white parasol along the embankment. The vague image of a feeble woman arouses a fantasy which contradicts the traditional family system based on heterosexual unions. Minee's fantasy falters and her feelings are hurt when she finds out that Ogawa Naoko has a sibling, and similarly other objects of her admiration—an unni and Japanese female teachers—turn scruffy with freckles all over their face or grow huge bellies in their pregnancy. Also, Yoshino-san, a student-turned-gisaeng, hides her face almost from shame under an umbrella. The story suggests two different futures for women, one where women become consumed by the patriarchy, producing offspring, and one where they fail to belong to the system and end up becoming a courtesan. Given these circumstances, it is understandable why Minee fears growing up. Therefore, S-relationships seem to be presented as an alternative beyond a heterosexual family system that has strengthened the binary view of women. The deep, intimate relationship between teenage girls inherently transcends patriarchy, not to mention Japanese imperialism.

After Seoul and Tokyo normalized relations in 1965, people began to pay special attention to "The Era of Fantasy," as it shed light on memories of the colonization era. Yet, the literary establishment criticized the fact that although the girls long for friendship beyond national boundaries, the story actually draws no concrete conclusion. The critics also thought "The Era of Fantasy" was too personal and private to be understood in any historical context. However, in that it focuses on the intense homosexual intimacy among teenage girls, the story needs to be read again as an account of resistance against both heterosexuality and national borders. Minee consistently perceives herself to be shameful and tortures herself, and although "The Era of Fantasy" allows her a glimpse of what lies beyond ethnicity and heterosexuality, it does not simply offer a utopian vision. Instead, the powerful personal memory—as opposed to anti-Japanese ideology—creates a special, meaningful space and time which resists being incorporated into a national narrative. This is a new political arena that romantic love cultivates, and the place where the reader can absorb Pak's story in a contemporary sense.

Pak's last story in this collection is "The Sickness No Medicine Can Fix," which was published only ten months before the first book of *Toji*, basically acting as a prequel to the epic novel. Set in Pyeongsari, a small feudal village, at the turn of the twentieth century, the story has a different tone from others in the collection as it attempts to adroitly depict not just a single character but the whole village. The perspective freely moves back and forth between a third-person limited and an omniscient viewpoint, a method demonstrating the strong oral tradition in Korean villages.

The story deals with a forbidden love between Wolsun, a shaman's daughter, and Yongi, a married man. Unable to overcome social conventions and taboo in the strictly patriarchal and Confucian society, their love was destined for failure. Yongi has a feudal duty as husband to Jungnim-daek, whom his parents chose for him, but his life focuses on the voluntary, romantic love toward Wolsun. While Jungnim-daek's jealousy is described as annoying and unsightly, Pak focuses on Wolsun's fair skin and tender heart, which, to some extent, justifies the love between Wolsun and Yongi. Although Wolsun's fragile beauty and obedient personality may embody the virtue of a traditional woman, it is noteworthy that Yongi's love is based on an individual's free choice as opposed to the strict Confucian order. In this sense, the way the story approaches love cuts across the pre-modern and modern eras, and Wolsun and Yongi's love is destined to remain a sickness that is incurable with either a pre-modern method (a shaman's gut-ritual) or a modern method (medicine). Their love represents a social crack in the turbulent times, but it shows extreme romanticism: the two, captivated by fateful passion, refuse to obey the worldly life and dare to reach the threshold of death together. However, in the end, when Wolsun leaves Yongi, he obeys fate and accepts their parting.

"The Era of Fantasy" (1966) and "The Sickness No Medicine Can Fix" (1968), both written later in Pak's writing career, are closely related to her masterpiece, *Toji*. In fact, the plot and characters of "The Era of Fantasy" are repeated and expanded in the *Toji* chapters titled "Red and Black" and "Confrontation," and "The Sickness No Medicine Can Fix" was later inserted into the first volume of *Toji*.

According to Pak, *Toji* was in her mind even before the Korean War, and she reeled in the tales that she heard from her grandmother on Geoje Island. Once, when the yellow-ripe rice grains fell on the endless land, cholera was said to have swept through the village, killing nearly everyone. Only one girl survived and remained to protect her home. Then, a man came and vanished with the girl. Some villagers later said that they saw her wearily doing dishes at an inn. This story stuck so vividly in Pak's mind throughout her young days that she could not expel the image of the yellow rice grains representing life and vitality, and of the bloody red death spread by the cholera. Likewise, "The Sickness No Medicine Can Fix" is full of romantic love, challenging death (despite the acknowledgement of life's barriers), mysteriously twisted fate, and the faint traces of those who disappear into somewhere unreachable. This kind of love, accompanied by the inevitable denial and destruction of the secular world, is a mixture of the two colors stuck deep in the writer's mind: the yellow of life and the bloody red of death.

In an interview, Pak stressed that she had to keep away from fantasy in times of difficulty lest she fall apart, and her thirst for balance kept her characters—Pak's alter egos—at objective distance. Indeed, no Korean writer has better objectively depicted how mortification and violence affected the survival of women characters in the postwar than Pak Kyongni. Instead of letting her ego compromise reality, Pak pursues human dignity and fascinates herself with romantic love, going beyond fate and social institutions. The short stories in this collection show how

Pak Kyongni overcame her personal tragedies, moved Korean people's minds, and further became a seminal figure in Korean literary history. I hope the readers will be able to confirm Pak's ever-expanding and deep perspectives through these stories.

Professor Kang Ji Hee
Hanshin University
Translated by You Jeong Kim

honfordstar.com